TEEN
MACHINE

TEEN MACHINE

Ishita Agarwal

Published by
Rupa Publications India Pvt. Ltd 2022
7/16, Ansari Road, Daryaganj
New Delhi 110002

Sales centres:
Allahabad Bengaluru Chennai
Hyderabad Jaipur Kathmandu
Kolkata Mumbai

Copyright © Ishita Agarwal 2022

This is a work of fiction. Names, characters, places and incidents are either the product of the author's imagination or are used fictitiously and any resemblance to any actual person, living or dead, events or locales is entirely coincidental.

All rights reserved.
No part of this publication may be reproduced, transmitted, or stored in a retrieval system, in any form or by any means, electronic, mechanical, photocopying, recording or otherwise, without the prior permission of the publisher.

ISBN: 978-93-5520-559-9

Second impression 2022

10 9 8 7 6 5 4 3 2

The moral right of the author has been asserted.

Printed in India

This book is sold subject to the condition that it shall not, by way of trade or otherwise, be lent, resold, hired out, or otherwise circulated, without the publisher's prior consent, in any form of binding or cover other than that in which it is published.

To all those who feel they'll never be good enough.

Contents

Part One: The Stream Question

1. Previously Perfect — 3
2. A Ray of Light — 9
3. 'Stop Acting Like a Child' — 16
4. Pathway to Success — 22
5. Dinner Table Fiasco — 35
6. Gatekeeping — 41
7. What If? — 47
8. Comfort Zone — 54

Part Two: Swimming with Dolphins

9. First Day — 63
10. Am I Getting *Punk'D*? — 74
11. New School — 85
12. Playing Truant — 92
13. Not My Best Moment — 102
14. 'So Much Pressure, Yaar' — 113
15. My Resolution — 120
16. Avik's Non-Hobbies — 128
17. Big Day — 137
18. 'Congrats on the Wreck—Rank' — 147
19. Indian Inadequacy — 154
20. Vacation — 160
21. Putting the Past Behind — 170

Part Three: The Final Struggle

22. There is No Try	179
23. A Second First Day	185
24. Familiar Feelings	191
25. 'Why Do You Like Me?'	202
26. Not Going to Lose	210
27. My Chemical Romance	216
28. Confrontations	222
29. Trying My Best	228
30. The Top	236
Epilogue	248
Acknowledgements	253

Part One

The Stream Question

1

Previously Perfect

When I woke up yesterday, life was much simpler. In the unforgiving cold of mid-January, I had dressed up in my school uniform. It was a foggy morning, sure, but still bearable.

I had happily sung the prayer in the morning assembly, standing next to my half-asleep tenth-grade peers. I was so overjoyed to be back in school after the winter break, to see my friends and even my teachers again!

Today, though, was a whole different story. I woke up with the same tenacity as yesterday, ate my breakfast and merrily made my way to the car. However, today the cold air hit my face like a ton of bricks. Our school uniform was not very appropriate for the Chandigarh Januaries. Yesterday, at dinner, Dad did say something about a 'cold wave' hitting North India around this time. The entire car ride to school, I couldn't see more than 10 metres in front of me, and the car slowly snaked along the hazy road. I wanted the driver to speed up, but I held my tongue. Surely, getting into a car crash had to be worse than getting scolded by the teacher for being late, right?

When I finally reached my school, even the board that read 'White Meadows High School' was barely visible in the fog. As I sprinted across the lonely hallways, gasping for air, I knew I was late. Oh, how I missed my winter vacations now: waking up late in the morning, slovenly backyard lunches under the pleasant sun, followed by books and podcasts and some writing work for a school column and for my ongoing fan fiction.

The class monitor was distributing small slips of paper to every student in the class.

'Avani, you're late,' the substitute teacher glared disapprovingly in my direction.

'Sorry, ma'am,' I said, pressing my lips in my best 'good kid' smile. 'The fog was too dense today.'

'No excuses. I'm marking you down as absent for the first half today.'

The smile on my face disappeared quickly. You know the sinking feeling in the pit of your stomach that comes with the anticipation of a day about to go wrong? I was starting to feel it. God, I missed my regular class teacher. She never treated me like this. She knew I was a good kid.

It's okay, Avani. I told myself. *You have full attendance anyway. So, how much does this deduction of half a day even matter?*

I sighed as I sat down next to Parnika, my best friend and deskmate.

'Wow, she's a piece of work,' Parnika said under her breath, giving the teacher the stink eye.

'It's my fault. I should've been on time,' I said, hiding my face under the pretence of finding a book, trying not to show how upset I actually was.

'*Psssh.* It's not your fault. I mean, you can't control the weather, can you? Come on, cheer up,' she said, punching my arm slightly.

I smiled back at her, 'Thanks.' I spotted some papers on her desk. For a moment, I was swept by panic, thinking I'd somehow forgotten we had homework to turn in today, 'What are you up to?'

'Oh, this? I'm just working on my coaching assignment. I better get back to it. It's due tonight,' she said, rearranging the loose sheets in order. I sighed in relief.

Averting my gaze, I focused my attention on the class monitor distributing those slips to each student. Were they permission slips? Were we finally getting to go on a school trip? A tiny sliver of hope made its way into my mind. Maybe this wasn't going to be a bad day.

A small slip of paper with unruly edges, no doubt torn with a metal ruler, was passed on to me. Printed on the slip was a form:

Dear student,

Please return this form by 30 January with the following information:

Name: _____ Roll No: _____

Class: _____ Section: _____

Stream: (tick one box)
- ☐ *Non-medical*
- ☐ *Medical*
- ☐ *Commerce*
- ☐ *Humanities*

_____

Signature of Parent/Guardian

You know how people say some moments define your life? How your life has a pre- and a post- era? This was one of those moments. First, my hands and the back of my knees began to perspire. In no time, I was reduced to a huge, sweaty mess despite the sudden onset of the cold wave.

'Class, you must have all received the forms by now,' the substitute teacher announced. I was starting to dislike her more with every passing minute. 'You must decide your stream for class eleven and turn in the forms to me by the end of the month—that is, by next Friday. Do you all understand?'

Forms, with their defined columns and graduated blanks, are an ideal of definitiveness and comprehensiveness. Everything is standardized and made official. But right then, the little slip of paper stared at me with nothing but defiant uncertainty.

I looked around. The whole class was quiet, with the usual amount of indifference in the air.

My hand shot up.

'Yes, Avani?' She stared at me, her face visibly bored.

'Ma'am, when will our class teacher be back?'

'Oh, she's not returning from Canada for this session. I'm your new class teacher now.'

That was it. Today was officially the worst day ever.

'Stream? You're going to choose non-med, right?' Parnika spoke, looking over at my side of the desk. My sweaty hands had softened the form already, causing it to crumple lightly.

The question of choosing a specialized stream for the last two years of school had haunted me throughout the year, and now, it was here for the reckoning in the form of this...form, which was staring me right through my soul. Those four tick boxes with the streams written next to them had me overwhelmed, stressed and confused. Had the time finally come?

'Hey, Avani?' Parnika spoke louder, waving her well-manicured (school-approved clear nail polish, of course) hands slowly in front of my face. Parnika had her shit together—school, friends, boys and even her *nails* were always on point. I wondered how she did it all and stayed relatively sane.

'I'm still thinking about it,' I blurted. I guess my dilatory excuses weren't going to cut it anymore.

'But we have to decide soon. Don't forget that we have to submit this form in two weeks,' she reminded.

'Yeah, I know,' I said, shoving the form into my bag. 'Have you decided?'

'Yes, I've already filled the form. I just need to get it signed by my parents. I'm taking non-med, *obviously*. Didn't have to think too much about it,' Parnika announced, very matter-of-factly, tucking a stray curl behind her ear. This is the kind of foresight that had won her numerous awards.

But I had already known what Parnika would choose. She had been attending extra coaching classes to prepare for the IIT exam since we were in sixth grade. How she was able to decide that she wanted to pursue a degree in engineering at the age of 10 was beyond me. Like I said before—award-winning foresight. The only reason I knew about IIT was her obsession with getting into the top engineering college in the country. A few years ago, she actually left my birthday party early so that she wouldn't miss her classes. My parents sat me down afterwards and explained to me the prestige that comes with an IIT admission and education. Your admission is predicated on one of the most challenging and competitive exams in the world, which is why students choose to go to coaching centres. These coaching centres have specialized instructors, many of whom are graduates of IIT themselves, so they teach only the syllabus covered on the entrance exams. So, naturally, when the time comes, these students obviously choose the non-medical stream, as it would allow them to study maths, physics and chemistry in school along with their coaching classes, which have advanced classes for the same subjects.

Yes, that was my version of 'the birds and the bees' talk.

'I...don't know. I know I'm not going to take medical or commerce because biology is the one subject that scares me, and economics bores me. So that leaves me two options—the humanities or non-med,' I said, absentmindedly shuffling the pages of my chemistry notebook—the substitute teacher was becoming suspicious of me and how much I was talking. I wasn't going to give her another reason to hate me.

'But you're so smart. Why do you want to study humanities?'

I exhaled loudly, raising my eyebrows at her. I hated the prehistoric perception that people had about any stream that didn't include the natural sciences. Sometimes, though, I wondered if those perceptions had inadvertently become part of my mental process as well.

'I'm sure there are smart people in the humanities class as well,' I said, looking her in the eyes with a deadpan stare.

'Hmm, maybe. But statistically speaking, most school toppers take one of the sciences. Why waste all that capacity for rigour by choosing humanities, a less competitive stream, right?'

I was speechless. What was I supposed to say to that? Apparently, Parnika had done her research.

'Anyway, I'm so excited about the farewell party two weeks from now! I heard we're going to a club,' she whispered to me as the substitute teacher continued to stare daggers at us.

'We are?' I asked.

'Yes! Oh my God, I have to get a dress, find the right shoes and accessories! So—much—work!' she said, not looking too disappointed about it either.

'That's...nice,' I mused. I really did try to be supportive.

She gave me a sympathetic look. 'I know you don't like parties, Avani. But I'd really like it if you'd come. It could be our one last chance to have fun together before coaching starts.'

One last chance—as if our lives were ending and this was a party to celebrate the occasion.

'Hmm...'

'Plus, we'll shop for dresses and the shoes to go with it—oh, and don't forget the makeovers.'

'Okay. I can work with that.'

'Yay!'

It seemed like things might not be so bad after all.

2

A Ray of Light

As the school bell rang, signalling the end of the day, I felt a wave of calm wash over me. It was strange; when I left for school in the morning, I was quite excited not to be at home. But now, I was not excited to be at school either. I was officially stuck between a rock and a hard place.

Like most of the students, my classmates who took the bus left in droves, as the buses ran on tight schedules. The fog had died down, and there were even some stray sun rays.

I waited for my mom to pick me up, standing in a small patch of sun, hands shoved in the pockets of my ill-fitted blazer, figuring out how to while away the rest of my day. Unlike Parnika, I didn't have demanding coaching assignments to fill my time. I typically felt proud of my free time, but now I was regretful of it.

'Hi, Avani,' a deep but hesitant voice called out to me.

I looked back and was utterly surprised at whom I saw.

'Oh hey, Shiv,' I smiled sheepishly.

Was a *boy* talking to *me*? Did he want to copy my homework? Or maybe he wanted my friends' numbers. That was usually why anyone of the opposite gender talked to me in school.

'School was so boring today, wasn't it?' he continued, smiling at me—more like smiling down at me. This guy was like a foot taller than me. In the much-dreaded regular 'health' checkups we had at school, I'd set a record for the shortest, at a good five feet, whereas Shiv had set the record for the tallest.

A million alarm bells went off in my mind. But my first thought was: what if my mom saw me talking to a boy? I would never hear the end of it.

'Yeah. It's been a bit difficult adjusting to school after the break,' I said. School was definitely not boring, per se. It was more existential-crisis-inducing, I would say.

'Everything's a bit bleak,' he commented, looking around. I'm sure he meant the weather. But for me, the meaning was completely different. Bleak was an understatement. But why was everything bleak for *him*? He was one of the all-rounder boys. The only 'shortcoming' I could think of was that he had poor vision, ergo, the glasses. Other than that, everything was perfect. Good grades, cool friends, athletic, nice hair—wait, why did I think of that last part?

I nodded, trying to peek over his shoulder to check if my mom had arrived.

'So, how did you spend your winter holidays?' he asked, shifting his weight between his legs. Was he nervous talking to me? We had been in the same class for a few years, yet we had never talked before. Surely, he wanted something from me.

'Uh…' I fumbled, wondering if two weeks of basically sleeping, eating and continuous media consumption was something to brag about. 'Not much…you know, the usual stuff.'

'So, basically watching movies?'

'Yeah, sure. I just watched the entire *Harry Potter* series again,' I said, giving him a sympathetic smile. It was the one book-to-movie adaptation I thought had been done well.

'Oh, I like Harry Potter too! Who is your favourite character?' his whole demeanour changed—he looked way more relaxed. Kind of the way he looked playing basketball with his friends during PE.

I pretended to think deeply about this. I already knew Snape was the obvious choice, but I didn't want to blurt out the answer and look too eager. Plus, I wanted to know if he made the right choice. People tend to agree with others' opinions when they make small talk.

'Mine's Snape, obviously. He's the best character,' he said, smiling.

'Oh! He's my favourite too,' I said, smiling back, peering at him through the sun's rays. I guess I was the one agreeing with his answer now. Wonder how that made me look.

'Um, Avani, I missed a few days of school before we closed for the winter holidays. Actually, my dad retired from his job, so my parents are moving back to their hometown. I was helping them move.'

'Oh, you're leaving?' I asked. Wow, the cute guy who is probably going to leave forever decides to talk to me *now*. Why couldn't he talk to me last year or the year before that? That's just my luck.

'No, I'll continue to attend coaching classes here only. My hometown isn't that good for non-med coaching.'

'Oh,' I said, surprised that coaching could be qualified as 'good' or 'bad'. Didn't they all teach the same stuff?

'So, anyway, I was hoping to borrow your notes for social science. I missed the days they taught that chapter about cricket,' he fidgeted with his coat button.

There it was. The true reason he wanted to talk to me. I knew it.

'Sure,' I resigned as I unzipped my backpack.

'No, no, I don't want to take the notebook from you, I guess you have to study for the test next week. Can you text me the photos, please?' he asked shyly.

I hesitated, 'Oh...sure.'

'Your number? Can I have it?' his voice shook.

I scribbled down the number on his notebook. My parents had bought me a phone when I graduated ninth grade. I used it mostly to text Parnika or ask for her notes.

I felt awkward now. If he had just wanted my notes, then why did he waste time trying to make small talk? He should've gotten straight to the point; it would've saved everyone's time and energy. Did he want Parnika's number too? I would be more than happy to oblige. Surely, her phone must be blowing up all day with texts from all the other friends that she had.

'So, what stream do you think you're choosing?' Shiv asked, his head cocked to one side.

What I should've said: 'I haven't really decided. It's because I'm a confused piece of crap who defers decisions till the last moment. Well, better get going now. A delightful tête-à-tête we had! Ta-ta!'

What I actually said: 'Oh, sorry, I have to go. My mom is waiting for me in the car.' And then ran off towards the school gate without saying goodbye. That's right—I literally chose to run away from the most important question on everyone's minds. I could feel that this habit would not bode well for my future. Why am I like this?

Mom hadn't actually come to pick me up yet, which was quite unusual. But I had to make sure that Shiv thought I'd disappeared, so I did what any rational teen would do. I hid behind a tree and hoped he wouldn't see me. I know; am I not the smartest girl in class?

Shiv seemed like a nice guy, though. He didn't seem rowdy like the other boys in class. Parnika had mentioned him a few times since both of them went to the same coaching class. I wondered what it was like to attend a 'second school', as Parnika called it.

For a long five minutes, I had to endure the awkwardness

that came with being the strange girl hiding behind a tree. I had to commit to the act; I couldn't let Shiv know I was lying. Thankfully, soon after, the driver finally pulled up in our car. Mom was sitting in the back, scrolling on her phone.

'Mom, you're late! I've been waiting for a while,' I complained, with extra exasperation in my voice, brushing off the twigs and the stray leaves from my clothes.

'Yeah, I lost track of time. I came home late from the college, and then I was making *pav bhaji* for you guys,' she apologized, rummaging through my backpack for my lunch box. She always checked to see if I came home hungry. Yes, she was *that* mom.

Somehow, the prospect of pav bhaji made me forget everything that had gone wrong today. When Mom made pav bhaji, all was right with the world—even if it lasted for just as long as it took to wipe my plate clean.

'Avani, you didn't touch the green beans!' she scolded, shoving the tiffin in my face. The smell of cold beans wafted into my face. Immediately, my gag reflex kicked in, but I held my breath. I didn't want to argue today.

'I don't know, Mom. I just don't like it,' I mumbled, opening the window on my side and feeling the biting wind on my face as the car started accelerating.

Even though I didn't match her gaze, I could feel her disapproving glare through the back of my neck. As always, it stung, and I knew I shouldn't have said anything. *What a disappointment,* I could almost hear her thoughts.

'What's this, Avani?' she asked. I heard paper rustling and turned around.

The 'Stream Question' stared at me once again, this time accompanied by the quizzical look on Mom's face. Nothing could be worse than this—Mom, the Stream Question and us being in a moving metal contraption for 20 minutes.

She began to read the form aloud, and my mind switched gears to come up with a contingency plan. How bad would the situation be if I made a run for it right now? Like, straight up, open the door and roll out of the car?

I shook my head. I couldn't do that. I still had pav bhaji to live for.

'You've already made your decision, right?'

'What do you mean?' I snapped back to reality.

'I thought you'd already decided—humanities, obviously,' she said, smoothing out the creases in the form and putting the paper back neatly between the pages of a notebook.

She sensed my dithering and continued, 'Beta, you spend all your free time reading novels, watching movies and doing God-knows-what on that laptop of yours. To seriously consider non-med, one needs to be devoted to their *academic* books, not the novels lying around the house. You won't be able to spend your time like that anymore if you take non-med. Besides...'

'Besides, what?'

'Beta, I don't want to hurt your feelings, but I honestly don't think you can do well in non-med,' she said, looking at me sympathetically. She had never looked at me like this before. Usually, it was, what I assumed, an expression of utter disappointment.

'What? Why?' I shot back.

'You're just not made for the constant hours of studying, hard work and mental toil. You're too...' she paused, weighing her next word carefully, 'delicate.'

'Oh!' My heart sank. *Delicate*. Was this how she really felt? Was I, indeed, not made for this? I could feel tears welling up in my eyes and a lump forming in my throat. I couldn't argue without my voice breaking. Maybe she was right. I was delicate.

I sighed, looking out the car window. I knew I finally had

to stop running from the Stream Question and decide, but I didn't realize the process could be so demoralizing. Mom was thinking along the right lines. I had to take a fully informed decision. I needed to know if I was ready for what awaited me on the other side.

'You've made pav bhaji today?' I asked, turning back to look at her when my eyes had stopped stinging.

She nodded and smiled.

I had had enough of decision-making for today. I just wanted to go home, eat pav bhaji and do my homework.

3

'Stop Acting Like a Child'

My dad and I often went for walks to Sukhna Lake. We'd try to solve each other's problems: he would discuss how his work was going as the managing director of a government department, and I would discuss what was happening at school. He wasn't the one with most of the issues, though. Usually, he'd help me create study plans for upcoming tests, and before the said tests, when I would inevitably freak out, he would reassure me that I'd studied enough to score well. After the tests, we'd discuss my score and how well I'd done in class. Sometimes I'd joke that my dad could most definitely earn good money as an unqualified but effective therapist. He was kind of the opposite of my mother in that way—his advice was usually encouraging and didn't annihilate my self-esteem.

We would try to squeeze these walks into our extremely busy schedules on most days. Oh, who am I kidding? I wasn't busy at all. I just did a very good job of pretending to study, reading or doing important 'research' on my laptop, i.e. working on my *Harry Potter* fan fiction.

Today, I was dying to go on a walk with him. My mind had been swarming with so many thoughts, and my usual outlet of writing in my journal wasn't helping. I needed 'professional' help.

'Ready, Avani?' he asked, walking into my room, his slightly rotund figure looking even more expansive, bundled up in a puffy jacket and wool scarf. I wish they'd allow this kind of garb at our school, instead of the polyester garbage we had to wear.

Sukhna Lake, though it looked beautiful and pristine in the day, had a different vibe to it when the darkness set in. The knee-high lawn lamps lining the road lit up only half of the path, leaving the people wandering by the lake as shadowy silhouettes. In a way, it was really calming not to evaluate strangers' appearances and not be evaluated yourself.

After walking quietly for a while, the Stream Question festering in my mind, I decided to finally attack it. Dad was my last option, the only voice of reason.

Looking into the distance at the locked-up tower, which had been named the Suicide Point, I began my briefing.

'So, Dad, today we were given a form in school. We have to fill our preference for streams in eleventh class and submit it at the end of this month.' I let all of it out in one breath, adding, 'Parnika has already decided.'

I don't know why I said that last part. Perhaps it was to address the severity and urgency of the situation since my super-smart best friend had already decided and I hadn't.

'I thought you had decided your stream?' he asked.

'Nope,' I declared gingerly. He was the only one I could be honest with, but I was still scared of his response.

'Okay, so what are your options?'

I'm pretty sure Dad knew all the options. He always followed a very logical decision-making process and always started from the basics. It's one of the things I admired most about him.

'Non-medical, commerce, medical and the humanities,' I counted my options on my fingers.

'And are there any which have been completely eliminated from our choices?' he asked. I liked how he said 'our', like we were in this together.

'Yeah, well, I don't have any interest in economics or biology. They are probably the two subjects I dislike the most. So, we can eliminate medical and commerce. So, it's either non-med or humanities.'

'So, why don't you want to take non-medical and do IIT coaching?'

I cringed at how quickly he chose to ignore humanities. I wasn't sure how to articulate my feelings about IIT coaching to him—my fear of not being good enough, not being able to work hard enough and subsequently failing.

'Why does choosing non-med translate to coaching for IIT?' I asked in earnest.

'After your class 12 board exams, you'd have to sit for the Joint Entrance Exam—or JEE as you may know it. The results of JEE will decide what engineering colleges you apply to. And IIT coaching will prepare you for these entrance exams,' he said.

'I'm not sure that I like science,' I admitted.

'Why not?' he asked sincerely.

'I mean, I do like learning new concepts at school. It is satisfying when I finally understand something difficult.'

'And you get good marks in school.'

'Well, yeah. But…' I trailed off. How was I supposed to explain that I felt like I wouldn't be good enough for IIT coaching? I had seen the questions on Parnika's coaching assignment. They seemed otherworldly and scary. I wouldn't know how to begin to solve them.

Before I could formulate a response, Dad abruptly paused our conversation and took his phone out of his pocket to answer a call. I was annoyed. We were having such an important conversation about my future and a decision that could alter the whole course of my life, and here, my dad had paused that conversation to talk to a guy from his office who wanted his opinion on planting some *trees*.

Okay, I know climate change is real, and his job is really important. Maybe, like me, everyone at his office also thinks he's a great voice of reason, and being who he is, he helps them as he helps me. He *is* very logical.

I tried to calm myself down, using logic, i.e., the Dad way. I should look at nature—that always works. I stared to my left at the dark lake, but it didn't offer even a semblance of comfort. Instead, it filled me with fear. What lurked in the darkness?

A few metres ahead, some children were playing on the stone seating area that separated the walkway from the lake. Gosh, I wish I was like them, not knowing what lay next—and not caring for the most part either, just making up new games to play in the park every evening, going home to eat home-cooked meals and watch cartoons, going to bed at 9.00 p.m. looking forward to a new day and then doing the same things over again. My life was exactly like this before today happened.

'Where were we?'

'Uh…IIT coaching?' I offered.

'Yes! By the way, a few days ago, I met Parnika's dad. He was telling me about a prominent coaching centre's orientation class on this Friday. It's open to all students in tenth grade who are looking to take up non-medical. Perhaps this orientation will help you figure out what the preparation is actually like. You can ask them all the questions you have and decide after that.'

My dad and Parnika's have been friends since college, where they'd both studied engineering.

'No. I don't want to go,' I complained. Thinking about going inside a coaching centre made me feel nauseous, not the excited-in-a-good-way kind of nauseous but in a doomsday-is-approaching way.

'Why? It's a great opportunity.'

'I don't know…I just don't feel like it,' I murmured. 'I'd rather stay at home on a Friday night and browse the internet for hours on end. Like a normal teenager, you know?'

'Avani, come on! You need to stop acting like a child now. You're going to be 16 this year,' he protested.

I don't know what came over me, but I just wanted to run away from him. I began to walk faster, determined to reach the other side of the lake even though it was a good 500 metres away. I wasn't able to exit the horrible conversation with Mom earlier in the day because we were in a moving car, but here, I had free rein.

You're going to be 16 this year. I felt like the protagonist of a Disney movie who's about to be cursed.

Stop acting like a child? Where did that come from? I was acting the same as yesterday and the day before that. Why did no one say anything before today?

I was convinced that there was something very wrong with the day, or perhaps my stars weren't favourable, whatever that meant. I wasn't into horoscopes, but I would definitely go home and look up when this 'bad time' would pass.

'I think it'll be good for you!' Dad called out, trying to catch up with me.

I looked back and couldn't help stifle a laugh at Dad with his various winter accoutrements falling off as he tried to run. I really couldn't stay mad at him for more than a minute.

I thought Dad would help me decide right then. I did not want to attend some weird 'orientation session' in some shady coaching centre to help me decide. I wanted Dad to just *tell me* the right thing to do. Why couldn't he do that? My parents and teachers had always told me what to do, and despite insistent protests from my end, I would do whatever they asked.

Was I just supposed to magically start making decisions for

myself once I was about to turn 16? If this is how it was, I absolutely hated it.

'Avani, I'll come with you if you want,' he said between breaths. I slowed down and allowed him to catch up with me.

'Okay, I guess I can go if you're also coming,' I relented.

I felt like a clingy kid on their first day of school. I would probably do much better if I could take all my exams with my dad just sitting next to me—not telling me the answers but just being there.

On the other hand, Mom would probably sit next to me and complain about the parts of the syllabus that I had glossed over and how much time I had wasted reading the newest release of *The Hunger Games* trilogy.

4

Pathway to Success

I'd checked my horoscope on Tuesday, and it turned out that the stars would not be in my favour for a while. How long, you ask? Well, two years, to be exact.

Shiv: Hey, you there?

I glanced at my phone and I rolled my eyes. It was Friday afternoon. I was finally back from school and ready to sleep off my headache, which I'd acquired the moment I woke up today.

Avani: What's up?

Even after I'd supplied him with all the notes that he had asked for, Shiv had been trying to make more conversation with me throughout the week. He would ask me questions about my favourite colour or my favourite movie. I wondered if he was trying to figure out the answers to my 'forgot password' questions. Was he going to ask me my grandmother's maiden name next?

Shiv: Not much. I'm going to the orientation for a coaching centre tonight.

Avani: Which one? Is it Hellen by chance? I'm going there tonight.

Shiv: Yes, Hellen. That's unexpected LOL. I thought you'd

planned a Harry Potter movie marathon for today.

Avani: Well, yeah. That's how I usually spend my Friday nights. But coaching is more exciting, isn't it?

Shiv: Ah, I see. Yeah, I guess I'm also somewhat excited.

He wasn't very good at catching sarcasm. But then again, text messages are hardly the best medium to convey tone.

Avani: How do you usually spend your Fridays?

Shiv: I usually spend them completing coaching assignments. Or hanging around my family when I'm lucky enough to not be given any assignments.

I was hoping that today would be the day that would bring the much-awaited clarity to all my doubts about the mysterious 'IIT coaching'.

I wondered why they call it 'orientation'. It's not like I was a part of their institute yet. In the books I've read, colleges and universities have orientations with coffee or punch or a cheese plate and crackers. However, I had a feeling that would not be the case here.

The anxious, nerve-racking wait began as soon as I got home from school. When my dad finally showed up, I rushed out to his car.

'We're going to get late,' I muttered, looking at him with my eyes narrowed.

'It will be fine, Avani,' he shifted his attention to his phone.

I know he was trying to reassure me, as he often did before my exams, but it didn't help. The thought of walking in late and all eyes being on me—even with the comforting presence of my dad—turned my stomach into knots. To be honest, being late was only the tip of the proverbial iceberg of my worries.

I took a deep breath as our car lined up behind several others at the Sector 17 intersection. The timer read 200 seconds to go. I looked at the cars beside me. The passengers looked mellow. Some of them were listening to soulful Punjabi music. Why couldn't I be chill like them?

When we finally reached, I slammed the car door shut and ran towards a monolith of a building. In my hurry, I didn't even notice the big lit-up sign at the top, which read 'HELLEN', with the 'EN' part not lit up. Dad trailed behind.

'We'll get a seat, Avani. Relax,' he attempted to calm me once more.

That's exactly what didn't happen, though. A receptionist sitting at an unnecessarily large desk directed us to a classroom in the basement—nothing if not a sinister beginning. The classroom was chock full of students and parents rifling through brochures and discussing tips to increase productivity. Since we couldn't find a place to sit, two chairs were brought in from the next classroom and dragged to the very front, next to the dais. *Wow, great*. Front row seats are *never* a good idea. Cricket matches? Honestly, I'm never going to a cricket match, so it doesn't matter to me. But I assume you're more likely to get hit by the ball. Water parks? You get the most drenched. Zoos? Most chances of being eaten alive. Classrooms? Same as zoos.

As we walked from the back of the classroom to the front, I saw some familiar faces in the sea of students—particularly Shiv and Parnika. I sat down on my seat, realizing my heart was beating extremely fast. There were so many people around me, almost 150 students stuffed in this damp, almost prison-like classroom. The bad lighting made everyone look a bit ghastlier than they would've looked normally.

Why were there so many people here? Wasn't this just some shady coaching centre Parnika's dad recommended? A shady coaching centre wouldn't have a reception like a hotel lobby or a big banner with the word 'Shark' hung up across the blackboard. Were they asking us to be sharks or were we actually in a shark enclosure? Was I about to get eaten up?

A tall, lanky, clean-shaved man with thick glasses—who honestly looked like he hadn't seen the sun in months—walked to the front of the classroom, his back a little hunched, and adjusted the microphone attached to his half-sweater. Wow, they had microphones in classes! Was it really that big of a deal?

'Good evening, students and parents,' he boomed uncharacteristically, and the room fell silent. Once everyone's eyes had turned towards the dais, he continued, 'I'm Sahil, one of the teachers here at the Hellen Institute.'

He really enunciated every word quite strongly, making everything sound more official than it actually was.

'We have produced 2,000 students in IITs in the past few years, more than 100 of them graduating with computer science degrees from the top IITs. These students, from Hellen centres all over India, have gone on to work at renowned tech companies and earn crores of rupees per year. Many of them have also pursued master's and PhDs in their respective fields at internationally top-ranking universities.'

I straightened up in my seat. It didn't seem *so* lame now. Still, I couldn't help but find it funny when he said that they had 'produced' students in IIT. Where did they originate from—the ground? Did they just pop up from the ground like moles into an IIT? I chuckled slightly.

The teacher, probably used to spotting troublemakers in class, located me in a flash.

'What's so funny?' his eyes narrowed. Instinctively, I shot up out of my seat and stood in rapt attention.

Suddenly everyone's heads turned towards me. All 150 eyes, most of them spectacled, peered at me judgmentally. My cheeks burned, and I could feel my face go red. Would it be weird if I made a run for it? Move to Mexico, learn Spanish and maybe become a Hindi teacher. I could live among the alpacas and limit my social interaction.

In a thin voice, I replied, 'Nothing, sir.'

'What's your name?' he asked, still looking at me with a weirdly amused expression on his face. Why couldn't he just continue prattling like a normal teacher? Why was I suddenly the object of all these teachers' animosity?

'Avani,' I said, looking at the whiteboard behind him, not able to maintain eye contact. I couldn't bear to look anywhere else, especially not at a particular someone from my class.

'Ms Avani,' he said, putting one hand on his hip and wading through two rows of chairs, closer to where I was sitting. 'I've never seen you before. Were you a part of our foundation course?'

'Sorry, what course?' I blanked out.

He turned to look at the class. 'The foundation course at Hellen is for those who decide early on and commit to their goal. Students from sixth class onwards can opt for it. Foundation courses help to develop your IQ, and logical and analytical thinking. Compared to freshers, students who have sat for a foundation course tend to have a much better understanding of basic concepts and are able to grasp and master IIT prep much faster.'

I stood at the front of the class, like the before picture in his advertisement about the foundation course that could've made me smart enough to know that I should not have laughed during the first few minutes of the orientation.

I remained silent, hoping he'd move on, but he decided to make an example out of me.

'So, Ms Avani, how did you do on your maths midterm?'

He expected me to divulge my marks in a room full of overachievers—the audacity!

It took a while for my brain to register that he actually expected an answer. I'm sure that helped convince the class that a foundation course is absolutely necessary. *You're welcome, sir.* I could hardly remember when I scored well on tests, it was always when I did poorly that my brain decided to make the feeling a core memory. For example, the time when I scored 85.5/100 in Hindi in seventh class is ingrained deeply in my mind, still haunting me from time to time.

'Probably 95/100,' I said, finally meeting his gaze, my voice not so feeble now. Hey, they were good marks, I was proud of myself for working hard.

Unfazed, he replied, 'That's great. However, with our foundation courses, we strive to make sure our school students always score above 95 in their school exams, and most of them actually do! We hope we can take that 95 to 100 if you join our JEE prep course, Avani. We strive to achieve nothing but the best here at Hellen.'

I'd always thought 95 was good enough. Wasn't it?

'Okay, sir. Thank you,' I said, plopping back down on my seat, silently praying that this fiasco would be over soon and the ground would open up and swallow me whole.

Next came a video of testimonials from students who had scored top marks in the JEE Advanced examination. One after the other, adolescent boys introduced themselves along with the college they'd been accepted into like it was their last name. They ended their introduction with a beaming, 'Hellen is the pathway to success,' as the inspirational piano music grew to a crescendo and the screen faded to white between each success story. Behind the lenses, their eyes looked exhausted. Why weren't there any testimonials from female students? Why did everyone follow a template just to introduce themselves? Why were they convincing us in such an emotionless, almost machine-like manner?

What was I getting myself into?

The piano music blared loudly out of the ancient speakers for the last time, and Sahil sir returned to the front of the class once again. He went on to talk about the two-part national entrance exam called joint entrance examination or JEE, 'The first exam, called JEE-Main, is a kind of standardized examination to get accepted—no, to even apply—for undergraduate programs in engineering, architecture and the natural sciences. This exam is held after the twelfth class board exams. Many colleges and universities accept or reject students based solely on the score and rank obtained in the JEE-Main.'

He stopped and took a sip of water from a glass of water that was kept on the teacher's desk on the dais. Then, he spoke with renewed enthusiasm, 'But for the best of the best—the Indian… Institutes…Of…Technology—' he accentuated each word with a pause and gestured wildly with his hands, '—the game has just begun. See, for IIT aspirants, JEE-Main is simply a qualifying examination. The JEE Advanced exam comes next. This is the big league. This is a six-hour-long exam with a two-hour lunch break in the middle. *This* determines whether you get into an IIT or not. Only around 1 per cent of the lakhs of students who take the JEE Main make it through to the IITs—the hallowed halls of Indian technical education, the place where everyone wants to get into. You'll spend the next two years preparing for those six hours.'

He stopped and breathed into his mic as the sheer enormity, or perhaps the scarcity of the numbers washed across the room. Someone actually gasped in the back.

If Sahil sir's roasting didn't scare and intimidate me, this barrage of information surely did. Sitting in one place for six hours for an exam? I could barely do three hours at school.

My breathing finally returned to normal when he finished his lecture. The whole time, I was afraid that he'd call on me again, finding some other way to disparage my self-esteem. He had already succeeded to quite an extent. A few students and parents raised their hands into the air and waited eagerly as he answered each of their questions.

I sat quietly, stunned by the information overload. One question echoed itself louder and louder into existence: could a person like *me* do this?

'Okay, students, the talent hunt test will be starting soon. Parents, please leave the classroom.'

Suddenly, the entire atmosphere changed. There was a palpable buzz of competition in the air, as everyone around me took out their stationery boxes and scrambled to find good seats. Students took out their notebooks and started revising; others smirked overconfidently at them. Someone even started chanting prayers.

What the hell?

I looked at my dad quizzically. My heart rate, which had finally returned to a normal pace at the end of the session, now skyrocketed again. I thought I was safe now. I guess I thought wrong.

'I'm sorry, I had no idea there's a test today,' Dad said as he got up from his chair. 'It's okay, I'll wait outside. It's just two hours. Maybe I'll have a little chat with Parnika's dad.'

Yeah, go have a little chat with him. Why don't you have some tea and crumpets together?

'I'm not prepared, Dad! I can't take the test!' I protested.

'I'm sure it'll just be a normal test. You'll do great, beta. Give me a call when you're done, okay?' he patted me on the back and walked away. I couldn't believe it. How could my dad, the most logical man on earth, not know about the test? Or did he hide it from me on purpose?

Sahil sir walked to the front of the class with a big stack of question papers. 'Attention, students. Now that the parents are gone, we can finally have some fun!'

I heard some laughter from the back. I prayed to God that that was sarcastic laughter.

'If some of you still don't know about the talent hunt exam, let me explain: The first 30 highest scores will get coaching scholarships, and the first 100 will get into our top batch. But don't worry, even if you're not one of them, most of you will be included in our other batches!' he said, handing me a sheet of paper and moving past.

'Think of this test as an opportunity to study among the best students within the country. The test will be in multiple-choice questions format, similar to JEE-Main. You have two hours starting...' he looked at his watch, 'now!'

Talent hunt? Was answering MCQ questions some kind of talent?

I focused my attention on the paper and realized that most of the questions were from the concepts that had been taught in the ninth and tenth grades. Hey, maybe I had a chance. Some questions seemed to have familiar words. Plus, it was MCQ, so I already had the correct answer in front of me—how hard could that be?

As I began with the physics section, I knew something was wrong. The words were familiar, I understood the questions, but I had no idea how to solve them. All I knew were the basic formulas, which surprisingly kept me going in circles. This wasn't like school exams, where I'd be able to quickly figure out the solution, mentally referring to similar questions I'd practised as preparation. At the very least, I'd write some part of the solution and get partial marks. I was really starting to see the downsides of MCQs.

After two hours were up, I slumped in my seat, feeling like someone had just boiled my brain for the duration of the exam. I was overheated, uncomfortable and dejected. Was this a glimpse into my life for the next two years?

∽

I made my way up the basement stairs to the lobby, hoping to find Dad somewhere in the midst of the sea of students, all chattering amongst themselves. Under different circumstances, I would've too, but I was incapable of forming coherent sentences at that point. Everyone seemed excited and relieved as if they'd expected the test to be harder than it actually was. My stomach dropped as I saw someone very familiar looking directly at me.

'Oye, Avani!' Shiv waved from behind a group of students. It was unusual to see him wearing something other than our school uniform. He looked very relaxed, like he'd just returned from a vacation in the Caribbean. In comparison, I looked like the unfortunate soul caught in a tidal wave on the said vacation. He sifted through the crowd to reach me. 'I didn't notice you in class.'

After the disaster of a test, I was completely defeated, but no way was I going to let that show on my face.

'Oh, I didn't notice you either!' I lied, with what I hoped was a confident smile on my face. It was quite strange talking to him in person—we'd been texting each other but hadn't really spoken face-to-face since the day he'd asked for my number.

'Yep. So, you're doing this too, huh?' he said, chuckling casually. He looked happy. Like today was just another day.

I shrugged. 'I might.'

Awkward silence. I looked around the reception area and saw

imposing standing posters of kids wearing grey T-shirts which read 'Hellen: Pathway to Success' and doing the victory sign. Various ranks and names of entrance exams were plastered on the pictures. I wonder if they ever felt confused or unsure about their life choice to do IIT coaching—probably not. They probably knew they were destined to do this since the day they were born.

'How did the test go?'

'It was fine, I guess. What about you?'

Maybe my test actually did go fine. Maybe it was this way for everyone. In that case, relatively, I could've done well too.

'It was quite easy. Most of the questions were similar to those in the practice book we'd got in our foundation course,' he said dismissively.

'How long have you been going here?' I asked, finally mustering up the courage to ask something useful for once.

'Since sixth class,' he shrugged.

'Even Parnika has been taking coaching since then.' I blurted out.

He nodded. 'Yeah, I know. She and I usually sit together in class.'

'That's cool, I guess,' I said, looking down at my still-clammy, sweaty hands. 'I've never been to a coaching class before, so this is all a bit new to me.'

'A bit new' was an understatement.

'Oh, that's okay. You do pretty well in school, anyway,' he said, smiling at me.

'Oh. Thanks,' I said. Did I do well at school? Probably yes. But was I going to do well in this test or these classes? The thought was enough to send me into a downward spiral.

It was hard for me to maintain eye contact with most people. Instead, I fixated my eyes on his chest, which was weird, but I just couldn't bring myself to meet his eyes and attempt to read his expression. It was too overwhelming.

'Hi, Shiv! Avani!'

I broke my borderline-creepy gaze and looked up to find Parnika looking fabulous in a pink crop top, high-waisted white jeans and heeled boots, making her seem even taller than she already was. Who wears white jeans anymore except the Real Housewives? It's a disaster waiting to happen. She still managed to look great, though.

'Hey, Parnika, I like your—'

'So, Shiv, will you apply here to be coached for JEE?' she ignored me completely.

Standing next to Parnika and Shiv made me feel like an oaf. They were tall, graceful and smart, whereas I was quite literally and figuratively the complete opposite.

'Yeah, I'll try it out. It's been good so far till the tenth grade. So far, the teachers are actually good at their jobs, unlike at school. My older brother tells me that a good teacher can be the difference between simply qualifying and actually getting into IIT. I've heard that Sahil sir teaches really well, but he only ever picks the top batch,' Shiv explained. 'I just hope I get in.'

'Oh, of course, you'll get in. We'll all get in!' Parnika said shrilly, punching his shoulder. 'And yeah, sir is *great*.'

This was their world, and I'd just mistakenly stepped into it, kind of like Alice in a dystopian Wonderland. How were they so sure? So confident? Meanwhile, I was directionless and confused.

'You okay, Avani?' Parnika butted into my inner monologue, giving me the side-eye.

'Yep. I'm great,' I said, nodding a bit too eagerly.

'By the way, are you guys excited for the farewell or what? I heard there will be a couple's dance as well,' Parnika said. Why would she choose to say that now?

'When is it, by the way?' Shiv asked, looking directly at me.

'Uh...' I murmured. How would I know?

'It's in one week from now—the weekend of next week. Before we break for the preparatory holidays for board exams,' Parnika said. She had all the answers.

'Oh. Nice. I am looking forward to it, actually,' Shiv said, still looking at me. Okay, how could this guy maintain eye contact for so long? I could learn a thing or two from him.

'Avani'd rather stay at home. Isn't that right?' Parnika said, elbowing me in my stomach. *Oof*, I did not expect that. She was always so high-energy.

'I mean, yes, I'd like to. But there's no way Parnika would let me.' I smiled. I was kind of grateful to her for that. I got dragged to so many social occasions because of her.

'That's right,' she said, switching to business mode. 'So, Shiv, did you complete that advanced calculus assignment? I wanted to ask a few questions about that.'

'Yeah, sure. Let me call you once I reach home, and we can discuss,' he replied.

∞

When I was finally able to exit the overcrowded hall, I spotted our car and quickly beelined towards it.

'So, how did you like it?' Dad asked once we were in the car, away from all the mess in that weird Hellen hell.

'Oh. I'm pretty sure what I'm going to do now. Thanks,' I said, turning to face the car window, looking out at the topiary on Matka Chowk, the landmark Chandigarh roundabout, trying to forget today ever happened.

5

Dinner Table Fiasco

I spent a good amount of time updating my Harry Potter–Draco Malfoy fan fiction over the weekend, trying to ignore everything else around me.

> Parnika: Hey Avani, want to hang out on Sunday and pick our dresses for the farewell?
>
> Avani: Hi, sorry, can't do. I have an upset stomach.
>
> Parnika: Oh, take care!

I don't know why, but I didn't want to deal with her high-energy self this weekend.

> Shiv: Hi, sup?

I groaned, going 'offline' real quick.

I had no idea why he was still finding new ways to talk to me. I suspected he still wanted my civics notes. He could just ask. Plus, it wasn't like my notes were all that great. Once my hand would start cramping up while copying down the answers, all the letters would look the same. Also, I had a habit of listening to the band My Chemical Romance while writing down the answers, leading my notebook to be sprinkled with some unconsciously written emo lyrics.

My Sunday evening blues set in quickly. I wasn't really looking forward to going to school tomorrow. I had to submit the form by the end of this coming week. Plus, the farewell party was next weekend, and I didn't even want to think about that.

As I made my way to the dining table, I realized my dad would be back from the gym, and I could bet a lot of money that he would want to ask me the Stream Question. Suddenly, an uneasiness filled my stomach, making me feel not so hungry anymore. But I knew what to do now, and I had faith Dad would take my side. We were all in this together, right?

'Avani, how are you?' Dad asked from the bathroom in the hallway over the noise of the faucet.

'I'm okay!' I replied. What else could I say? That I was writing a *definitely PG-13* fan fiction story about two *Harry Potter* characters for most of the weekend while listening to obscure Lady Gaga songs from her meat dress phase? It was the least I could do to avoid thinking about the important life decisions that had been forced upon me.

After we were all seated, the usual silence filled the room. Well, apart from the whirring fans of the oil heater in the corner. Typically, Dad and I would discuss some current world news. I mean, I would much rather discuss the latest YouTuber scandal, but I don't think anyone in my family would appreciate the intricacies of the social dynamics between a particular pair of beauty gurus. Mom would sit in silence, adding nothing to the conversation and quietly judging us—I was sure of it. The only time she would speak would be to ask if we wanted more lauki, the worst possible vegetable to ever exist—it was mushy and tasted like nothing.

Though today Dad didn't continue our ongoing riveting discussion on the possibilities of a deadly virus taking over the world. Instead, he abruptly spoke, 'Oh yes, I forgot to tell you—today, I got a call from Hellen, and they said that they would be

Dinner Table Fiasco

releasing the results of the talent hunt exam this Friday.'

He dug into the lauki. Mom had asked me a while ago for my sabzi choice for dinner, and when I said paneer, she told me that she'd be making lauki instead. I mean, why ask at all?

'Okay...so?'

Dad had a bemused expression on his face. 'We can admit you in the centre after that!' he said, as if it was a hospital or a psych ward.

I guess this was the time to let the bomb drop. Finally. I'm sure Dad would understand. He was just that kind of guy—he'd always been on my side so far. Still, the uneasiness refused to leave the pit of my stomach.

'Papa, I don't want to do non-med. I'll take humanities,' I blurted.

Mom was unfazed, slurping on some tomato soup. On the other hand, Dad's mouth had dropped opening into an O and his eyebrows were raised like he'd received some critical news about a project going down in flames back in the office. Was I that project? Had I messed things up?

'Look, Avani, there are a lot of options for college if you take non-med. You can basically do anything other than becoming a doctor. If you take humanities, your options after school are limited. Think about your future,' Dad began to convince me, his eyes intently gazing into mine. Did he not hear me?

'I don't get it. Dad, you're the one who told me to stop acting like a child. I'm trying to be mature and take my own decisions!' I said, feeling the heat rise up on my cheeks.

'No, it's not that, Avani. You can't just make this decision on a whim. You should understand the severity of this choice you're making right now. It could change your entire path for the future, and—' Dad started with his lecture. I knew how this would go. I had heard him sermonizing on his opinions for hours and hours, until the people around him would just give up and agree.

Then, I did the unexpected. I cut him off. 'I've made my decision, Papa. You are forcing your ideas on me! Stop lecturing me like you always do. I don't want to take non-med, I don't want to do the stupid, depressing IIT coaching. I want to take humanities. It's final.'

'Avani, come on. You are being illogical, and you're not thinking about your future. Give non-med a chance. You should think about your life and your career,' Dad said.

'I don't know what my future career is!' I blurted out.

'In that case, it is most logical to take non-med. You can do anything you want after the twelfth grade. You can even figure out what you want to do after finishing your BTech degree. Think about your future salary, if not your career. Engineering graduates get paid really well. Whereas if you pursue humanities, you'll find it extremely difficult to get a well-paying job.'

Why was he making this about money? I was about to add more fuel to the fire, defending myself, when Mom interrupted, 'Let me say something for once? Avani, I think you should take humanities.'

I couldn't believe this conversation was happening. But the most unbelievable thing was my mom actually taking an interest in the conversation. Although, it was more of an argument at this point.

'What?' Dad gave a quizzical look to Mom. Some lauki dribbled down his chin. Ugh.

'I do agree with you on the jobs and salary front. But preparing for all the engineering entrance exams is really hard, and we all know that she is too soft, too delicate, too sensitive for the competition. Besides, you already know how much she likes to spend her time reading fiction novels, watching movies and writing stories. There won't be any time for all of that if she takes up

JEE coaching. She won't be able to do it. She'll be much happier and more comfortable in humanities. We can afford to support her financially if she needs us to do that for a while.'

That hurt. She really didn't believe in me.

'What do you mean she won't be able to do it? She always scores top marks in the school exams. She's a diligent student. If she can't do it, who can?' Dad persisted, a stern look on his face.

'Dad, do you know how terribly that Hellen test went? Those were the worst two hours of my life.' I felt strange talking about my 'failure' in front of him. I'd never had one to talk about before.

'It was just one test, Avani. I'm sure it was not as bad as you're making it out to be. Besides, you weren't prepared. I'm sure you'll do great in the future tests.'

'*No, I wouldn't*. I'm just not as smart or prepared as the others. Didn't you hear what that teacher said during the orientation? He said that foundation courses were really important. Do you know some of my classmates have been going to coaching since the sixth grade? I'll never be able to compete with them. What's the point of going to JEE coaching now?'

Dad scolded, 'Avani, you're the one who didn't want to go to coaching. You remember we asked you when you entered eighth grade, right? You said that you were already doing so well in school, so you didn't need coaching.'

'We can't do anything about it now. Now I'm one month away from graduating tenth grade, and I'm not prepared for this,' I mumbled, looking at my ghee-soaked roti, which was cold as papad now.

'But you've always done so well in school exams. You didn't need that foundation course!' Dad said, the amount of exasperation immeasurable on his face.

'There's a lot of difference between school exams and JEE questions,' I said, holding my voice to a medium. I didn't want to raise my voice. Instead, I wanted to minimize it. Disappear.

'You're smart enough to learn things now, Avani. I believe in you!' He looked at me with hope in his eyes.

'No, I'm not,' I said, my voice starting to break. 'I really can't. Mom is right. I can't.'

I had made my decision. I was going to choose humanities. I was going to stay in school and attend classes. I would do very well in school exams, as I've always done. I wouldn't have to attend JEE coaching or go into that scary underground classroom ever again. I wouldn't have to become a part of Parnika and Shiv's world of complex maths questions and unknown Greek alphabet variables. I wouldn't have to compete to be in the top 1 per cent. I would go to a nice college for the humanities in Delhi perhaps; maybe I could take up English as a subject.

Yeah, that sounded nice. It sounded familiar, safe and easy. Even Mom would be satisfied with my decision, for once. I'm sure Dad would come around.

I couldn't do non-med and JEE coaching. I knew that I just wasn't good enough.

6

Gatekeeping

On Monday, I woke up with a headache. Again. Was this going to be a frequent occurrence now? I'd made a special ponytail today—as much as was possible with my shoulder-length hair. I was hoping the high ponytail (with a side braid, yeah, I went all out) would serve as a distraction from my swollen eyes.

Parnika was absent. I was left feeling slighted that she didn't tell me she wasn't coming to class today. I could have stayed at home too, or at least I would have mentally prepared myself to be alone in class. Well, not really alone, the rest of the students were there—but still, I didn't have many friends other than her.

Although, I guess it was karma for lying to her about my sickness.

As I was rummaging through my backpack, looking for the history book for the next lecture, there was a tap on my shoulder.

'Hey Avani,' Shiv said, looking down at me as he stood in the aisle.

'Oh, hi,' I said. Why was he always so interested in talking to me? It was kind of annoying. But also, I didn't mind. What the hell?

'I see Parnika has left you today,' he said, smiling.

'Yep. She's absent,' I said, finally finding the book.

Suddenly, the teacher walked into the class. Shiv was still standing in the aisle. He glanced over at the empty seat next to mine and raised his eyebrows at me. Damn, this guy was smooth!

I nodded lightly so as to not seem too eager. I'd been dying of loneliness the entire four hours I'd spent at school so far.

The teacher started with the lecture, which could've made even an insomniac fall asleep. The thing was, I hated my history lectures—but I liked reading the textbook. But only when it was not for an exam.

I was suddenly very aware of Shiv's presence next to me. Slowly, I turned my gaze to him, still facing the class so as to not make Shiv aware that I was checking him out. It was wrong, I knew. I should focus on history and my studies, especially since final exams were coming around.

But there was something about Shiv—his black, straight, well-groomed hair and his bright smile. He had semi-muscular arms, probably since he was very into sports.

I shook my head. This was not the time to like a guy.

'You okay?' Shiv whispered, looking at me.

'Yeah,' I said, quickly bringing my gaze back to the teacher.

'So, how's stuff?' Shiv asked, glancing at me. Did he know? That I was awkwardly looking at him? Ugh, kill me now. Send me to hell already.

'Stuff is fine.' Not really. I had cried for so long after last night's dinner fiasco that I could hardly keep my eyes open now. 'What about you?'

'My parents vacated their house yesterday,' he said, his voice solemn.

'Oh,' I said, not expecting this serious turn. 'So, where are you going to live now?'

'I'm going to live as a paying guest in this room that's pretty close to Hellen,' he said.

'How is it?'

'Well, it's a room with two single beds, a cupboard and a

study table. I may even get a roommate soon,' he said, a slightly dejected look on his face. 'It kind of sucks, to be honest.'

'Oh.' I didn't know what to say to make him feel better.

He was fidgeting with the eraser I'd lent him a few minutes ago.

'I wanted to ask you something,' I said.

Shiv immediately froze. 'Okay. Go ahead,' he said after a few seconds of quiet.

'I wanted to know, how did you decide on taking non-medical and going for JEE coaching?' I asked.

He unfroze, shrugged, saying, 'There was nothing to decide. I like maths and science and do well in exams. I mean, I knew I was going to do it since sixth grade.'

I also liked maths and science and got decent marks in exams. But I didn't know if that was enough for non-medical and JEE coaching.

'My brother is a few years older than me, and he guided me a bit,' he continued.

'What is he doing now?'

'He's a software engineer in New York. He earns more than three crore rupees a year, you know?'

'So, he's your inspiration.'

'Yeah, you could say that.'

'What else has he told you about JEE coaching?' I kind of felt like I was interviewing him.

He hesitated, 'It's just that it's quite intense and cut-throat. He told me that it was very draining. There is hardly any time for anything other than studying and attending classes.' His words reminded me of what Mom had said.

'Do you think the humanities are easier?' I mumbled.

He chuckled. 'Definitely. Non-med isn't a good choice if you aren't mentally prepared for it. Be prepared to fight the odds.

That's what my bhaiya told me. I mean, with only around a 1 per cent acceptance rate, getting admission at an IIT would be definitely more difficult than getting into a decent humanities college.'

He sounded like he was trying to gatekeep non-med from me by scaring me with statistics. Was I scared by him?

The window was open, the cool winter air was flowing in, but somehow the seat I was sitting in started to feel stifling. I squished myself between Shiv and the desk to get out of my seat, not saying a word to him.

'Sorry ma'am, I need to go,' I said to the teacher, walking swiftly out of the classroom.

The hallway outside was deserted. Looking outside a window, I saw the busy streets of Chandigarh. People drove on the streets in their two-wheelers and cars wearing puffy jackets and monkey caps. The sky was grey and the trees, although abounding with leaves, seemed colourless and dull. The cold wave was in full swing now. I couldn't remember the last time I'd seen a blue, sunny sky.

Mom's words rang in my head. I wasn't made for the cut-throat world of non-med and JEE coaching. I was delicate and soft, and such people couldn't survive there. How could I ever be in the top 1 per cent? I would never be able to get admission at an IIT—it almost seemed a fact. What Shiv said, about fighting the odds, scared me. Why should I do something I was most likely going to fail at? I knew wasn't as prepared or smart enough from the way the Hellen talent hunt exam had gone. I wasn't a study machine like everyone at Hellen seemed to be.

Humanities, on the other hand, seemed easier. I wouldn't have to attend the extra coaching classes. I'm sure I'd be able to get by, attending lectures at my school and hopefully getting good marks in the humanities subjects would be the same as it had been so far.

I could see a girl like me succeeding in the 'safe' stream that humanities seemed like. I couldn't see that in non-med. But was this the right train of thought for choosing streams? What about what Dad said yesterday about having the most career options if I take non-med? That seemed enticing, considering how clueless I was about my future career. The hopeful gleam in his eyes when he said he believed in me was ingrained in my mind. What if he was right?

'Avani?'

I looked back. It was Kavita ma'am, my English teacher from the ninth class.

'Oh, good morning, ma'am,' I said, very conscious of the fact that I probably looked like a weirdo if Kavita ma'am had managed to spot me staring outside a window in the middle of an empty hallway.

'Are you okay?' She asked, furrowing her brows.

I put on my best teacher-pleasing face and said, 'Of course, ma'am. I just had to…find my watch.'

She smiled, looking at me. 'But you're wearing your watch.'

'Oh. I didn't notice,' I said, 'Thank you, ma'am.'

I turned around, ready to beat myself up because of this cringeworthy conversation. What was wrong with me these days?

'Avani, I wanted to ask you for a favour,' she said.

I turned around, facing her again. I'd already destroyed my reputation as a smart kid in front of her. Was she going to roast me like Sahil sir did last Friday? I didn't even care anymore. She could have roasted me all she wanted. I'm pretty sure I was immune by that point.

'I had to talk to you about your column for the school magazine this year. Do you mind coming into the teacher's room at lunchtime?' she asked, a knowing smile on her face.

'Oh…of course, ma'am,' I said, smiling sheepishly. 'I mean—I don't mind. I'll be there.'

She shook her head. 'Okay, I hope to see you right on time.'

I nodded, scuttling away before she asked me other things, like what was I doing roaming around in empty hallways like a madwoman. I was actually glad she'd called me during our lunch break. Otherwise, I'd have to spend it alone since Parnika wasn't available, since I wasn't sure I would be able to handle talking to Shiv after my horrendous exit.

7

What If?

Walking into the teacher's lounge seemed surreal. I'd been in there many times but only for short durations. Today, I was able to take it all in. It was full of dusty cupboards, which would trigger a sneeze-fest if I got too close to them. There was a decent-sized conference table in the middle, full of stacks of notebooks and test papers.

'May I come in, ma'am?' I stood in the doorway, tiffin in one hand, notebook in the other. I always carry a notebook—just in case.

'Come in, Avani.' Kavita ma'am was the only teacher in the lounge, which made me feel much calmer. I didn't feel ready to face anyone else right now. 'Please, dear, sit. Don't look so nervous.'

My heart melted a little. She spoke with so much care and deliberation. I didn't know how much I needed that 'dear' until she said it. I wanted to hug her and tell her that I missed her so much. But that would be weird.

'Thank you, ma'am,' I said, sitting in the plush chair next to her. Damn, why did the teachers get the good stuff? We were paying to go to school, shouldn't we have got the good stuff? 'You called me about the column?'

She paused and thought for a few seconds, trying to recollect our meeting. 'Oh, that!' She exclaimed, leaning back in her chair.

She was quite lively for an old-looking teacher. 'No, everything is great with the column. As always, your work is immaculate.'

I smiled, remembering how much fun I had over the winter holidays working on the column.

'I could see that something was bothering you. Even though I'm not teaching you and your class this year, I still care about my students, especially a brilliant one like you,' she began. She waited a few moments for me to reply, but I couldn't possibly think of anything to say, not even a thank you, so she continued, 'I'm guessing it has something to do with eleventh class?'

I nodded, slightly stunned at the direction this conversation had started going. No offence, but I really didn't see Kavita ma'am as a potential career counsellor. I'd always seen her as a soft-hearted and inspiring English teacher. How could she know what I was going through?

'Let me guess some more. Are you confused between humanities and science? I know you enjoy writing—and I also know how much you enjoyed doing your science projects during the summer holidays, since you'd written about it in your English report.'

I nodded some more, amazed at how attentive she was. I thought teachers didn't care at all about their students outside of the classroom, only about the bad stuff so that they could berate them.

'I've already decided, actually. I'm going to choose humanities,' I said, hearing the tone of dejection in my own voice.

'Oh? You have? That's great!' she said. 'Why the long face then?'

I shook my head. 'It's nothing, ma'am. I'll be fine.'

She was quiet for a while. I guess she was coming up with a way to excuse herself from this conversation. I get that. If a whiny, self-absorbed teenager came up to me and started sulking, I'd tell her to grow up and stop being so tragic.

'Avani, are you hungry? It's lunchtime. We should eat before the period gets over,' she said, taking out her lunch box.

We both sat in silence, chomping down our respective lunches.

'Those science projects were stupid, anyway,' I mumbled.

'Sorry, what?' She looked askance at me, interest causing her eyebrow to shoot up.

A thousand alarm bells went off in my head. I back-pedalled. 'I'm sorry. I shouldn't have said that.'

'No, really, I want to know more. I swear I won't tattle to Ahuja ma'am.' She had a mischievous glint in her eye.

'What I meant was, those science projects—the ones we were assigned for our holiday break were useless. Sure, I learnt about how electricity works and made a pretty diagram for it. I enjoyed reading the chapter and answering all the questions. I even got really good marks for that project. But that didn't help me solve those difficult coaching questions. *I'm just not good enough.*'

She was silent for a long time. I don't know why I said what I said, it's not like she would understand the context of 'difficult coaching questions'.

'If you enjoyed the process of doing the project, why would it be useless?'

'Because there's no point to the projects. I don't know why I even try so hard at school activities. I should've spent my time going to coaching like my other classmates who were so obsessed with taking non-med, practically since the day they were born.'

'May I ask why you didn't go to coaching like these classmates you speak of?'

I shrugged. 'I don't know. Maybe it was a mistake on my part. I guess I thought it was too difficult, too much work. Besides, I already understood and enjoyed the science and maths lectures at school and through self-study. It was easier to just avoid all that and stay at home, read or write.'

'Oh, I see.'

'Anyway, ma'am, I don't want to take up more of your time. I am pretty decided on taking humanities.'

'Why do you want to take humanities? Is there a particular group of subjects you are interested in or a potential enticing career?'

My career was a long shot. I knew the reason why I was comfortable taking humanities, though, 'Because it seems like a less scary, less intimidating option where I can see someone like me succeeding.'

'I see. So you're not taking non-med because you're scared and think you'll fail?'

'...Yes.'

'And taking humanities feels safe, even though you've no particular interest in any subject?'

'...Yes. Many people around me seem to agree with my choice, given my *personality*, so I am fine. I'll be fine,' I said. I wasn't sure if the last part was true.

'What personality? Who are these people deciding for you?'

'Timid, soft, emotionally fragile, scared.' I might've been paraphrasing, but that's what Mom meant. I was sure of it.

She was silent again for a bit, mulling over something in her mind.

'Do you also believe those things are true about yourself?'

I was shaken. 'I...I'm not sure.'

Was I timid, soft, emotionally fragile and scared? Maybe sometimes. But wasn't that true for everyone? I was strong too. If I weren't strong, I would've run away the second they started distributing those coaching tests. But somewhere, somehow, I found the strength to carry on in that difficult moment. Even when I had to stand up for myself to my dad, I did it.

'Avani, look, I'll just tell you what I think, okay? First, you are very wrong in underestimating humanities. It requires fervour and passion like any scientific subject. Maybe even more, given the difficulty in finding well-paying jobs. If you don't have that, your life can easily become hellish, even in humanities.

'Second, your fears of failure are universal. Many people face them. But heroes don't run away from situations. Instead, they fight. Whether they win or not is a different and irrelevant topic. The important thing is that they fought the battle. They didn't give up before the battle began. And that is the most important thing.

'If you don't want to do non-med, don't. But is it justified to leave a subject you're interested in just because it's going to be difficult? Is it justified to give in to your self-doubt? How will that serve you as a person?'

Taken aback at her in-depth response, I blurted out, 'Why should I do something I'm most probably going to fail at?'

She chuckled, 'Because if you don't do it, you'll always wonder what if. What if you could actually *succeed*?'

The bell rang, signifying the end of the break period. I snapped out of my vulnerable state and switched to a more palatable version of myself. 'Thank you so much, ma'am. Really, I am very grateful you spent this time to address my questions,' I managed to not say 'the reason for my existential dread' instead.

She nodded, 'Of course, Avani. I wish you the very best for the future, dear.'

I almost wanted to hug her but only just managed to stop myself. *Be professional, Avani.*

∽

That Monday night, as I lay in my bed after an extremely quiet dinner with my parents, I started contemplating my actual motivations. Streams, at the end of the day, were created for students to gain specialized knowledge in their respective career fields. For a person who did not have a specific career they aspired to, what were they supposed to do? Logically, it would make sense to choose the stream that leaves the most choices open so that they can decide later on.

I was scared of non-medical because of the accompanying, apparently non-negotiable, IIT coaching. It seemed cut-throat competitive to get admission to an IIT. *What is the point of doing something I was most likely going to fail at?* That was the first thought in my head when I heard Sahil sir mention the abysmally low acceptance rate. But what Kavita ma'am said seemed correct, at least in my case. If I didn't take non-med, I would wonder 'what if' for sure. Besides, what was my alternative? Taking humanities? It was completely possible that it would be a big challenge as well. My assumptions about humanities being 'easy' was wrong, as proved by Kavita ma'am.

My second thought on hearing Sahil sir mention the acceptance rate, which I had quickly dismissed at the time, was, *what if I could do it?* It sounded ridiculous for sure, probably even foolish, but maybe I could study hard, traverse the 'pathway to success' and reach the destination? Dad believed in me, and he was the smartest person I knew. Surely there was something he saw in me. I wanted to make him proud. I wanted to prove my mother wrong. I wanted to prove my self-doubts wrong.

I had to do it even if I was scared.

I tore out a page from a stray notebook and started writing.

> ### Avani's Guidebook for Surviving Hellen
>
> 1. Just as I was at White Meadows, I want to be at the top of the class at Hellen. I will do the best job I possibly can; anything less would be unacceptable. I have to beat the odds and be in the top 1 per cent.
> 2. Perform on par with Shiv and Parnika. Try to become even better.
> 3. Prove to Mom that I am not a delicate or weak person who cannot survive JEE coaching.
> 4. Prove to Dad that he was correct—that I am as smart as he thinks I am.
> 5. I will not shy away from doing things that I want to do but seem scary. I can't be afraid of failure anymore. Don't ever be left wondering 'what if...'

8

Comfort Zone

I woke up on Saturday with the same thoughts that I went to sleep with: I am really doing this. I am taking non-med. I could still recall the entire scene from yesterday: checking the non-medical box on the crumpled, almost decrepit form, adrenaline pumping in my veins as I walked down the aisle to submit it to the teacher. Every step of the way, I was both freaking out over my decision but also silently confident about it, having mulled over it enough the past week, ever since that 'counselling session' with Kavita ma'am. The only major hurdle remaining in my school year was today's farewell party. You know, apart from the board exams, but I wasn't nearly as stressed for that.

At around 10.00 a.m., Parnika barged into my house with what seemed like a cavalry of bags—a handbag, make-up bag, and two dry-cleaning bags. I emerged from my room in pyjamas and sleepy eyes.

'Avani,' Parnika said, looking me up and down. 'I thought you'd have at least taken a shower by now!'

'Chill, Parnika,' I said.

'How? How am I supposed to chill? The party starts at noon. It barely leaves us time to do our hair properly.'

'I already took a shower last night. I'm good to go,' I lied.

She looked at me with her eyes narrowed, investigating my

hair, 'Hmm. I'm pretty sure you didn't, but I'm going to let it slide. Your hair has a special ability to look freshly washed all the time. I'm kind of jealous, honestly.'

'Uh...wow, thanks,' I was honestly speechless. I couldn't believe it was possible for Parnika to be jealous of me. If anything, I was the one usually silently envious of her, although I tried to never let it show. She was my closest (and only) friend since a very young age, and we'd just stuck together.

'Why are you like this, Avani?' she asked as we walked up the stairs to my room.

I thought she meant it as a joke, so I said, 'You mean, why am I the human embodiment of a sloth?'

She didn't laugh, 'Why aren't you looking forward to this party?'

'Because I'm not confident like you are, Parnika. I'm just constantly tripping over myself and fumbling. I don't thrive in huge social settings,' I said, quickly throwing the clothes strewn around my bedroom into the laundry basket.

'But don't you ever think that you deserve to enjoy yourself once in a while?' she asked, plopping her bags on my bed.

'I do enjoy myself. I just enjoy different things. I'd rather not go to big parties and dance with a boy who may or may not be cute. It just sounds scary,' I said, mumbling the last part.

'Maybe you should try stepping out of your comfort zone. See what's out there,' she said, fidgeting with one of my books on my desk.

'I don't know, maybe you're right,' I muttered, sitting cross-legged on my bed.

'I'll help you,' she said, putting the book down on the desk, smiling at me.

'Oh God, no. Please, don't help me.' I joined my hands in front of myself as if praying.

'You can't stop it now. I've got a plan,' she said, with a mischievous glint in her eye.

∽

'Blend this, please. No, ew, don't rub it. Tap it! Gently tap,' she said, flitting around my room, taking out stuff from her bags. It had been two hours since she barged into my house, and we were still on the make-up stage.

'Where would I be without you, dude?' I said, 'gently tapping' the liquid onto my face. It quickly disappeared, along with some of the darkness under my eyes. This was sorcery.

'Purgatory, probably,' she said, fidgeting with the neckline on her pink bodycon dress. She had a look of contempt on her face.

'What's wrong?' I asked.

'Nothing.'

'What's wrong?' I asked again. I was wearing a frilly white top tucked into a black skirt with leggings. It didn't compare with Parnika's dress, but it felt the most comfortable out of all the clothes I owned. I guess I really liked to look like waitstaff at a fancy restaurant.

'Okay,' she said, looking outside my bedroom door, probably to check the coast was clear. 'So, you know how I was absent this Monday? Well, I'd taken the day off to sew a dress for today. I know, I'm a bit extra, but I had this vision in my mind that I just really wanted to bring to existence.'

'Valid reason for taking a day off,' I concurred.

'Yes! That's what I told my dad. But no. He took away my sewing machine! Can you believe that?' she said.

'Oh. That—'

'He told me I shouldn't waste my time on stupid stuff like "making clothes". That I could get a tailor to do it for me,' she said. 'A tailor wouldn't know what's in my head!'

I nodded. 'So then, what did you do?'

'Well, I couldn't sew, obviously. So I bought this online. This hideous, pink, body-hugging monstrosity. The polar opposite of my vision. I wanted something flowy. Something ethereal, you know?'

'You look like you're punishing yourself,' I said, wanting to say something more comforting but not sure exactly what.

She sighed, 'Let's go. We're late.'

'No, wait,' I said, walking to my closet. I pulled out a beautiful, flowy lilac dress from my closet. 'Remember this?'

Her expression changed to one of recognition. 'Of course. It's the midi dress with puffed sleeves that I stitched for you for your last birthday. Isn't the fabric amazing?'

'Yes, it is quite amazing. Here, you can have it,' I said, handing it to her.

She hesitated. 'Avani, I can't. It was your birthday gift.'

'Fine. Borrow it, then,' I said, physically putting the dress in her hands.

I saw a slight smile on her face. 'Thanks, Avani.'

∽

'Oh God, it's so dark here,' I mumbled as we entered the club. Our class had managed to reserve a club for three hours in the middle of the day. I thought the club would be brightly lit during the day for some reason. It just felt odd for it to be dark.

'Well, yeah. That's the way clubs are supposed to be,' Parnika said, grabbing a free soft drink can from the bar. Wow, I felt like a real grown-up. 'Dark and mysterious. What happens at the club, stays at the club.'

'I've literally never heard anyone say that,' I retorted.

'Hey, Parnika. Avani,' Shiv approached us. He was dressed smartly in a button-up shirt with a tie and dress pants.

'Oh, hey Shiv!' Parnika said.

Another classmate of ours came up to us. 'Hey, should I take a photo of you guys? I'll be uploading them online.'

Everything happened like clockwork. I was on one side of Shiv, and Parnika was on the other. Parnika linked her arm with Shiv's, striking a side pose. Meanwhile, I stood with my arms by my side, a veritable amount of distance between Shiv and me, forcing a smile.

'Uh... Avani, you're not in the frame,' the classmate mumbled.

I stiffly shifted a bit closer to Shiv, my arms almost touching his. Oh my God! This was so awkward. Within a split second, Shiv put his arm around my waist. Before I could react, the picture was clicked, and the classmate disappeared.

'I'm gonna go meet some other people, okay? You kids have fun,' Parnika trotted away before I could say another word. Now I was left alone with Shiv and an overwhelming feeling of awkwardness. Remembering the impending couple's dance did nothing to alleviate my nervousness.

'So...' Shiv trailed off, 'you're taking non-medical?'

I immediately started to panic. *Calm down, Avani.* I had practised this. 'Yes. And I'm going to Hellen, the whole shebang.'

'Nice,' he said, smiling at me.

Silence.

'So how do you and Parnika know each other?' I said, desperately trying to fill the awkward silence but instantly realizing it was a dumb question. They knew each other from the coaching they'd been doing since they were kids.

'Well, it's a funny story, actually. I met her in coaching in sixth class when our teacher forced us to sit together. She was paired with me because she was too talkative and kept doodling dresses in her notebook instead of paying attention,' he said, a vacant look of reminiscence on his face.

'So, you were supposed to be a good influence on her?' I asked, a hint of sarcasm in my voice.

He didn't get that, of course. 'I guess so. I told her that she should study if she wanted to impress her dad and get a good, well-paying job. Her dad was the one who put her in the coaching, from what she told me.'

I nodded. Parnika's dad was a bit intense, like Parnika. But not friendly intense like her.

'Enough about Parnika and me. What about you? When did you meet her?' he said.

'Well, her dad is friends with my dad. So, yeah, we are childhood friends, really. She kind of adopted me, to be honest,' I said, shrugging.

'Oh, okay,' he said, looking around the dance floor. A new, slower, more romantic song started playing.

Was this the couple's dance? My eyes darted around for Parnika. I finally spotted her, standing in a corner, drink in one hand, talking to some other girl. She winked at me.

'Do you want to dance?' Shiv asked.

My jaw dropped. I looked at Parnika, desperate for her to save me. Instead, she just waved at me, a knowing smile on her face. Oh God, was this her plan all along?

I tried to think about the situation objectively. Did I want to dance with Shiv? My mind immediately went into defensive mode. No, I was way too shy and scared to even think about it. What if I looked super awkward? What if I messed up the steps? What if I stepped on his foot and he had to go to the hospital? The probability of me messing this up was large.

Then, my goals for the next two years popped into my head. If I wasn't scared, I'd probably do it. It was like non-medical, where the probability of success was abysmally low. I was scared of failing, scared of messing up. But I had still opted for it because if I didn't do it, I would wonder 'what if'. If I didn't dance with Shiv, I definitely would also wonder what if. I could almost imagine myself as an 80-year-old, sitting in my rocking chair, creating some digital knitting pattern probably, wondering if life would've been different had I danced with Shiv that afternoon all those years ago. Okay, that was a stretch, but I knew I'd regret not doing it.

I had to do things out of my comfort zone. I had to try now.

'Okay. I'll lead the way,' I said, walking towards the dance floor, not looking back. *Let's do this.*

Part Two
Swimming with Dolphins

9

First Day

I opened my eyes and instantly regretted it.

'Avani, get up! You have to leave in an hour. You still have to take a shower and eat breakfast. Come on, get up!' Mom pulled off my blanket.

I groaned as a headache set in. I stumbled out of bed, turned off the air conditioner and moved towards the bathroom. A strange face stared back at me—this one had dark circles and unkempt hair from tossing and turning last night.

The holidays after my tenth-grade finals had gone by pretty quickly, with me spending most of my time similar to how I had in my winter break. I'd treated these 10 days akin to how I imagine death-row inmates treat their last meal—decadent, luxurious and almost debaucherously, or, in my case, watching random YouTube videos of goats getting petted, eating an unceremonious amount of Italian food and sleeping till noon.

But last night was horrible.

I kept checking my clock again and again. I don't know when exactly I fell asleep, but I could feel the aftermath today. My hands and feet were cold, even though the temperature had done almost a complete 180 from the cold wave back in January. It was 11 April. This day would go down in history as the most nervous I've ever been.

When I came out of the bathroom, my mother was still in my

room. She was setting down two cups of masala tea on the desk.

When I'd finally told my parents that I'd changed my mind about taking humanities and I was going to take non-med and everything else that came with it, Dad's response was as ecstatic as I had expected. Mom, however, didn't have much of a reaction. Since that day, she'd been behaving a bit differently. A bit kinder and softer—less lauki, more paneer. We hadn't talked about this, of course. Mom and I typically didn't discuss our true feelings in our free time.

'Have some tea,' she gestured towards the desk.

Warily, I took one cup and sat down on my desk chair. I didn't like tea very much.

'I'll drop you at Hellen on my way to work,' she said, picking up her cup and sitting opposite me, on the edge of my bed. She smoothened out the sheet next to where she sat, which I'd crinkled by my tossing and turning last night.

Coaching. The sequel to school. What was next? College? Office? Retirement home? Crematorium?

'Mom, I'm nervous for my first day,' I blurted out.

She smiled at me knowingly. 'I know.' She put her arm around me, engulfing me in a side hug. 'You know, I had the same feeling when I started my job. But now it feels normal. And it will be the same for you.'

I sat there, quite astonished at her sudden hug—which had to be one of the first hugs we'd ever had. 'I hope so,' I murmured, with my head on her shoulder.

She smiled a bit and said, 'Go on, drink the tea. I think you may like it this time, I went easy on the cardamom.'

She never did this in the past. She would always continue to make tea like she always had. Why did she put less cardamom this time?

Gingerly, I took a small sip. A strong flavour filled my taste

First Day

buds. It was equal parts sweet and spicy. As the tea went down my throat, I could feel it soothe my throat and, somehow, my nerves. I could feel my hands beginning to warm again. 'Wow,' I looked at Mom's expectant face, 'it's really good.'

I wasn't lying this time.

Her smile grew bigger, and I could feel my heart expand and ache. It was a strange thing to see her smile. For one, I didn't see it very often. She was always stretched so thin with her teaching job at college or cooking meals for us at home. I looked at her closely and saw the bags under her eyes, similar to mine but much more pronounced.

I said, 'I'll just skip the shower today, I think.'

'No. Go take a quick shower, I'll have your breakfast ready,' she said, walking out of the room with the two empty cups.

∽

It really felt like the first day of school. My hands were sweaty, my backpack was full of three new notebooks—one for each subject, physics, chemistry and maths—and I was surrounded by people I didn't know. At least in school, I knew half the people in my class. Even if I ignored most of them, I knew their faces. I looked around in the sea of students, trying to spot Shiv or even Parnika. Where were they? All the people looked like I should know them, but all of their faces drew a blank. They were all alien.

I tried to sneak a look at the people sitting around me without being too obvious. I decided to take an aisle seat, which was probably not the best idea. People were walking past me all the time, brushing against my shoulder, and I was already so nervous about first impressions. What if they thought my shoulder wasn't a good enough shoulder?

I bent over my seat to retrieve my water bottle from my

backpack, when a guy walking down the aisle tripped and fell right onto me.

'Oh my God,' I said, in a low tone, even though everyone was looking at us now, 'I'm so sorry.'

The boy was a student. He was kind of skinny and had a fluffy head of hair and a blank look on his face.

He said nothing—not even an obligatory 'it's okay', completely avoiding eye contact with me. He looked at the ground and walked off like nothing had happened. My eyes were glued to his back—a blue button-up shirt that was also kind of sweaty—like me. What kind of person completely avoids eye contact? Actually—me. I do that. Wow, a self-burn.

Before I could dwell on this strange encounter, a middle-aged man walked in the room with a gusto I'd probably never seen in a man other than my dad. Was he a student too? I stifled a chuckle. *Remember what happened the last time you chuckled in this place, Avani? Never again.*

'Hello, students. I am Dr Khanna, one of the senior mathematics teachers at this institute. I am here to welcome you all to Hellen, your pathway to success, where you are most likely to forge a bright future for yourself if you stay determined and free of distractions.'

Well, that sounded promising and quite encouraging.

He continued, 'First, I have to ask all of you some questions.'

The next thing I know, notebooks were flying open all around me and pages were getting ruffled faster than you could say 'IIT'. Instead of taking out my notebook from my backpack, which was now on my lap, I just stared at my neighbour's desk, which had a closed notebook on it. She had marked it explicitly as 'algebra Notebook I' as though there were going to be multiple volumes and as if she knew what was going to be taught.

'There's no need to take out your notebooks, we don't have

a written test today. My first question to you guys is: why did you decide that you would like to become an engineer?'

I kid you not, the girl next to me actually wrote down the question—verbatim. And I thought *I* was the people-pleasing nerd.

I knew better than to share my life story with a bunch of indifferent 15-year-olds. They probably had a less complicated reason. They probably had it all figured out since the day they came out of the womb, like Parnika and Shiv.

The thin, dark-skinned girl with big, eager eyes sitting next to me raised her hand. 'Hello sir, my name is Meenal. My reason for deciding to become an engineer is that from a very young age, I have had a strong passion for engineering. I have always been very interested in it, so I had no doubt in my mind about what would be the course of the next two years of my life. I want to become an aerospace engineer and dream of working for the Indian Space Research Organisation (ISRO) or NASA one day.'

Wow, she'd thought it out that far ahead? Seriously, how could people have the conviction to decide on their dream workplace so early on? I couldn't even think of what I wanted for my next meal. Seriously—aloo parantha or paneer? This was a tough decision to make.

My reason for taking non-med was probably the worst. If I was being honest in class, I would've said something lame like this, 'To prove to Mom that I could do it, to make my dad proud and live up to his expectations, to prove something to myself—that I *can* do it. Also, I don't know what else to do. I don't hate maths or science. Although my love for it is probably not comparable to Meenal's.'

'Wow, that's great, Meenal. I appreciate your passion and enthusiasm for engineering. It's something that is absolutely necessary to be committed to the goal these next two years, plus another four years in engineering! Without passion, where would we be? Any other answers?' he looked around.

It was the blue-shirt guy who had tripped and fallen onto me. Wow, I would *finally* hear him speak. *How tantalizing.* Seriously, he didn't even say an 'ow' when he fell.

'I've always had an interest in building things from a young age. I remember taking my elder sister's mechanic set and making different gadgets. After I learnt about electricity, I would build different devices—like a mechanized dustbin. Also, I was inspired to take non-medical after my parents had motivated me.'

'That's amazing, young man! What's your name?'

'Av…ik. Avik, sir,' he spoke with a slight stammer in his voice. I didn't care what his name was, for me it would be Dustbin Guy.

'I am sure all other students are also full of inspiring, passionate stories about why they decided to take up this stream. It is important to be motivated in this rigorous field of study, arguably the most important aspect.' Sir continued, 'Now my second question is one which you *most definitely* should know. If you don't, it would be quite shameful, actually. I'll pick one of you to answer it. Let me see…'

My heart sank. I was actually looking forward to answering the first question now, since I'd fabricated a pretty good fake story about me.

I'm Avani, a descendant of the inventor of the fulcrum. It was always destined in my stars that I get into this coaching centre and get into mechanical engineering at IIT Bombay, after which, like my great-great-great-great-grandfather, I, too would get absorbed into the Secret Society of Fulcrums.

He scanned the room, his beady eyes looking for his new victim. I avoided eye contact, instead deciding to harden my focus on Dustbin Guy's back, who was sitting a few rows in front of me. I could feel his eyes like lasers, hoping they wouldn't land on me.

First Day

Well, I guess my eye contact circumvention plan was a bust because of the next thing Dr Khanna said: 'The girl with her head down in the red-and-white shirt.'

My gaze shot up, and my body automatically lifted up from my chair.

Why was I getting like this? Whenever I was called upon in school, I was confident, my knees never shook and I never had tunnel vision.

'What's your name?' he asked.

'Av...Avani.' I stuttered. What was happening? He had only asked for my *name*.

'Okay, Avani, my question for you is...'

I closed my eyes for a second, bracing myself for the question. If I would get it wrong, it would just be another nail in my coffin, just after the Dustbin Guy tripped over me and getting roasted by Sahil sir. I hoped I'd get it right.

'What's the full form of IIT?'

My mind went blank. Oh my God. I could hear some murmuring coming from the back. Even Dustbin Guy had turned around and was staring at me.

What was it? I'd just read the full form on Wikipedia the other night, when I had ended up on a page about some entrepreneur from the same place.

'Indian Institute of Technology. I think there are about 22 of them right now. It's a collection of colleges where people go to study engineering,' I said, regaining the majority of my School Confidence. I was right. I knew it.

There was muted laughter coming from all around. Even Dr Khanna chuckled. What the hell? I was pretty sure that I was damn correct.

Once the class regained its composure, sir—who still had a slight smile on his face said, 'Correct, Avani. Though it is a much bigger deal than just a group of engineering colleges. Those students end up becoming the new leaders of the world, bosses of most people—perhaps even you, one day. You may sit down.'

Wait, did he mean that I would be the boss of someone one day, once I got into IIT? Or was he implying that the IIT people would boss me around? I stopped my head from spinning any further. God, these people were so pernickety—just take my answer for what it is. I crashed into my seat, just glad to not have people staring at me. This would've never happened to me at school. I missed it. Where were Parnika and Shiv?

Sir continued, talking about the curriculum and what the next few weeks were going to be like.

'By the way, your class is the Dolphin batch. There is another batch in the room above you, called the Shark batch, which has the students who scored in the top 20 per cent of the entrance test we had a few weeks ago. Your teacher for maths will be Shruti ma'am. She is a brilliant teacher who has been a part of our institute for quite a while now.'

My heart sank deeper and deeper. I wasn't in the best batch? The results for the talent hunt exam were released in late January. I hadn't bothered to look at them because I knew I'd bombed it. Still, I had held out some hope in the back of my mind that maybe everyone did poorly and my relative performance would be good enough to get into the best batch. In the past, whenever I thought I'd 'bombed' a test, it didn't turn out to be that bad. I guess this time was different.

Soon enough, sir disappeared and was replaced by the new teacher—another unfamiliar face. My heart sank at the sight of her. She wasn't my school teacher—even though I tried to imagine my favourite maths teacher or even Kavita ma'am at her place—I couldn't. I was an alien to the new teacher, full of alien people around me.

First Day

With only a brief introduction about herself and no effort to ask for introductions from us, she began to teach. What did she teach? That's right, algebra. Meenal was definitely a fortune teller.

At the one-hour mark, I expected Shruti ma'am to walk out of the class. Instead, she stopped teaching and gave us a few questions to solve.

I started reading the question slowly, racking my brain for the solution. Thankfully, it wasn't as bad as last time when I was taking the test here. I tried to apply what she had taught us and was able to figure out the solution. When I got to writing my satisfied answer, a hand beside me shot up in the air.

'Ma'am!' Meenal exclaimed.

Soon enough, a couple of more hands went up in the air, all yelling out the same thing. Shruti ma'am walked around the aisle, checking each student who'd raised their hands' solution. She said stuff like 'Good job!' and 'Yes, absolutely correct', which was pretty nice of her to say.

By the time I would finish solving the question, she'd dictate the next question. I was too slow to even note down the next question, partially due to my ridiculously sweaty hands, barely holding on to the pen, as I copied the question from Meenal—who wasn't very excited about me looking into her notebook, as she was actively trying to shield her notebook from me like I was going to shoot lasers at it or something. I wasn't going to copy her plans to fly to the moon or something.

I wanted to get just one 'good job' but wasn't fast enough.

At the two-hour mark, I begged to God for this torture to end. It took two and a half hours for my brain to actually turn to mush, and thankfully she stopped then.

Was this how coaching was going to be like? Sitting for nearly three hours, listening to some alien teach one subject? My heart stopping every time they would dictate a question, and students raising their hands even before she'd finished dictating it? Would the other subjects be the same? This wasn't fun or exciting. This was nerve-wracking.

When the class got over, I wasn't sure what to do. Was I supposed to wait for another teacher to come and traumatize me some more? Or was I supposed to run back home? Because I definitely preferred the latter option.

'Hey, I'm Avani,' I turned to my right, speaking to the girl next to me.

'Oh, hello. I'm Meenal,' she spoke.

'Which school are you from?' I asked. Was this how conversations went?

'I'm not from here. I'm from a small town in Punjab, you've probably not even heard of it.'

'Try me, I think I'd know,' I said, cockily.

'Okay, do you know where Sangrur is?'

My cheeks burned. 'No, sorry.'

'Yeah. Well, it's a small town,' she said. 'Big city people like you wouldn't know.'

Great. I'd managed to offend her town already. 'By the way, how did you know they were going to teach algebra today? I saw you'd already written the topic in your notebook before they introduced the topic.'

Maybe this was an interesting conversation choice? Maybe she really had prescient powers? I could ask her about my fate. Hmm, probably not a good idea.

'Actually, my brother studied here too, so he gave me his notes,' she said, matter-of-factly, holding a worn-out notebook in her hand.

'Oh, that's so cool,' I said. 'Could I see it?'

She hesitated, and that's when I knew I'd messed up. 'Actually, my friend is waiting for me. She must be outside. Maybe some other time?'

Immediately, I blabbered, 'Yeah, of course. Sure. It's okay, cool.'

Real smooth, Avani. Real smooth.

Without saying a word, she left and I was left alone in the uncomfortable wooden bench, wondering how I ever made friends in my life.

I missed Parnika so much. She was so easy to talk to. I never had to try hard with her. Why was it so difficult to talk to new people?

10

Am I Getting *Punk'D*?

Given my trepidation in the last three hours, I decided to stay put in my seat for an extra while, taking in the classroom around me. Maybe it would help my hands to finally stop perspiring, and my heart would return to a normal resting rate. The room was well-lit, but it still felt dark. Perhaps because of the fact that there wasn't a single window. The walls were bare, no bright bulletin board full of colourful drawings like there used to be back in school. The benches were straight-backed, wooden and hard to sit on for longer than two minutes. They resembled an uncomfortable, purgatorial version of pews in a church. I mean, the bench didn't even completely support my butt. Yes, part of my butt was in the air for three hours. No wonder I couldn't move now even if I wanted to.

I couldn't imagine myself doing this for the next two years. I couldn't even imagine doing it for another day, to be honest. Everything about it screamed depressing. Even though I knew depression happens from the inside and it can happen to someone living in the fanciest of places, this place looked like it could induce depression.

When there were only a few students left, I suddenly felt more uncomfortable in this hellish version of a classroom. Just as I was about to get up, though, a middle-aged man walked into the aisle and kept walking till he reached a few benches in front of me, where Dustbin Guy was sitting. I quickly scooted to the corner of my bench, preparing to leave from the other side, putting back all my knick-knacks into my backpack.

'Here you are. I was looking for you everywhere, I thought you were *somewhere else*,' the man spoke gravely.

'I'm sorry,' he said, his voice solemn.

Was Dustbin Guy…Avik alright?

'You lied to me, Avik. You told me you'd gotten into Shark batch,' the man cried.

I looked around the classroom, only to realize that I was the only one left—apart from those two. I should leave, I should walk out as quickly as I can and not look back. But for some reason, I couldn't bring myself to move. Maybe it was because my butt was really numb from the horrible bench or maybe it was because I was somehow concerned about this stranger whom I'd meanly nicknamed after a dustbin.

'I'm sorry,' he repeated. 'I didn't mean to. I didn't want to make you worry-'

'I didn't raise you this way! I didn't make you become a liar, this is all on you. What are you going to do next? Steal perhaps?' The man continued, 'You should be ashamed of yourself.'

'Sorry,' he said. 'It won't happen again.'

'It better not! Do you want to be known as a spineless, worthless, incompetent boy? Because that's what you seem like right now. You have no motivation to do anything, you're going to end up like your useless sister. You are just wasting our money.'

'I promise you, Dad, I will never end up like her, okay? Please don't worry about that.' It was strange, even though the man, his father, was raising his voice, Avik's was steady and calm.

An uncomfortably long pause followed, after which the man looked at Avik and said, 'Come with me!'

Avik soon followed suit, looking down at the ground as he

walked behind his father.

Even though I didn't know him at all, something just felt off about the whole conversation. Who talked like that? How could Avik just bear it? How was he so calm, as if it had happened multiple times before?

When I finally got out of the classroom, I bumped into Shiv. *Oh, great.*

'Oye, Avani,' Shiv said, looking at me, smiling, eyes twinkling. Oh my God, his eyes were literally twinkling! 'It's so great to see you.'

Why was he happy? There was nothing at all to be happy about here. Definitely nothing to cause your eyes to twinkle, for God's sake.

'Hey,' I said, raising my eyebrows at the sight of a large folder in his hand. It had a ferocious shark on the cover, rising out of the ocean water like it was desperate to escape.

'All the Shark batch students got this folder. They even gave us some advanced problems to get us started.' His voice was bubbling with delight, 'I'm looking forward to working on my first assignment. I'd already started studying some topics in our post-boards exams because I was just so excited!'

I really wasn't sure if he was being sarcastic or actually serious. I paused, waiting for him to start laughing or say 'ha, punk'd!' but it never came.

'Well, that's great for you. I'm glad you have so much enthusiasm,' I said, looking down at my shoes.

I guess I finally understood why I hadn't seen him in my class. It's because he was in the *better one*. I don't know why, but that affected me more than it should've. It hurt me more than when I got to know that I'd gotten into Dolphin, i.e. not the best batch.

Why were they even segregating us based on our academic performance? That never happened in school. In school, we were all equal and were taught the same things. It wasn't like some of us were given more 'advanced' lessons. I missed school, damn it.

I couldn't believe he'd already started studying in the post-exam holidays. Weren't we supposed to not do anything in holidays? Enjoy, relax, partake in debauchery—well, in my case that would mean reading dystopian novels, but I thought that was the way to spend our much-earned free time? Not studying for the next class. What the hell?!

'So…how was your class?' He asked, still intently looking at me. I think I was going to be sick.

'Class was…great,' I said, in the most confident way possible.

I didn't have the nerve to tell him I was in Dolphin.

I don't know why it pained me to even think of telling him—it ashamed me so much to admit it. I was a Dolphin, not a Shark. I felt incapacitated, standing there in front of him. I was a lowly Dolphin, while he was a fierce Shark. I felt *small*. What did he think of me at this moment? *Avani's downfall has started. She will never be able to keep up here.*

Wait, weren't dolphins smarter than most mammals? Didn't that make us the smarter batch? Wow, these Hellen people were really flawed in their thinking.

'Did you see the shirts we have to wear?' he said, smiling, pulling a grey polo shirt out of his backpack.

It had the Hellen logo on the middle, plastered across the chest as if it was a Nike t-shirt. God, was this for real? If this was a nightmare, this is the time to wake me up.

'Oh, I didn't know…' I trailed off, spotting Parnika charging towards us with a force I'd only seen in a bowling ball.

'Hey Shiv, where did you disappear?' Parnika said, putting her arm around Shiv's shoulders. Wow, they seemed like really good friends.

'Ohhh, hi Avani!' She seemed shocked, like she'd just remembered I existed.

I smiled and spoke, 'Hey Parnika. I missed you so much!'

I actually was quite happy to see her. Seeing her familiar face made me feel a little less alien, even if we weren't in the same batch. Maybe this could be my new friend group? Me, Parnika and Shiv? Perhaps I would get over the embarrassment and shame of being in Dolphin one day or I'd get promoted to Shark soon enough?

'You didn't get the folder?' She asked, an exasperating amount of concern on her face.

'Nope. We didn't get one in Dolphin.' Because we are apparently second-class citizens. I felt like my soul had left my body, overcome by shame. Was it possible to die of embarrassment?

'How was class, Avani?' Parnika asked. I looked at her, wondering if she was taunting me or just asking a normal question.

'It was good. The teacher was good. I made a friend as well.'

That was kind of true. Meenal could count, right? If you ignore the whole 'running away from me' thing that happened. We would be besties in no time.

'Wow, that's great,' Shiv said.

'Well, our class was so much fun! Sahil sir gave such an interesting lecture. Did you know he's also from an IIT?' Parnika said, looking at me.

'Wow, that's great for you guys.' I tried my best to keep my smile. I wasn't going to stop smiling.

Shiv looked at his sports watch, 'Sorry, Avani, I need to run. Got to meet Sahil sir to ask some concepts I need help with.' He looked at Parnika, 'Parni, coming with? We had to ask the infinite solutions algebra question.'

'Yep. See you, Avani. Let's hang out sometime yaar. We totally lost contact during the boards. Come over anytime on weekends, okay?'

'Sure.'

Even though they both were familiar faces—it didn't feel the same. They were on a different level from me now.

⁓

I walked to the entrance of the building, eager to get home and dive into some kind of activity that would make me forget today. I saw a few stray students standing next to a huge crate.

It was full of grey polo shirts, same as the ones Shiv was raving about.

All the good sizes were gone—so I was stuck with an oversized polo shirt. Great. The only thing worse than a polo shirt was an oversized polo shirt. There went my dreams of wearing different outfits to class every day. I could actually imagine Future Me attending three-hour classes, vacant look on my face, wearing that dull grey shirt with some grey sweatpants, wearing brown Crocs and having at least 20 grey hairs. What had I done in my past lives to deserve this hell?

As I was power-walking to the exit of this damned institution so that I could cry in peace, I spotted someone in the corner of my eyes—it was Avik. My legs instinctively turned in his direction. He was sitting alone on a bench, his backpack next to him. Thankfully, his dad wasn't there anymore.

'Hey Avik, are you okay?' I asked, looking down at his dishevelled, fluffy hair. The volume was seriously unbelievable.

No reply. It was like he didn't even notice I was there.

'Hi, I'm Avani,' I said, sitting down on the other side of the bench. It was 7.00 p.m. and it was the weird time when the sky had almost lost all of its light and the streetlights hadn't been lit yet. Maybe he just didn't see me.

His round eyes stared back at me with a blank stare. 'I'm fine. Thanks.'

'Okay.' I didn't know what else to say. How could I say, 'How are you okay if your dad talked to you like that,' without sounding weird?

'What do you want, Avani?'

I was a bit taken aback, but I blabbered, 'I just wanted to make sure you were okay. After you…' I paused, thinking about whether I should mention his father shouting at him or not, 'tripped on my backpack. It seemed like it hurt.'

'I'm fine. It's nothing,' he said, still looking down.

'Are you sure? We could go to the doctor or—' I pushed.

'Yeah, I'm sure,' he proclaimed.

He added, in a lower voice, 'Besides, I fall all the time.'

I wasn't sure what he meant by that.

'Sorry, I didn't mean to overhear your conversation with your Dad.'

He looked shocked, 'Oh. I didn't see you.'

'You know, I didn't get into the Shark batch either. It kind of sucks.' I slumped back on the bench, crossing my arms. What was I doing? I thought I had to go home, not tell my life story to a stranger.

No reply. He just looked at me. I couldn't read his expression. What was he thinking of me? Then I realized, he didn't know me. He couldn't judge me in the same way as my parents or friends probably did. Or it was possible he just didn't care. Maybe I wanted to comfort him by sharing my misery. Either way, I was compelled to tell him more.

I continued, 'My friends from school are in Shark. They're probably judging me super hard because I was one of the smart kids till tenth class. Now I just want to leave and never look back.' I looked at the grey Hellen polo shirt in my hand. 'Besides, I'd rather be caught dead than wearing this thing.'

'So, you're thinking of leaving?'

'I might. You know, this horrible thought has been running around in my head. What's the point of taking non-med if you're not even in the top batch at a small institute in a small city in such a big country. I know. I hate how I think sometimes.'

He chuckled.

'Hilarious, am I?'

'It's funny. My dad said the exact thing to me today.'

'Oh.'

He sighed. 'Well, since I'm probably never going to see you again, I should tell you my truth as well. You know, just to keep things even. As you can see, I got into the Dolphin batch too. I knew I would, my test didn't go too well that day. I had it all figured out—Dad wasn't supposed to find out, I was going to study hard for the next test and get promoted to Shark, and he'd never have to know. But he found out.'

'Oh…' I mumbled. His truth was way worse than mine.

'It's like he wants me to succeed but then he says things like this. And I can't help but believe him. Maybe he's right.'

'No way. Look, I don't know you at all but I heard you talk about your—'

'Mechanized dustbin?' He chuckled. 'Sadly that has no value when you want to get into an IIT. The only thing that matters is how many questions can you answer correctly and how fast.'

'Oh. Well, if you can build a mechanized dustbin, I'm sure you'd be able to do that as well.' It was like I was reiterating Dad's words: 'If you're scoring such good marks in maths in school, why can't you do non-med?' Was there some truth to it?

'You know, I wish your words were true. They definitely sound comforting. But everything's really going wrong right now,' he said, slumping on the bench.

'I wholeheartedly agree with that. Things haven't gone right since January for me,' I said.

'For me, since the start of ninth class,' he said, looking at the cloudless, purple-pink sky.

'Why?'

Not answering my question, he said, 'I think you shouldn't let your friends' supposed opinions get to you. If they're good friends, they wouldn't judge you. And you definitely shouldn't judge yourself,' he said, getting up from the bench, wincing as he shifted his backpack to his other arm. 'Anyway, take all this with a grain of salt. I don't want you to hang around, especially because I told you all this on the premise of you leaving Hellen.'

'Right...' I said, staring at him as he slowly disappeared into the dark.

I didn't know what had just happened. Did I really just pour my heart out to a complete stranger, and did he just do the same? Although he was kind of elusive about his life sucking after ninth grade, rightfully so, why would anyone reveal that to a stranger?

By the time I reached home, I could hardly think straight. So many things had happened—so many alien faces.

I took a deep breath, setting down my bright pink backpack on the floor. Dad was having his evening tea in the verandah of our three-bedroom house. I didn't want to disappoint him. I didn't want to tell him what a failure his daughter had been on her first day at coaching—she didn't even get a single algebra question right in time, whereas her hyper-focused neighbour, a future Kalpana Chawla, got every single question correct. Most of all, she didn't even get into the best batch.

'So, how was your day?' Dad said, leaning forward in his chair, looking at me with a sparkle in his eyes, similar to one I'd seen in Shiv's. Ugh, Shiv. Why did I hate everyone all of a sudden?

'It was fine,' I said. The less I say, the better.

He looked at me expectantly, as if waiting for me to tell him how I got every question right, how the teacher was so proud of me and everyone already loved me and I was going to do amazing.

'How was the batch? Did you meet Parnika? Her father just called me up to tell she'd gotten into the top batch.' Ugh, why did he have to be friends with Parnika's dad? Now he looked so excited to hear about my 'amazing' first day. A complete 180 from the day I told him didn't want to do non-med.

A feeling of dread filled my stomach. 'Yes, I saw Parnika as well. We…we were both sitting together, actually.' It felt so easy to lie, especially when his eyes shone and he broke out in a smile.

'Oh, that's great, beta! See, all your worries were for nothing. You'll do amazing, I am a 100 per cent sure of it,' he waved his hand around so fast that some of his chai splashed on his shirt. *White shirt.*

'Look what you've done now,' Mom said, giving him a disapproving glare. She then turned to face me, the disgusted look on her face quickly fading, 'Avani, do you want some paneer today? I bought some on my way home from college.'

'I…of course,' I looked at her and then my dad, who was busy with his futile efforts to do damage-control on the stain. We both knew she was the one who was going to be handling it.

'So, tell me more about the class. How was it?' Dad asked, once Mom had gone back to the kitchen. My gaze was still fixed on the tea stain on his shirt, the one he had spilled due to excitement from a lie I'd told him. A lie that was going to get bigger and bigger.

'I told you. It was fine.'

'No, but I want to know more. Did you enjoy it?' he asked, as Mom poured some more tea into his cup.

'It was… challenging,' I said, looking at his leather shoes, ones that had a really pointy front part. They looked uncomfortable.

Why did he still wear them?

'That's great! Challenging is good. What is life if not a challenge?' he exclaimed. 'I'm sure, being the best student that you are, you'll come out on top!'

Come out on top? Ugh, that made me so miserable.

'Avani, you look tired. Why don't you go and rest? I'll call you when dinner is ready,' Mom said. 'Don't forget, you have to go to school tomorrow. I've already ironed your new school uniform.'

I quickly made my exit, feeling like I was out of an interrogation. Why did I just do that? Why did I have to lie? I was sick to my stomach. Seeing Mom act so nice, make paneer for me made it even worse. I felt like I deserved eternal damnation.

I wanted to tell him what a horrible day I had had today, all of the mean-looking people around me, about my laughable attempts to have a normal conversation with strangers, my lack of ability to solve basic maths questions within a set time limit, my overall incompetence at existing.

But Dad always thought I was so perfect at everything. The few times I had faltered—that day while we were walking in the park, he'd told me to grow up. Or the dinner. He just couldn't understand that even I, yes, his *perfect* daughter, could fail to be the best for once.

I hated myself for lying, but it was just a little fib. I'd soon enough get promoted to Shark. I would work hard for it.

11

New School

'Avani, have a good day at school! I'll come to pick you up at noon, okay?' Mom said.

I entered the gates of a completely unknown place, wearing a salwar-kurta, without knowing anything about where to go or whom to meet.

I had dubbed it Fake School. I missed my old crappy school uniform, I missed the small playground and the basketball courts that I was too intimidated to play on. I was never going back, was I? Why did that make my heart hurt more than I thought it would?

I stood in front of the small administration block, watching younger students in their salwar–kurtas and boys in their shirts and pants, propagating the pre-existing gender disparities in our education system by enforcing gender-specific uniforms. They were chasing each other in the ground, playing a game from a myriad of childhood favourites. Well, at least the look of excitement on the kids' faces was the same.

I remember when that used to be the way I used to spend my free periods in school. It was a pure time in my life. Though I was unaware of it at the time, Shiv and Parnika had probably been going to coaching even then.

'Hi, are you from Hellen too? I saw you in Dolphin yesterday.'

I turned back. There were two girls walking towards me,

wearing the same Fake School uniform.

'Um...yes,' I uttered, wondering if Hellen would be the thing where I'd be *from* for the next two years. Not from White Meadows High School, like I was for many years of my life.

'We're in Dolphin too. My name is Riya, and this is Smriti,' she said, gesturing to the spectacled girl next to her. Riya was taller than me and had her hair tied in a long side ponytail. Smriti was almost my height, had a sensible bob cut and wore spectacles.

'Oh hi, I'm Avani.' I was finally making friends. It. Was. Happening! I tried to look cool, maybe even unfazed some would say, but mentally I was doing cartwheels. They didn't look like they were going to run away from me, like Meenal did.

'I think we should go to class. It would have already started.' Smriti said, adjusting her glasses. She looked like the more serious one for sure.

'Which class?' I asked, genuinely having no idea where I was supposed to go.

'All Hellen students are in the same section. Didn't you know that?' Riya said, a bit shocked at my ignorance.

As we were walking to said class, in the corner of my eye, I spotted Avik. The last (and only) time I talked to him seemed so long ago...although it was just yesterday. He was all alone, walking to the same classroom. If this was normal school, maybe I'd gossip to Parnika about him and we'd make lame jokes about his strange hunched walk.

Parnika would say, 'Is that the new 'rapper walk'? I heard Post Malone has already started practising.'

I'd joke back, 'Maybe he's his personal walking trainer. Every rapper has one, these days.'

I sighed. It felt like it would never be the same between us now. Entering the classroom, it felt like a weird sense of deja vu. Looking at the gaggle of students seated in a familiar column style, talking to each other loudly and unabashedly almost made me feel at ease and reminded me of the comfortable, assuring past that was a part of me until recently. *Almost*. There was something off-putting about the entire situation. It was like there was an air of subtle hostility in the room. I couldn't see any camaraderie or potential pen-fights breaking out any time soon.

The three of us took a seat moderately in the back, although I would have preferred a seat much more in the front—where the quieter people were.

I took a deep breath. These girls were being nice to me. I should at least sit with them and reciprocate their kindness. Apart from them, I really didn't know anyone else in the room. Except…maybe Avik, who was sitting in a corner right near the front door (this guy was a genius; good idea for a quick escape) and Shiv, who was sitting in the back as well, talking to a bunch of guys around him. Parnika was sitting next to him, all of them talking amongst themselves as if they were an elite, untouchable clique. The seats next to them were full. I wondered if I asked, would they make space for me, a Dolphin?

Our class teacher came to discuss how this whole non-attendance thing would work. She told us we would need to come for the midterm and term end exams and apart from that, it was up to us to attend or not. They simply didn't care.

When my parents first told me about this non-attendance option, I was shocked. I had no idea that such schools existed. How were they even allowed to function? It was the day I realized I was really saying goodbye to the familiar. School had been a part of my life ever since I had the capacity to store memories in my brain. Even though Hellen was somewhat of a substitute, it would never be able to replace school in my mind.

'I bet Hellen's paying them in crores. That's probably how this school's still operating…' Riya murmured to us, as the teacher told us about the syllabus for the midterms.

I nodded. Wow, it seemed like these girls really did know everything.

'I heard that the school asks the non-attending students to come to the school sometimes, so no one suspects anything when the authorities come to visit.' Smriti whispered.

'Apparently they pay the authorities too…' Riya said—a bit louder than Smriti—which was probably not such a good idea.

'You two girls!' the class teacher spoke, looking directly at us, 'Get out of the class. Wait, take your friend with you too, she seems more interested in whatever things you were talking about. More interested than in what I was saying anyway.'

Oh God! This was my absolute worst nightmare. This had never happened to me before, except once when I was in the second grade and my class teacher asked me to stand for the whole class period for sneezing too loud.

Somehow, I managed to quietly scurry out of the class, trying to preserve whatever dignity I had left, not making eye contact with anyone, praying no one saw my face. Especially not Shiv or Parnika. I would be horrified. Even though Avik had said that good friends wouldn't judge me, I was so embarrassed. As I left the room, my gaze met Avik's, who was sitting right by the door. Surprisingly, though, I didn't really care what he thought of me—at least not much as Shiv or Parnika.

As soon as we were out of the class, the two girls burst out laughing.

'Oh my God, that was hilarious,' Riya wheezed, barely able to contain herself. Seriously, tears were leaking out of her eyes.

'I know!' Smriti spoke.

Riya studied me for a moment, punched my arm lightly and said, 'Avani, you need to lighten up. Stop being so serious all the time! Didn't the class teacher look hilarious when she was scolding us? Damn, her voice got so shrill all of a sudden!'

'Yeah, she sounded exactly like Janice from *Friends*!' Smriti spoke, still giggling. I couldn't believe I thought she was serious and innocent because of her glasses and her 'sensible' haircut.

'Isn't she our class teacher, though? Shouldn't we make a good impression? Or at least not a bad one,' I said.

Riya gave me an incredulous look. 'We're not in kindergarten anymore, Avani. She's a teacher from a low-grade school whom we probably won't see again. It doesn't matter. You need to chill out a bit. Hang out with us, we'll teach you how.'

I forced out a laugh, not knowing what else to do.

It felt wrong. I wanted to apologize to the teacher, even if I wasn't going to see her again. Even if she was from a 'low-grade school', whatever that meant. All teachers deserved respect.

I wanted to escape from this place. I wanted to go somewhere and hide. Forever. And never have to come out. Ever.

I knew I couldn't do that, so I decided to do the topical equivalent of it. Hide in the bathroom.

When I reached the slightly foul-smelling girls' bathroom, I burst out in silent sobs, quite akin to how they had burst out in laughter. Was my personality so depressing and serious that I felt so out of place? Everyone else seemed to be having a better time. These girls, Shiv, Parnika, and all the other laughing, gregarious faces I saw back in class. Only Avik seemed miserable, and that was probably because he was so grim as well.

Just as I walked out of the bathroom and into the now-busy corridor, I bumped right into someone. My vision was still a bit blurry because of the tears, but I could make out that it was Shiv from his casual walk.

'It's funny how we keep continuing to meet like this,' he smiled slightly and looked straight into my eyes. My stomach did a weird flip—like it would minutes before the distribution of the exam paper at school. I wasn't sure if it was a good feeling or not. It just felt strange and uncomfortable.

'Yeah, it's *hilarious*,' I said, fighting my facial muscles to muster up a smile. I hoped my red-tipped nose didn't give it away that I'd been crying. It was one of the telltale signs—at least my family could always recognize it.

'I was wondering…do you maybe want to go out sometime?'

'Oh, um…' I said, extremely confounded at the direction this conversation had taken. 'Where do you want to go?'

'Why don't you think about that?'

I mentally rolled my eyes at him. *He* was the one who asked me to go out, so shouldn't he have had a location in mind? Wait… did he want to go out with me, as in 'go out' with just *me*?

'What about other friends? Are you bringing Parnika along? Why don't we ask her what she'd be interested in as well?' I wouldn't mind all three of us going for a movie. It'd be like a school reunion.

He shook his head, still smiling slightly, 'I'm not bringing Parnika along.'

'Then who else?' I asked, my voice getting shakier and smaller, dreading the answer.

'It's just gonna be you and me,' he spoke so casually, so confidently—like it was no big deal for him. Like he'd done it a thousand times before—and always been successful.

'Oh. I see.' I hated this. I hated having to make decisions on the spot. Why didn't he ask me over text? Then I could've made a pro-con list like a normal person.

'So, you'll decide the time and place,' he wasn't asking me—he was telling me. Like the IITian boss that Khanna sir was talking about.

After a long pause full of conflicting thoughts in my head, I finally agreed, 'Okay. I guess I can do that.'

'Okay, see you on the date!' he turned around and walked away to join his group of friends.

Did he just say *date*? When did we agree on that? Just because we were going somewhere, just the two of us, made that outing a *date*? The mention of that word made me sick to my stomach. Either that or the fumes from the women's bathroom still lingering somewhere in my nose.

I mean, we danced together at the farewell. Was this the natural progression of things? Where were they going to progress to? I could feel my breaths getting shorter as the cogs in my mind whirred.

Oh God, what was I getting myself into? First getting kicked out of class with my new friends and now going on dates? Mom would literally explode if she got to know.

But...maybe this was good for me. Maybe I need to just be chill and do things differently now. Venture out of my comfort zone. I didn't have Parnika around to force me to do 'scary' things anymore.

12

Playing Truant

The next day, I scrambled across the hallways of the coaching centre, trying to locate my chemistry classroom. It was already 2.55 p.m., and the class started at 3.00 p.m. By the time I reached, all the good front row seats were already taken. I scoured the classroom for the frontmost empty spot in the girls' section.

For some strange reason, girls and boys had separate sections in the classrooms at Hellen, i.e. gender-based seating segregation. I was quite astounded and enraged at this 'unspoken rule' but chose to silently accept it for the sake of my sanity.

The girls' section was really small. There must have been 25 girls compared to about 100 boys? Yeah, that seemed accurate. And this was only the Dolphin batch. I had no idea about the Sharks. I hated using these words in my everyday life. Made me feel like I was in kindergarten again, or part of some really weird army contingent.

The frontmost available seat was the last row of the girls' section—which also happened to be the infamous 'co-ed' row (Riya had told me about this, of course).

As I slid into the aisle seat, I spotted three familiar faces. Riya and Smriti were sitting in the same row, though not directly next to me.

Instead, another familiar face sat next to me. Someone about whom I'd almost forgotten—Avik. Why was he sitting in the co-ed row anyway? I had a feeling that only 'couples' or 'almost couples' sat in that row.

I shuddered at the thought of me and Shiv on the date, sitting together all cutesy with each other. I coughed, like I was about to puke.

Before I could ponder any further on *that* issue, Avik said, 'Are you okay? You look like you're going to be sick.'

Avik conspicuously scooted away from me, at least as far as he could manage in that already overcrowded bench.

I smirked, 'That was my plan all along.'

Avik looked at me, his eyes narrowed, 'You coughed on purpose so that I'd move away from you and you'd have more personal space?'

Well, that wasn't the reason why I coughed, but I could pretend. I nodded, raising my eyebrows slyly.

'Genius,' he shook his head in disbelief. 'You're not...really infected, are you, though? I don't want to catch whatever...disease you may have.'

'Rude,' I said, glaring at him impishly.

He scooted back to his original position so that we almost touched shoulders.

'By the way, I'm not sitting in this row to talk to *girls*. I just sat here because it was the closest seat I could find to the front of the class.'

'Sure. You tell yourself that,' I said.

'No. I have no interest in getting distracted by *girls*,' he said, putting an emphasis on the word 'girls' like it was a bad word.

I don't know why I got so angry at that comment. Maybe all the frustration from the week, and it was just Wednesday.

'I also don't have any interest in getting distracted by *boys*,' I retorted, trying to replicate his tone.

Avik was silent. After a few moments, he said, 'I'm sorry, I didn't mean to be sexist. It's just...something that was told to me by my parents: don't talk to girls in coaching. They will distract you from your goal.'

I chuckled, 'So, your parents think girls are like sirens ready to pounce on unsuspecting, innocent boys?'

He snickered. 'Pretty much.'

'Glad to know we hold so much power,' I smirked.

'By the way, nice job getting kicked out of class first day of school. You must've been a "Cool Smart Kid" back in tenth, huh?'

'Oh. You saw that.' I was mortified. But not as mortified as I would've been if Shiv said the same thing to me. I wondered why. 'My best friend, Parnika, fits the definition of Cool Smart Kid. I was on the un-cooler side of the spectrum.'

'Where is she now?'

'She's one of the Shark batch students.'

'Oh—'

Before he could add anything, our chemistry teacher glided into the room. She actually *glided*. She was a fast-talking, short, stout lady—she scared me, that's for sure. It was hard to keep up with her, but from whatever knowledge I was able to glean, it was obvious—she was an expert at her field, a far better teacher than any we had in school.

'We have a test in the next class. Come prepared!'

I was jolted back to reality. A test *already*? It was just the first class! What kind of new method of torture was this?

Avik let out a very audible sigh. He slumped back into the cold, hard, unforgiving bench.

'You tricked me, you know,' he looked askance at me.

'What?'

'That day when we talked. I told you what I did thinking that you'd never come back.'

Involuntarily letting out a small chuckle, I said, 'Well, I'm sorry if you feel bad that I'm still here.'

'I don't,' he murmured.

'What was that? You say something?'

'Nope.'

∽

I had physics class for the first time today. Finding my class quickly in the dark Hellen hallway, I took a seat comfortably in the front, grateful to arrive early compared to the others.

After a while of sitting alone, I turned back to see where the other students were sitting—and everyone was sitting two rows behind, chattering to each other. In the corner of my eye, I spotted Riya talking with Smriti. They waved at me, and I quickly beelined my way to them, almost running into a guy who was walking to the front with his backpack.

The teacher soon walked on the dais (seriously, they had a *stage* for the teachers in this coaching centre). He sort of resembled the pigs from Angry Birds—he might've been a great guy, don't get me wrong, but I couldn't shake off the resemblance.

'Hey, why'd you sit on the front bench?' Riya smirked.

'Why, is there a problem with it?' I asked. Didn't everyone want to sit in the front?

'I've heard this physics teacher isn't as good as the Shark one. So, I guess no one wants to sit in the front.' Riya shrugged.

How the heck did they have so much information about everyone? I hardly knew anyone's names yet. Well, I guess it was a good thing I knew these girls now, they'd teach me.

As he started droning on and on about vectors, I lost interest and started idly doodling in my notebook. Riya was right, he did teach really poorly. Instead, my attention was fixed on their muted conversation going on to my side.

'Do you know who topped the Hellen talent hunt test?' Riya asked.

'Who?' Smriti said.

'You know, they guy who always tops almost all Hellen tests.'

'Oh. *Him*. Of course.'

They turned to face me. I looked at them with a forced, lost expression on my face, as if I'd not been overhearing their conversation so far.

'So, Avani, how do you know Shiv?' Riya asked.

'Umm…who?' I asked, dumbfounded. Did I hear them right? Or was I just hearing his name everywhere now?

'Yeah, Shiv, the guy you were talking to at school yesterday?' Smriti asked.

'Oh…' I replied, not knowing what she wanted out of this conversation. 'He and I were classmates at our previous school.'

'Is there something going on between you guys?' Riya chimed in. Meanwhile, the physics teacher droned on and on about magnitudes and directions. Gosh, I think I gave up on understanding this lecture at the 10-minute mark.

'No. He's just my classmate,' I replied firmly. Why did they care anyway? Doubt creeped into my mind. Was it really that obvious? Had they seen us together? Had he told anyone anything about us? Ugh. There was no 'us'.

'It's cool that you know him,' Riya said. 'He's one of the smartest guys here. We were in coaching together for the past four years…so that's how we know him and his *reputation*,' she replied.

'You guys have been going to coaching since sixth grade as well?' I asked, partly intimidated and partly horrified. Even my new relaxed, chill friends were more 'advanced' than me. Was this the norm, and was I an anomaly?

'Yeah,' she replied in a tone that felt like she was just stating the obvious.

My thoughts were interrupted by the teacher, who said, 'We'll be taking a short 10-minute break. Then, I'll start teaching the topic "Pulleys and Levers".'

I sighed with relief. His weird droning voice would've soon put me to sleep, if it weren't for my new friends' gossip. For most of the lecture, I'd been doodling, similar to how I'd spent most of my time during the talent hunt exam back in January—drawing an intricate city with octopi as residents. I looked around the classroom as everyone broke out in a buzz of conversation—everyone was engaged in some sort of dialogue. Everyone except one person. Avik was sitting alone on my previously occupied front seat, two rows ahead of anyone else in the classroom. He was sitting alone, staring at his notebook full of notes about today's class. I glanced at my notebook that contained nothing other than today's date, some initial scribblings of the physics topic we'd been taught today and an extension of my imagined underwater octopus city.

I was about to get up to give him some company (and maybe learn something from him) when Riya suggested, 'Do you guys want to go to the shops across the street?'

I assessed her proposal, then concluded, 'We won't be able to make it back in 10 minutes.'

She replied with a wry smile, 'We don't really need to come back.'

'But what about—'

'Avani, the attendance is already done. No will notice and no one cares. Chill, your parents won't get to know,' Smriti said knowingly.

I stood there, quietly, with them looking at me expectantly, as if to say 'What's wrong with you, *loser?*'

They really wanted me to miss this class, huh? Well, I'd already missed the first half, at least mentally, so I don't think I'd understand much in the second half anyway. The teacher really wasn't that good, I would probably understand more when I'd go home and have a glance at the textbook. And I finally had some friends. I couldn't disappoint them. Somewhere, deep inside, I felt so validated that I'd managed to find friends even in this hopeless setting. That someone still liked me. All the people here were so strange and new. Not to mention *competitive*. It was nice that someone was talking to me, at least. I was glad my social life wasn't dead. I was glad I wasn't *boring*.

I glanced over at Avik. He'd just make snarky comments about me anyway. 'Let's go,' I said, picking up my backpack and leaving the classroom with my newfound friends.

∽

The outside of the coaching centre was deserted. It felt like leaving school early because of a sick day—but this time, I was doing something wrong.

'Let's go to the samosa shop. I just really have a craving for the masala aloo samosa with the mint chutney!' Riya exclaimed, as we started walking across the huge parking lot.

'I'd love that. Remember when we used to skip all the time back in ninth class? Gosh, that algebra teacher we had was *so* boring. We used to sneak into the teacher's room afterwards, mark our attendance,' Smriti added.

'So our parents wouldn't find out, yeah. Fun times.'

'It was all fun and games until that supervisor caught us that one time. Gosh, my parents took away my phone till the school year ended.'

Wow, these people were seasoned professionals. I definitely wasn't.

I could feel the panic rising up in my chest. What was I doing?

'Riya, I forgot my wallet. You guys go, I'll catch up with you,'

I said, running towards the classroom. Maybe I could still make it. I could go and sit next to Avik on the front bench.

By the time I reached the classroom, I heard the teacher's droning voice booming on the mic. I was late. I couldn't walk in now. The door was right next to the stage, everyone would look at me. I didn't want to have the orientation situation again, where someone points me out.

My breathing shallow, I perched myself on a bench near the entrance of the coaching centre, taking out my phone.

'Mom?'

'Avani? Is everything fine?' She sounded concerned. I'd never called her before actually. Maybe once to ask her where she kept my favourite socks but other than that, never.

'No... I'm not feeling so good.' I added, after a moment of hesitation, 'Could you come get me? Like, as soon as possible.'

'Are you okay? Did you hurt yourself?'

'No, no. I'm sitting outside the building,' I said.

'I'm coming to get you, beta. I'll be there in 10 minutes. If you don't feel safe outside, go back in the building. What are you doing out anyway? Your class was supposed to go on for... another hour, right?' She was getting into her car, I could hear the door open and close.

'Talking while driving isn't safe, Mom,' I said, consciously evading her question. Wow, was I actually lecturing my own mother? I wondered what lie I would have to cook up to tell Mom.

'Okay, I'll be there in 10 minutes,' she said. 'Why don't you take deep breaths and listen to some music in the time being, it'll make you feel better. You know...that band which is related to death and chemistry.'

I chuckled. 'Okay, Mom. Thanks.'

I put on my earphones. Listening to My Chemical Romance always made me feel more badass than I actually was. I mean, on the outside, I was a girl sitting all alone on a bench while skipping class and feeling extremely bad for doing so, but on the inside, I was a punk rocker flying on a private jet faster than the speed of light.

I don't know how or why Mom knew that I liked listening to the 'band related to death and chemistry', I don't know why, but when she finally arrived, I hugged her for probably the second time in my life and I don't know why, but I couldn't bring myself to lie to her. I didn't want to become like Riya or Smriti.

'I skipped class today, Mom. I skipped physics class. Well, half of it,' I said, once we were driving away from the godforsaken hellhole. I looked at the other side of the road, trying to spot my friends. Then I saw them standing with a boy, talking animatedly.

'You did? I didn't think you had it in you,' she chuckled.

'What?' I was shocked.

'You always follow the rules, Avani. I'm just surprised to see you break one,' she shrugged.

'I'm surprised to see you *not* lecturing me,' I blurted out. 'Sorry, shouldn't have said that.'

She shook her head. 'No, it's true. You're right, I lecture you a lot.'

'No, Mom, it's okay. You're my mom, you're supposed to lecture and scold me. It's your right.'

'It's not. I...I'm surprised you called me and not your father, honestly,' she stammered.

'It doesn't matter. You're my mom,' I said, tears brimming in my eyes.

'Avani, what's wrong?' she asked, still keeping an eye on the road but trying to look at me as well.

'Nothing, you should focus on the road. It's nothing, I'm just getting too emotional,' I said, trying to blink my tears away.

She chuckled. 'Did your dad say that to you? You're too

emotional? Yeah, I've heard that one before.'

'You have?' I asked.

'I think he can be painfully logical at some points. Too pragmatic. Sometimes he forgets to be subjective,' she said.

I looked at her with amazement. Did he also say that to her? So, I wasn't too emotional? I was just normal?

'So, I'm not too emotional?' I asked her, I don't know why.

'No, of course not. You're a normal person. Normal people have emotions,' she said.

'I…I lied when I said I was in the same batch as Parnika. She's in the top batch and I'm in a lower batch than her,' I blurted out.

I couldn't believe I just told the truth to Mom. But I knew I couldn't have told Dad. I didn't want to face him one-on-one again after I lied to him that day about my batch. He wouldn't get it. He was too much of a proponent of following the rules. I almost shuddered at the thought of how he'd react to this situation. He would judge me—because he had a different image of me than the one I was currently portraying. And Mom? What did I have to lose with her? I was sure she already kind of hated me.

'Okay,' she replied, her voice not showing a hint of emotion.

'So? Are you gonna scold me? Throw me out of the car?'

'I'm obviously not going to throw you out of the car, Avani. I'm not your enemy, *I'm your mother*,' she said, her voice strained.

I looked at her. She wasn't angry, like I'd imagined. Instead, she had a slight frown on her face, as she stared vacantly at the car front of her.

'I'm sorry,' I quickly said and looked away from her. I couldn't bear to look at her any longer. Her frown was different from the one she'd give me when I'd leave some of the lauki uneaten on my plate, which I'd deemed her 'Lauki Frown'. Instead, she just looked plain disappointed.

'I'm sorry you had to lie,' she mumbled.

13

Not My Best Moment

When we arrived home, we quietly parted ways: Mom, to the kitchen, and me, to the safe haven that was my bedroom. I couldn't bear to look at her any longer. I was afraid I'd say something else that would make her frown like that. It's just…I'd never seen that look on her face before. I was used to angry, disapproving Mom—but this was different. This was Mom full of grief.

I knew I had to distract myself—and I knew I had a fresh sheet of chemistry homework already waiting for me, so I knew what I should do—*not* play *The Sims 3*. I couldn't resist the temptation of playing my favourite video game, though, so I booted up my computer and waited for the game to load. *The Sims 3* was a life simulation video game, where we could create characters and control their lives, right from the imaginary worlds where they could live to what they ate and their career. I liked it because it offered me an escape from the real world. It was like doing a soft-reset of my brain. I set a timer on my phone for half an hour and lost myself in the game.

After half an hour, as promised (even though I wanted to continue playing), I sat down with the assignment.

Two hours later, I heard a knock at my door.

'Dinner?' Mom was standing at my doorway with a tray of casseroles. 'You didn't come downstairs to eat with us today.'

'Oh. I totally forgot.' I looked at my watch, it was 10.00 p.m. already. I was too preoccupied by the empirical formula to remember about hunger.

Her face was unreadable. The look I'd seen on her face a few hours ago was gone. The normal, lauki-frown Mom was back. I wasn't sure if that made me happy or sad.

'Just keep it over there, I'll eat it after solving one more question.'

'Also, your phone was lying downstairs…you had multiple calls and messages from someone.'

'From whom?' I really didn't want it to be Shiv. I hadn't decided on the time or the place for our 'date'—honestly, at this point, I was disappointed that he didn't know about my sheer incompetence in making even the smallest of decisions. The thought of him made my stomach feel weird. Or was that hunger?

'Riya…I think. Also Smriti, some other girl. Here, I got your phone for you.'

She placed my phone on my desk, which was full of open assignments with tick marks on solved questions, circles on doubts/unable to solve questions and multiple question marks on questions that didn't make any human sense.

'Thanks, Mom. I'll eat my food soon.'

'It's 10.00 p.m., Avani. Please eat it soon, otherwise it will get cold.'

She gave me one last look, closing the door behind her as she left.

I mentally berated myself for being so direct with her. She was surely disappointed in me. Hell, I was disappointed in me for lying about my batch and skipping class. This was getting too much.

I quickly replied to a text from Shiv, who was asking me about my favourite phone brand (I think it was safe to assume he was running out of random questions now). I also had a few missed calls from Riya and one from Smriti. I called up Riya.

'Hey Avani, I thought you weren't picking up because you were mad at us or something,' Riya said.

'Sorry, I didn't have my phone with me.' It was better to not have my phone nearby, lest I'd get distracted by another text from Shiv. That guy really liked to text.

'Have you started the chemistry assignment?'

'Yes. I'm on question 35. Still so much to do,' I flipped the sheet and saw that the list of questions went on till 50.

'Wow! Smriti and I are just on question 15. You've done a lot, Avani,' she exclaimed.

'I have?' I perked up.

'Yeah...anyway, I had some doubts in the assignment. I was hoping you'd help me clear them?'

'Sure.' My work *was* worth something. Someone actually needed my help. I thought I'd never be asked for help after my genius phase, that is, my time at White Meadows, ended. It had all been going downhill since then.

Finally, after explaining at least five questions' answers, I got a chance to ask something for once.

'I skipped all the numericals related to mole concept for now. Do you have any idea how to solve them? I think I'm still unclear on the whole topic,' I asked.

There was a long pause on the other side. 'No yaar...I was hardly able to get past question 15. The movie and bowling really tired me out.'

'You guys went for a movie *and bowling*?'

'Yeah,' her voice perked up, 'we ran into some of the Shark batch students across the road. You know, you made a huge mistake by ditching us. It was *so much fun*.'

'Oh.' I wanted to cut the phone, not wanting to hear about

certain Shark (still hated using this word unironically) students whom they might've run into.

'Shiv was there too, in case you're interested to know. He won, of course. So was your classmate from school, Parnika. She's really fun! We should all hang out.'

I soon quit the call, with no answers to my mole concept doubts and just with an increased feeling of self-loathing and FOMO. My throat was dry, my head ached and my stomach twisted out of hunger.

∽

The next morning, a Sunday, I mustered up the courage to call up Parnika. Maybe I could go over to her house and discuss the horrible week. She'd invited me, casually and verbally, anyway. Maybe her week was horrible too? Probably not. She was Hellen royalty. Hesitantly, I picked up my phone and fixed up a time for us to meet. Like the old times.

I was at her door at noon sharp. I rang the bell to her massive three-storey home...mansion.

'Hello, beta! How are you?' her father was standing in the doorway.

'Hello, uncle. I'm good.'

'Parnika is upstairs in her room.'

'Thanks.'

'By the way, Parnika told me you're in Dolphin batch at Hellen?'

'Yes, Uncle.' Was that my identity now? The former smart girl who is now a second-class citizen.

'Oh, I see. Nice seeing you, beta.'

Walking upstairs, I saw various framed photos on the wall. Parnika holding trophies, all the way from kindergarten to now. She truly was an achiever. And I was proud of her. Sometimes, a bit jealous. But mostly proud.

'Hey Avani!' Parnika was out in the balcony.

'Hi!' I walked over to her. 'What's up?' I asked, standing next to her looking at a beautiful view of the Rose Garden. Wow, man, she was really lucky. My view was of the trash dumpster for our lane.

'You know. Same old, same old,' she said dismissively. 'You?'

I was hoping she'd say something like, 'My standard of living has significantly depreciated in the past week.' But I guess it was just me.

'Um… Getting used to it all. Everything's a bit new.' This felt like a lie. It was a lie. I wasn't used to it at all. Not even 1 per cent.

'Yeah. Coaching can be a huge kick in the face when you start with it,' she said, like she was a seasoned expert. I half expected her to say, 'This ain't my first rodeo.' Cause it wasn't. It was probably her sixth.

'Yeah, that's what I'm finding out now,' I said, laughing at my own misery.

'You'll get used to it,' she said. I was relieved. She was definitely the bigger, more seasoned person in this conversation. Actually now, every conversation.

'Thanks. I hope so.'

We both stared at her lush backyard, almost comparable to the Rose Garden with the amount of flowers blooming.

Maybe I could suck it up and clear my chemistry doubts with Parnika. Avik had said that good friends wouldn't judge me. I could try to let go of my ego in front of Parnika.

'Hey, could I ask you something?' I said. 'I had a few doubts about the mole concept. Could you explain it to me?'

'I really just want to take a break right now from this coaching shit. Want to watch a movie or something?' she said.

Oh. My stomach dropped. I had never heard her swear. Ever. Not even a mild one like this one. If anything, I was the swearer in our friendship. Was she ok?

'Sure. Which one?' My voice sounded a bit strained. Like I was trying to hold back a few tears. I wasn't sure why, maybe her tone felt a bit off. A bit rude—and not the 'friendly-rude' way we usually were with each other.

We went down to the lounge room, fully equipped with a surround-sound speaker system.

'*Harry Potter*?' She asked, a mischievous smile on her face.

'*Goblet of Fire*,' I said. 'I just really want to hear Dumbledore inaccurately shout, "Did you put your name in the goblet of FIRE??!"'

'Let me set it up.'

My mom had never let me buy any of the *Harry Potter* DVDs. Motivated by this, I had introduced Parnika to the *Harry Potter* series. Soon enough, she had persuaded her parents to get her the boxed set with all the extra bloopers and the deleted scenes.

Yes. I could be an evil genius sometimes.

Equipped with some macadamia nuts and popcorn, we started watching the movie. The opening score was enough for me to be fully absorbed in the darkness of the fourth movie and mostly forget about any of the previous embarrassing events like me getting turned down after showing an unprecedented amount of vulnerability.

Halfway through the movie, during the Yule Ball scene, Parnika paused the movie. 'You know what the real travesty is?' she looked incensed. 'Parvati and Padma Patil's outfits here. I mean, what kind of a look is that? Those pink and orange lehengas are almost a slap in our face. Who in their right mind could design that and deem it appropriate? I mean, I understand they are supposed to be students, but at least the designers could've gone for something less tacky and a bit cuter.'

'I know. Even the description in the books was much better.' I added.

'Uh-huh.' Parnika looked lost in her own world, barely registering what I said.

I said, 'By the way, made any new stuff lately?'

She was unusually quiet for a while. 'Um...no. I haven't done any stitching or designing. I'm focusing on studies for now.'

'Oh okay,' I said, observing her downcast expression. 'Are you...okay?'

'Yeah, I'm great.' She said, perking up, 'I should get back to some work. Is it okay if we hang out later?'

'Sure. I had fun hanging out with you again, Parni,' I said, using the nickname Shiv always called her with.

Maybe I just needed to try harder with Parnika. She didn't seem *too* different since coaching started. Maybe she really did just need a break from 'the coaching shit'. Maybe it was all in my head.

When the night rolled around, a feeling of doom filled me. Was this coming week going to be as challenging and tiring as the previous one? I shuddered at the thought of various upcoming events of this week—the chemistry test tomorrow, the grand test on next Sunday (yes, there was apparently a day dedicated mock tests in the JEE format—and they decided to use the only free day we had for it and called it the lamest thing ever) and, of course, the date with Shiv at the undecided place on an undecided time. I was glad that at least he didn't bother me later in the week to ask about my 'choices'. I don't even know why I agreed to go in the first place. The whole thing about 'stepping out of my comfort zone' was really coming back to haunt me now.

∽

On Monday, by the time the next chemistry class rolled around, I'd still not figured out the difficult concepts.

The thought of asking Shiv did cross my mind, but we didn't really talk about studying in our texts. Our chats were more along the lines of deep emotional topics such as: our favourite breakfast food (mine: upma), favourite flavour of biscuit filling (chocolate) or even the temperature at which we preferred to keep our ACs at (26 degrees). I know, *riveting*. Asking Parnika turned out to be a disaster. Maybe I could ask my new friends.

'Hey, Riya.' I slid next to her in the co-ed row, although I'd come early enough to secure a seat in the second row. The first was always full.

'Hi.' She didn't even turn to look at me, she had her spectacles on and was going through the chemistry worksheet. She looked like she'd pulled an all-nighter.

'Have you done the mole concept questions?'

'Na, yaar. I wasn't able to figure them out.'

I turned to Smriti who, equally disappointingly, had the same answer.

Maybe I should look at it in a positive light—if my friends didn't get it either, it meant that this chemistry topic was actually difficult for everyone. In school, they always used to re-teach the difficult topics, and put easier questions in the tests. I breathed a sigh of relief at this realization.

Suddenly, the chemistry teacher's assistant barged into the room. 'Quiz time!'

The decibel level of the class increased manifold. I breathed deeply a few times. It wasn't going to be difficult. I had read most of my notes. It was going to be fine.

I stared at the assistant, who really reminded me of Filch from *Harry Potter* during the Umbridge days, gleefully passing down stacks of the test papers. He could've had any other job, but he chose *this one*. He's probably been living for this moment. He probably feasted on the students' sadness. If Parnika were here right now, we'd roast him so hard.

As I got the test paper handed to me with an OMR (bubble filling answers) sheet, I was almost reluctant to open it. I looked up, all around me, kids were busy with their sheets. I had no other choice but to face the music.

I opened it and attempted to decipher the questions. The first few were all mole concept numerical questions, so I skipped forward. *It's okay, deep breaths Avani*. This had happened to me in school before. I'd get back to those later and it'd be alright.

'Oh, shit.' I heard Riya mutter, as she went through the paper in a similar fashion to me. 'Oh shit' was an understatement if anything.

In 15 minutes, I had answered all the theoretical questions. I was left with 55 of the 60 questions and still more than an hour to go. In the past, I would've breezed through tests confidently, there was more than enough time. This time, though, I was stuck. The only thing I could see clearly was the word 'moles' again and again.

Why hadn't I worked harder? Why wasn't I able to figure it out? Everyone doubted me. My mom, Shiv and Parnika, probably. Even *I* doubted myself. Why was I becoming so incompetent? What was I going to say to my dad this evening? Lie again? Tell him that his previously genius daughter was only able to answer 5 out of 60 questions, which may even be wrong?

As I was regretting all the life choices that led me to this unbearable moment, someone called out to me.

'Avani!' Riya whispered.

I leaned my head to her side in order to acknowledge her call. Did she want some water? I was actually thirsty myself; all this self-loathing was giving me a dry mouth.

'Did you solve question five?'

I nodded. It was one of the only five questions I knew properly.

'What's the answer?'

People cheated on exams in coaching classes?

I'd been a witness to cheating at school before. I never tattled on the people involved—of course, my parents didn't raise me to be a *rat*. I generally knew all the answers, so I did not feel the need to cheat. I was almost jealous of my past self.

'D.' I whispered. I felt a bit of pride, since I actually knew the answer to that particular question. I'd worked hard for solving it, and she wanted to know the answer. They'd been my only good friends here.

'Question 25?' she asked.

I shook my head, not daring to speak. I was afraid someone would catch us. That wouldn't be pretty.

She directed her question to Smriti, who was sitting next to her. I didn't dare move my eyes from my paper, but I could hear Smriti leaning back to ask someone in the row behind us.

'It's B,' she whispered back to me.

Before I could stop myself, the hand holding my pen filled in the 25th bubble.

I couldn't stop myself. I kept glancing at Riya's OMR sheet and copying the bubbles. She, in turn, was getting the information from Smriti—who was getting it from someone else. It was like a game of Chinese whispers.

At one point, I wasn't even sure I was filling the answers for the right questions. I just blindly kept filling them with whatever I saw on Riya's sheet. Just so I'd look like I had answered all the questions. That would at least look better than going through the shame accompanying submitting a completely empty OMR sheet. It seemed more socially acceptable to solve a question wrong rather than not have known the solution at all.

'Hey! Don't cheat!'

I looked up. It was the assistant, glaring at Smriti and me.

'I'll take away your IDs! You won't be able to sit for any more tests.'

He kept staring at us. His small, beady eyes were burning holes in my soul. My head was pounding with fear, adrenaline and shame. Was this really less shameful than submitting an empty but honestly filled OMR?

My heart rate finally returned to normal when he walked out of the room. Now, my eyes didn't wander. They were stuck to my own question paper partly because of fear, although mostly due to embarrassment. I was becoming such an absolute loser. What could be worse than this? Oh, how I was relieved that Shiv and Parnika weren't in my class for once. This was not my best moment.

Meanwhile, Smriti resumed her whispering with Riya.

I squeezed myself out of the bench, submitted my answer sheet to the assistant and walked out of the room before he or anyone else could say anything to me. I sat down in an adjacent empty classroom and just...broke down crying.

How could Riya and Smriti continue to cheat right after being reprimanded? Didn't they feel any shame, any remorse or any fear? My entire body was actually shaking from all of the above feelings.

I tried to register what had just happened. I just cheated in a test for the first time in my life because I was too ashamed to submit an empty answer sheet. How could I do this? First the lying to Dad about not being in Shark, then skipping class and now this? In my heart of hearts, I knew why. Because I desperately wanted to remain a perfect 'Smart Kid', like Parnika and Shiv. Like I used to be. I couldn't fail—instead, I had to be the *best*. The odds were already against me from the start. I had to be like them, even if it meant I had to pretend, apparently.

14

'So Much Pressure, Yaar'

I rested my head on one of the tables, trying to calm myself down by taking deep breaths. There was no one in the world I could talk to about my *real* feelings. Mom would be so burdened with disappointment in me that she'd spontaneously combust. Dad would be in denial, thinking I could never do that—I could never be so dishonest. Shiv or Parnika would just laugh at my inaptitude to do simple chemistry questions, which they probably learned to solve back when I was learning to walk. Riya and Smriti would tell me to chill out and stop being so uptight.

Amidst my silent sobs, I heard someone's footsteps into the room.

'Please, Shanaya, I can't talk right now.'

I looked up, my eyes still a bit blurry. I blinked away my tears. No one seemed to be in the room.

He spoke again, with stifled anger in his tone. 'No, you *don't* know what I'm going through. In case you don't remember, you very conveniently disappeared almost two years ago.'

I looked back—and on the bench right next to the door, I saw Avik sitting with his forehead on the table, phone to his ear. I could tell it was Avik from his fluffy, voluminous head of hair.

In a resigned tone, he said, 'I...I miss you. Take care of yourself, okay?'

I guess he was talking to his girlfriend or something. Wow,

even the loner had a girlfriend.

I remained motionless with my head on the desk, waiting for him to leave. Once he would leave, I could go back to my self-loathing.

'Hello, Papa? Sorry, my phone was busy,' he spoke again, his voice completely different from the last call he just made. It was more...panicky. He was quiet for a while, and I was too far from him to hear anything on the other side of the phone.

'No, I wasn't talking to her. It was just a friend I made in tuition. He was asking me a doubt.'

'No! You don't need to come back,' he sounded desperate, 'Please don't.' Then he attempted to compose himself, 'I'm not wasting my time. I will get better marks this time. And I won't talk to her, I promise.'

'Okay, I will send you the answer sheet with my marks when I get it,' he said in a resigned tone.

I think he cut the phone after that because he sighed really loudly while saying the word 'shit' again and again.

I couldn't hold it in anymore—so I let out a huge sneeze. Damn, these allergies are a real stick in the mud. In the corner of my eye, I saw Avik jump in his seat.

'What the hell? You were here the whole time?' He walked towards me, his eyes wide, eyebrows risen. He no longer sounded panicky, sad or desperate as he had a few minutes ago. He was embarrassed.

'Uh...yeah.' My nose was stuffy, making my voice sound really whiny, which tended to happen after I cried. 'Sorry...I didn't know you were here, I was just listening to music.'

'But you don't even have headphones on.'

I stammered. 'Uh...um—I just have really bad hearing, so the doctor told me not to use headphones. I'm actually just imagining the songs in my head.' Wow, I wasn't very good at this lying thing.

'Have you been crying?' His eyes were narrowed. 'Your voice sounds weird. And the tip of your nose is red—like Rudolph the deer,' he chuckled, as he took a seat on the bench across the aisle from me.

'No...I have a cold,' I said, moving my hand to cover my nose. How did *he*, of all people, notice?

'You have a cold in April?' His eyes were still narrowed.

'Allergies. You never know when they strike.' I tried to make myself sound as least stuffy as possible.

He remained quiet for a while. I could feel him studying me. Meanwhile I stared at my hands, unable to look back at him. 'Look, I don't mean to impose or interfere but is it because of the test?'

His voice was different now—it was softer and calmer. It was concerned, like my mom was on the phone, the day I'd skipped class. I immediately felt a bit relaxed.

I nodded lightly. How was this conversation happening? Since when had I started to confide in strangers?

'What happened, Avani?' Hearing him say my name made me feel *seen*. Like I was an individual, not just a kid in the sea of 'IIT Aspirants' here. Like I was human. Not a machine.

'I don't know. I used to be the best in school, but now I'm nowhere close,' I said. I wasn't sure where the words were coming from.

He mumbled, 'I knew someone who felt the same exact way.'

I looked up at him. 'Oh really? What did they do?'

He was quiet. 'Well, she uh—never mind. The thing is, if you really want to make it through the next two years here, you have to have tougher skin. Do you know what I mean?'

'Um, I guess,' I murmured. I was tough. I mean, I couldn't bench press anything more than a kilo, but I was tough. Right?

'There are going to be more than 200 tests in the next two years. Are you going to feel the same way after each test?' he asked. 'You won't be able to make it through it if you do.'

Who was he to tell me how to feel? 'I think I'm alright the way I am, thank you,' I said, getting up from the bench and getting ready to bolt. I was *not* going to listen to the preaching of a 15-year-old boy.

'Look, I don't know you at all but you seem like a smart and grounded person,' he got up too, standing just a few inches from me. He was quite tall. At least one-third more Avani. (Yes, that is how I measure heights). But he would be taller if he stood up straight.

Where was he going with this? Usually, people preceded something scathing with something equally nice. 'Thanks, I guess.'

'You know why you got caught cheating? Because you did it in the most obvious way possible. That's when I realized that you've never done it before.'

I looked at him in disbelief—but mostly in shame. He knew? Did everyone else know? Oh God, I was a human disgrace. 'I'm not a cheater.'

'I could tell,' he chuckled. 'Why did you even cheat?'

'I dunno. I don't want people to know I'm not…smart,' I mumbled. Who were these people? Did it mean my family and friends? Did it include someone else like *me*?

'You shouldn't pretend to be someone you're not. It doesn't pay off in the end,' he said, his face completely devoid of any humour. 'Sometimes, it's better to come face to face with what you actually are—before it's too late.'

'What are you, some saint?' I asked, chuckling a bit. This definitely sounded like some preaching, 'Why are you even telling me all this?'

'You remind me of someone,' he said, his lips pressed into a slight frown.

'Oh? Whom?' I asked.

He seemed hesitant. 'She lives very far away now.'

Was it the girl he was just talking to on the phone?

'This is for your *allergies*. I'm sorry if I said something wrong or if I was too forward,' he said, handing me a handkerchief.

'Thanks,' I took it from him and clutched it tight. It had a small musical note sewn into it, on one corner.

∽

When I walked into physics class, I was a bit late and my brain was still in a confused, post-cry haze. My eyes were stinging. Quickly, I found a seat at the back of the class.

I glanced at them, sitting a few benches in front of me—Riya was giggling about something with Smriti while the physics teacher droned on about pulleys. They seemed to have zero interest in the lecture. To be fair, I wasn't able to understand much either (he really *was* a bad teacher) but at least I was quiet.

I couldn't believe how I spent the last few days with them. I guess it felt good to have a few people who acknowledged my presence, who knew my name. Also, I didn't have to put up my 'Smart Kid' image in front of them. They didn't know how 'accomplished' I used to be back in school. But I couldn't be like Riya or Smriti, no matter how much I tried. If I really *had* to come face-to-face with who I was becoming now, I knew at least who I wasn't—I wasn't *them*. I wasn't chill and carefree, if chill meant not listening in class, gossiping, disparaging the teachers, bunking classes and cheating in tests. I know I was trying to get out of my comfort zone but these activities were a couple light years away from me. Also, me doing these things didn't make sense, because I wasn't content—not with the fact that I had cheated today. That *really* pushed my boundaries.

I wasn't sure how I would go through with our friendship. Perhaps I could spend a few days sitting apart from them, just to focus on the lectures. I wasn't going to ignore them completely, I would just try to be more *me*.

Though I really wasn't sure who this new me *was*. I could only try.

My phone chimed.

Shiv: Let's meet after class @6 in front of the shops, across the street.

Another consequence of me trying to 'get out of my comfort zone'. Still, I somewhat looked forward to it. He reminded me of school. The good old days.

By the time the class got over, I could feel myself getting nervous, and the feeling only multiplied second by second. I was about to meet Shiv, the Shark guy, the smart guy who would probably be surrounded by millions of people fawning over him. He was like a rock star here.

Was this what meeting your crush feels like? Or meeting someone you like a lot? Cause I just felt like I was going to pass out.

Getting up, I walked to the Hellen reception area and saw Riya and Smriti sitting in the waiting area. They gestured me to come over.

'Hey Avani. Where were you in physics class?' Riya asked, concern writ on her face.

'I was sitting in the back. I got a bit late,' I said, tersely. I wondered if they could feel the shift in my tone. Or maybe they didn't care enough.

'Shit yaar, my chemistry test went so bad,' Smriti moaned. 'My parents are going to be pissed at me. They already took away my laptop as punishment for not getting into the Shark batch. They say that they've spent too much money on me since sixth class for me to still be such a failure.'

'I know, I have the same crappy situation at home,' Riya slumped into her chair. 'So much pressure, yaar. It's like parents don't understand how difficult it can be for us. And then they compare us to the people who top.'

'Even after the cheating we did, I don't think I'll get a good rank. May as well forfeit my phone right now instead of when I'm forced to show the marksheet to them,' Smriti said.

I just stood there, speechless. If I'd told the truth to Dad, would he do the same? At least Riya and Smriti were telling the truth to their parents. My Dad trusted me so much he'd never ask for my answer sheets to verify my marks. I was worse, a cheater *and* a liar.

'Sorry, I need to go. See you later,' I said, quickly walking towards the exit, the pit in my stomach growing deeper.

15

My Resolution

As I walked out of the Hellen building, I saw a group of approximately 15 students standing together and talking loudly. I took a seat on the entrance steps, taking out my phone to text Shiv that I was too tired to meet him today. After all that happened today, I just didn't have the energy anymore.

'Yeah, man, they really should have more challenging questions on these tests,' one of the guys from the group said. Half of his face was covered with a beard, and the rest, with large, round glasses. They were standing a few metres from me, behind a car in the parking lot.

'Relax dude. This was only the first test. I'm sure it will get only more difficult from now on,' Shiv said. I could make out that he was standing in that group, too, somehow looking slick in his trademark grey Hellen polo shirt. I'd shoved that shirt way back in my closet and swore never to wear it. He was starting to grow out a stubble, looking like a genius Indian entrepreneur with millions in funding for his unicorn start-up. Weirdly specific.

Parnika said, 'Yeah, it better. Else I'll have to find another place,' she sounded gleeful today. A bit too much, if I'm being honest.

'Oh no, we'll miss you so much,' Shiv said sarcastically. Everyone in the group broke out in raucous laughter.

It was then I realized how 'out of place' I really felt. Riya

My Resolution

and Smriti weren't my type, I was sure of that now. And now these people? They were having fun in their loud, almost rowdy conversation about how the test was too easy. They really were an elite group of people.

'I woke up at 6.00 a.m. today to just revise for this test,' someone said. 'I didn't expect it to be so simple.'

Parnika spoke in a hushed tone, 'I heard that there was some cheating going on in the lower batches. Can you believe it? Those people feel the need to cheat on the first test? It's so sad.' She shook her head as if she were talking about something as tragic as the high unemployment rates in India or ever-growing corruption.

'Well, they are in that batch for a reason,' said a boy wearing a horribly fitting pair of pants. I had nothing against them apart from their egregious fashion sense. Maybe uniforms were a good idea after all. Some people just couldn't handle the freedom of choice.

'They're just squandering their parents' money,' Parnika chuckled, the haughtiness apparent in her tone. 'They should've just taken humanities instead.'

When did she become so judgemental? Or was she always this way?

'Hey, everyone deserves a chance. You never know who'll be at the top in the end. It's a two-year-long journey,' Shiv said. The others nodded along.

'Wow, look at you, Shiv. Saying all of these "enlightened" things. Are you sure you're not a monk in a teenager's body?' Parnika shrieked with laughter.

I felt so alienated. And ashamed.

Why was Shiv even interested in talking to me? I had a feeling he would be just fine with the group he was with. Why would he need me? I wasn't a genius like his friends. I was nothing.

I was in the process of making a quick exit to my car when Shiv called out, 'Oye, Avani!'

I wanted to keep on walking away from him, maybe even start running, not wanting to be seen by him or Parnika or any other member of their 'elite' group. But I turned around, with one hand on my hip, and stared at the ground, not able to make eye contact with him walking oh-so-casually towards me, hands in his jean pockets.

'How are you? I waited for you across the street, but you never came,' he asked, almost accusatorially.

I looked behind him at his Shark group, wondering if they could hear us. I'd rather not be heard or even seen by them, for that matter, so I walked a bit further away. Shiv followed suit. We were almost cat-and-mouse at this point.

'You okay?'

I don't know why, but I couldn't bring myself to look at his face. It was too much. He was so cool, and I was such a loser. He was popular, happy and smart, and I was basically friendless, sad and stupid.

'Avani? Did something happen?'

When I finally looked at him, I saw his confused, half-smiling face staring back at me. My stomach did a flip. He was perfect.

I was about to tell him about today—the fact that I was the one who cheated, and I was actually not as smart as I seemed back in school, just as I'd told Avik.

But I couldn't.

Instead, I softly smiled and said, 'No, no. I'm fine. I think I'm a bit hungry, actually.'

'Oh... Um, do you want something to eat? We could go across the street to the shops,' he gestured towards the busy road crossing.

'No, no! I'm just about to head home anyway. Mom made yellow dal today, my favourite,' I giggled, not feeling like my laugh was my own but rather trying to imitate Parnika's.

Yellow dal was not my favourite. The thought of going out to eat with a guy like Shiv was enough to make my stomach churn and for me to start spouting absurd lies.

'Yeah, it's my favourite too. Actually, I used to have it for dinner almost every day,' he chuckled with a reminiscent look on his face.

'Nice,' I continued smiling. My face had begun to hurt from the inauthenticity of my expression.

'Now I gulp down those rock-hard rotis with bland bhindi faster than 3×10^8 m/s,' he muttered.

I observed him as his expression changed to one of contempt. Wow, this was the only guy I knew who made physics references in complete seriousness.

'So...did you decide a time or place?' he asked, changing his expression back to one exuding confidence. 'For our date?'

'Oh.' I pretended to look surprised as if I just remembered that 'date' was even a word. 'No, sorry, I was too busy.'

Wasn't this a date? What was even considered a date?

'Umm, okay. Decide and let me know.'

Why was he giving me orders? It sure felt like he was my boss, and I was on a deadline.

'Why don't you decide? Since you're the one who asked me?' I raised my voice a bit.

'Why are you getting so agitated?'

The look on his face reminded me of my numerous recent conversations with Dad. It made me uncomfortable, to say the least. It was strange to see his 'nice guy' persona change into this. His eyes were narrowed and nose slightly scrunched upwards. It was almost like a look of disgust.

I wasn't quite sure either. Why was I getting so agitated?

'It's tough to adjust to this place,' I mumbled, telling him a half-truth, realizing how it was so much easier to talk about my problems with a complete stranger like Avik than Shiv, a guy I'd known for much longer. We'd texted a lot, Shiv and I, he knew my favourite colour and I knew his (blue), but we never talked about stuff like this. It was as if our texts were a safe haven from the reality of tuition, but when we met in real life, it was difficult not to be reminded of the Shark-sized chasm between us. It was like a huge elephant in the room for me—the fact that we used to be equals in school (I actually scored more than him in most subjects, not that I'm keeping record…I am) but now he was visibly smarter than me. I wasn't sure if he felt it too or was oblivious.

Shiv looked plain confused. 'But why? Hellen has the best teachers and classes. It's a hundred times better than White Meadows. It's home to me,' he shrugged. 'It's actually better than my current home.'

I stared at him, shell-shocked. Was he being sarcastic? I waited a while for him to start laughing or yell out 'psych!', but it never came. He was dead serious.

'Really?' I asked.

'Anything would be better than living with my weirdo roommate,' he said, kicking a stray piece of chipped concrete on the ground. It didn't go very far.

'Does your roommate go to Hellen as well?'

'Yes. He does,' he said. 'He's always on his phone, talking to some girl. Or he's staring out the window. He literally never talks to me. The worst thing is, he wants the fan to be switched off at night. He says the sound disturbs his sleep. It's April, for God's sake. If I were at home, my AC would be on!' He was incensed.

'Oh. Maybe you could ask for a change of roommates,' I said.

'I'd rather not talk about him. What about you? Why are you having issues adjusting here?' he asked, emphasizing the word 'issues'. When he asked me, he didn't have the sensitivity in his voice that Avik had. Wait, why was I even comparing them?

'It's tough to find good friends—and good seats.' I chose to tell him a moderate truth, similar to how I was with Parnika now.

His carefree look returned. 'But me and my bros—we have the first bench reserved for us. So both the problems can be sorted easily. Classes are fun that way too, and you get to sit nearest to the board.'

'Reserved?'

'Yeah, they reserve benches depending on your rank in your last big grand test. Right now, seats are reserved on the basis of the talent hunt exam. The first grand test is coming up on Sunday. So you just have to score the top spots,' he said.

Is that why the first few benches seemed to be always occupied by the same people? I thought I didn't get to sit there because I was always too late. 'What do you even talk about with your "bros"?' I asked.

Laughing, he said, 'Haha…bros. You're funny.'

I wasn't being funny, I was being sarcastic. Maybe he wasn't that smart after all.

'We were actually laughing because of our physical chemistry teacher. He kept talking about the animal "mole" instead of the chemistry concept!'

Was this the same guy whose favourite character was Snape from Harry Potter?

'Speaking of the Sunday test…why don't we meet after that? We can talk for a little while,' I said, almost as a joke, hoping he'd suggest something way better. Who meets for a date after a test? Who talks for a little while on the first date? That sounds so horrible.

'Sure, that sounds great,' he smiled again.

Honestly, I should have seen it coming.

After agreeing on the 'date', I was finally able to part ways with him and get on with my much-anticipated, merry ride back home. Except it wasn't merry at all. Instead, I was filled with thoughts of all kinds. Negative thoughts—shame, fear, doubt, confusion, anger, disappointment, sadness and frustration. It was a cocktail of negative emotions I was always under the influence of, at least since January, and now it was getting too much.

Why did I feel so horrible all the time in tuition and how in the holy hell did my classmates like Riya, Shiv and Parnika look so happy, whenever I saw them? My smiling muscles felt like they've atrophied or something. What was their secret to happiness and how could I achieve it? Why did only *I* feel like shit all the time?

Why did everything seem so demanding, all of a sudden? And why did it seem to be easy for everyone else? Those Shark people were actually *laughing* at the difficulty level of the test.

Was I even made for this? The 1 per cent that I was trying to fit into, how would I ever get there?

I could finally feel the dread catching up. The dread that had been following me all throughout tenth grade, and I'd ignored it throughout.

The dreadful feeling of knowing that I wasn't actually smart.

Ever since I was a little kid, I would be the one to get the best grades, and everyone would congratulate me about it. But when I was in the eighth or ninth grade, I didn't feel happy anymore being the top of the class at school. I saw kids like Shiv and Parnika, who were average in most subjects, except maths and science, where they were at par with me, I saw them beating National Science Olympiads, I heard that they were enrolled in Hellen foundation courses and were probably learning more advanced stuff than I was.

At the time, though, I passed them off as 'nerds' and something I could never be because I would rather remain at

My Resolution

home in my free time and pursue my side projects and hobbies, like writing my fan faction. I ignored the feelings of inadequacy, since I was in my little bubble of school and hobbies. I ran away from those feelings.

I wanted to stop running now.

I wanted to prove to Mom that I was made for all the hard work, mental toil and that I wasn't as delicate as she thought I was.

I wanted to prove to Dad that I was as good as he thought I was.

I wanted to prove to Shiv and Parnika that I was as good as them. I didn't want to feel inferior whenever I looked at them.

I wanted to prove to myself that I was good enough.

So, pushing my doubts aside, I resolved that if I got less than 150 marks (out of a possible 360) on the upcoming grand test, I'd leave non-med. No questions asked. But I'd try my absolute honest best for this test.

I needed this win. I needed it badly.

16

Avik's Non-Hobbies

I couldn't say I wasn't nervous walking into maths class the next day. Last night at dinner, I wasn't able to look my parents in the eyes. The guilt of cheating on the exam was eating me up. I wondered if the rumour had already spread and people would ostracize me like the outlaw I was. To my complete surprise, no one batted an eye as I moved to the front of the class and sat on a lone bench in the second, non-reserved row.

Revisiting the notes I made in class was strange and new. I'd never needed to do it before I joined Hellen, but it seemed important, since I'd seen Avik with his head buried in his notes till the teacher arrived.

'Hey, book brain.'

Someone tapped my shoulder (which is seriously annoying—just say my name, for God's sake). I turned around and found Riya and Smriti looking intently at me; both of them had their signature laid-back smiles plastered across their faces.

'Oh, hi,' I said, pressing my lips together into a thin smile. I remembered the missed calls accumulating on my phone because of them last night. I'd put my phone on silent, had a mini-meltdown, played *The Sims 3* for a while, completed the maths assignment and got ready for bed. Then I looked at my phone and saw the notifications piled up. *Too late to call them back*, I'd resolved and gone to sleep.

'You didn't pick up our calls last night!' Smriti exclaimed, an exasperating amount of worry on her face.

Riya interjected, 'Have you completed the maths assignment?'

Dumbfounded, I replied, 'Um, yeah.' I did it last night after getting off my rollercoaster of anxiety about the future. It took two hours, I slept at midnight, but I finished it. I was kind of proud of myself for going through the chapter on my own and being able to solve the assignment. I had finally caught up with the lectures and had no intention of slacking off in class again.

'Could I see it?' she said, extending her hand way into my personal space.

I wanted to tell her, 'No. You *can't* see it. You should have done it on your own, instead of probably going out bowling again with Shiv and Parnika, having the time of your lives.'

Instead, I reluctantly handed over my answers to her extended hand, hoping she'd remove it as soon as I did.

I sat quietly in my seat, hearing them click photos of my answers. I didn't feel proud to help them anymore. I just felt used.

'Thanks!' Riya returned my assignment and shuffled back to her seat next to Smriti.

Wow, did they just come here to take my answers and then leave once they were done? I couldn't tell how that made me feel.

I didn't want to abandon my front seat to sit next to them. To my surprise, they didn't even invite me.

Who were supposed to be my *people*? Who would be my Parnika? Who would be my 'bros', like Shiv had his?

∽

The maths class had ended a while ago, but I was still sitting in my seat in the almost empty classroom, going over my notes for the past few weeks. I had a bit of time to kill before my driver showed up.

'You know they're just using you, right?'

I looked up from my notes. It was Avik. He glided past me, taking the seat diagonally in front of mine, across the aisle seat in the boys' section.

'Avani? I'm talking to you,' he looked askance at me, eyebrow cocked. His fluffy hair and stubble-less face properly distinguished him from Shiv in my mind, who always had sleek, sorted hair and a bit of a stubble.

'Sorry, what did you say?'

'Oh, I forgot you have a hearing problem,' he said, his elbows propped on the tables on either side of the bench. Louder, he repeated, 'Your friends are *using you.*'

'*Oh my God!* Avik, quiet down!' I said, looking around the class. Some people gave us quick glances and looked away. I took a breath of relief when I saw my two friends weren't in class anymore.

He chuckled. 'I'm just telling the truth. They're *homework leeches,*' he muttered.

'*Excuse me?*' I asked, baffled at this boy's audacity to continue this conversation. Who was he to pass any commentary on my life?

'You've worked hard, completed the assignment all on your own, and now, they're just leeching off of you; therefore, they're homework leeches,' he said, casually shrugging.

'What, have you been stalking me or something?' I muttered.

He held his hands up in defeat. 'Okay, yeah, you're right. That's a bit weird. I was sitting near you and overheard your conversation with them. Sorry, I didn't mean to make you uncomfortable. I'll go,' He started walking out of the room.

I quickly caught up to him and said, 'You should really find another source of entertainment rather than my dumpster fire of a life.'

He started laughing. 'Oh God, a self-burn! Those are rare.'

'Self-deprecating humour is my *jam*,' I stated.

We were both laughing, walking out of Hellen, and I finally felt normal for the first time since before I was handed the Stream Form in January.

Sadly, it didn't last very long.

'Avani?' Dad was standing on the steps that led to the lobby. He seemed to be fascinated by the massive Hellen building as he kept moving his head from side to side, trying to take it all in, finally resting his eyes on us—on Avik.

'Oh, Papa, I didn't know you'd come to pick me up,' I walked towards him, feeling very awkward because of the boy a few steps behind me. 'This is—'

'Hello, sir. I'm Avik Chaudhry, a classmate of Avani's,' he walked towards us in a proper soldier-like fashion. I could sense the unease in his voice; his body was tense, especially his shoulders. He had transformed from his sarcastic self to this stiff soldier guy. Now, he sounded similar to the boy I had overheard on a call with his dad.

'Oh, hello, Avik beta,' Dad smiled warmly. His expression did not reveal much about his thoughts. Was he feeling awkward too? 'I'm glad to see Avani has made some new friends!'

If only he knew the truth. Although, Avik was probably the closest thing to a 'friend' I had.

Avik just awkwardly smiled, his lips pressed into a thin line.

He added, 'You're a local?'

Oh, who was I kidding—awkward silences? There were none if my dad was part of the conversation. He had a way of making everyone feel at ease, although I wasn't sure how at ease Avik felt. He had called my dad 'sir'.

'No, sir, I'm from Faridabad,' he seemed to be easing up. His shoulders seemed to loosen with each second. 'I live nearby as a paying guest. My grandparents live in Ambala,' he said.

'Wow, it must be tough,' Dad added. He was wholly invested in the conversation at this point. He looked at Avik with respect and admiration, as if he was an army veteran.

I could hear Avik sigh. He seemed different now—tired. His living situation was just like Shiv's. I wondered if they both knew each other. Avik didn't seem to be a part of Shiv's club, though.

'Yeah. I mean, the coaching here is the best in the nearby region. My parents couldn't afford to send me to Kota anyway, so I had to come here,' he said, shrugging. I had heard of Kota in the news as the mecca of medical/non-medical coaching. Somehow the only news that made national headlines was the bad kind, about student suicides.

Dad asked, 'So, what does your father do, beta?'

I squirmed when he asked that question. It made me feel very uncomfortable for some reason. Perhaps because I'd seen his father scolding him on the first day, and I was pretty sure that triggered some bad memories for Avik. Also, why didn't Dad ask about his mom's profession?

I quickly redirected my gaze to Avik, assessing his reaction to see if he felt any discomfort, but his face was undecipherable. He replied in the most typical way possible, glancing at me for some reason, 'Oh, he's a retired Indian Army officer. Mom's a teacher.' I was glad Avik mentioned his mom.

He quickly followed up on his previous statement by averting his eyes from mine and said, 'Sorry, I've taken up too much of your time. I'll get going now. Nice to meet you, uncle.'

Wow, he changed from sir to uncle that quick? It seemed like Dad really wasn't as intimidating after all, or maybe Avik was not one to get intimidated.

'How are you going to get home?' I blurted out loud.

'Oh, I've borrowed my grandparents' scooter, but it wasn't

Avik's Non-Hobbies

working in the morning today. I'll try to find a bus or, you know, walk.'

The bus? As in, the city bus? Before I could ask any more invasive questions, I was thankfully interrupted by Dad, who very graciously offered him a ride home.

'I don't want to impose,' Avik said.

'Of course not! Please, if you are comfortable, we'd love to drop you off. We are on our way home anyway, right Avani?' He nudged me.

'Um, yeah.' I mumbled. This was the strangest crossover I'd ever seen, stranger than the crossover between *Hannah Montana* and *The Wizards of Waverly Place*, even stranger than Katy Perry's collab with *The Sims 3*, called *Katy Perry's Sweet Treats*. I shudder whenever I think of the latter.

That is how I ended up sitting in the front seat, next to the driver and Dad and Avik were 'forced' to sit in the back. It was the most awkward seating arrangement in history.

'So, what are your hobbies, Avik?' Dad asked. He was doing his best to quell any awkwardness.

'Well, I've been in the top 10 ranks in the Maths International Olympiad four times in a row. I'm hoping for a fifth one this year.'

Really? That was impressive, but was that a hobby?

'Oh wow, that's great, beta!'

'I've also been the state topper in the Science Olympiad twice, and I'm an NTSE scholar. I'm currently preparing for the KVPY as well.'

What were all of these acronyms? I'd only heard about the olympiads and maybe about NTSE in passing. What about normal stuff, like video games or basketball?

'Do you like to play video games?' I asked, feeling like the dumbest person in the room. He just mentioned all of these competitive test acronyms he was preparing for, and look at me—

asking these caveman-like questions.

'Um, no, not really,' he mumbled as if he'd never heard of these activities, which, according to him, were probably meant for plebeians like me.

'Do you like reading, Avik?' I asked in a last-ditch effort, looking back in the car. Reading was intellectual, right? At least it was considered more sophisticated than playing video games (although I'd beg to differ—there are many video games better than books).

He was silent for a while, and I became hopeful. Maybe we actually had something in common. You know, apart from the strange circumstances that deemed us 'friends' now.

'Sometimes I buy books on astrophysics with my pocket money whenever I have some left. I love solving logic or maths puzzles—I'd bought a few before coming here just in case I ever got bored. That's about it,' he shrugged, smiling a bit.

I smiled weakly back at him. I shouldn't be too hard on him. 'I like reading, too. But I mostly read fiction. You like science fiction?' He seemed like someone who'd love sci-fi.

'I don't like fiction, no offence. I just don't understand—what is the point of imaginary stories that don't teach people about the technological advances around us?' he said.

'"Imaginary stories"? What do you—' I began to retort but was interrupted.

'Well, to each their own, right?' Dad glared at me, trying to placate the fire in me.

He doesn't like fiction? That meant he would hate any piece of writing I've ever written.

'Avik, you have some very interesting hobbies, son.'

'Thank you, uncle.'

And I thought we could be friends. How sad that it had to end like this!

Soon, we dropped him in front of his apartment, which looked like a normal multistoried house with external stairs to get to the upper floors without disturbing the owners.

After waving him goodbye, I turned to face Dad and rolled my eyes at him. '*Interesting* hobbies? Really, Dad? He has the most non-hobby hobbies I've ever heard of. You were just being nice, telling him he has interesting hobbies. Right?'

'No, I meant it. He seems like a smart kid, Avani,' Dad nodded, taking out his phone to reply to a text.

'So, you mean my hobbies aren't interesting?'

He didn't reply and continued tapping on his phone.

I repeated myself, a bit louder this time. 'I don't participate in NTSE or olympiads or KVPY, let alone score a good enough rank to show off about it. I'm not a smart kid, is that what you think?'

'Avani, I never said that,' he looked up from his phone to stare at me. 'Why are you getting so jealous of him?'

I scoffed, '*Jealous*? Me? Why would I be jealous of a nerd like him? Pshh.'

He was silent for a while. 'Of course, you'd know him better, but he seems like a good kid to me. You could learn a thing or two from him.'

'What things?' I stared daggers at him, wondering what got in him to behave like this. These 'arguments' were becoming a regular thing now. That's why it was better just to lie.

He shrugged, shaking his head. 'I don't know. I mean, he's very focused on studies.'

'So, you mean I'm not *focused* enough?' I could've expected to hear something like this from Mom, but never from Dad. He was supposed to be my cheerleader.

'Avani, what has gotten into you?'

'No, what has gotten into *you*, Dad?' I narrowed my eyes, feeling the tears about to overflow. 'Why don't you adopt him if you like him so much? He'll even call you sir if you want him to. He'll be a better kid than I could ever be.'

'Avani, what are you even saying? You are getting too emotional. Let's end this conversation now,' he stared at me for a second, an alien look on his face, and got back to his phone. When he stared at me, I felt like he was looking at a wild animal, full of pity and otherness.

'I'm not being emotional. I'm being a normal person,' I said quietly, reiterating Mom's words.

He didn't hear me, I guess. He was still typing something on his phone.

I was going to prove myself to him. I could be just as good as Avik, perhaps even better.

17

Big Day

Soon enough, Sunday, the day of the grand test and the big 'date' rolled around. I seemed to be prepared for one of these events more than the other—my overworn My Chemical Romance t-shirt (the only band merch I owned. I had cried with happiness the day my dad had gotten it for me on his trip to Berlin) indicated I wasn't mentally prepared for a 'date'. Even though I considered that t-shirt to be the best thing I ever owned, apparently, it wasn't very physically appealing—at least my mom said so when I left for the test.

As I approached the building, my breath quickened with each step. The area outside the building was swarming with students in various groups, talking animatedly with each other. I was never one of those people who could carry on a normal conversation before any test, so I entered the building alone, my mind buzzing with some maths, physics and chemistry formulae.

I'd managed to avoid most of the people I knew here for the rest of the week leading up to today. I was used to being quiet at this point.

I'd even sat by myself for many classes, not wanting to be around Riya and Smriti anymore. No, it wasn't that Avik's words about them had gotten to me. I just wanted to be alone and focus on the lectures since I was preparing seriously for the grand test. I had to score above 150 or I would leave non-med—I'd promised myself, and I always keep my promises.

The test was on the fifth floor, and I was pretty sure there was no elevator. Even if there was one, there was no way I would be going in it. That would be creepier than being alone in the maths classroom at 8.00 p.m.

As I climbed up the extremely dingy stairwell, noticing the walls coated with strange stains of all kinds, I thought about my previous test, and how I was compelled to cheat to keep up appearances as the 'Smart Kid'.

I wouldn't allow that to happen this time. I knew I had to prove myself to so many people around me, but I had to do it honestly. I had to score good marks on my own and prove that I was good enough.

By the time I reached the fifth floor, I was completely floored. Out of breath, I entered the massive exam hall—an endless sea of strange-looking metal chairs with metal tables in front of them. A large number of students had already occupied the chairs, mostly in the back.

I found a chair in the middle and sat down on the medieval torture device. Honestly, I'd never seen such an uncomfortable chair in my life. The table was too far away from it, and you couldn't pull it closer because the chair's architecture prevented you from doing so.

As the invigilators announced the commencement of the test, I leaned forward, my back in an awkward, rounded position, and started filling out my name and my other details.

'Shit, Smriti, there're no seats left in the back.' I heard Riya speak from somewhere in front of me. I kept my head down, hoping they didn't notice me.

How will we pass this test?' Smriti replied as they both whizzed past me. 'What will we show our parents?'

'Let's just sit here. There are a few seats unoccupied. This

Big Day

seems as close to the back of the hall as we can get.'

The two figures came near the seats behind me. I just wanted to take my test peacefully and not get into any trouble, so I paid no heed to them or the faint whisperings I could hear from where they were sitting.

I solved my way through the chemistry section, waiting for the horrible questions that would inevitably stump me and lead to my downfall, similar to the past Hellen tests I'd taken, but they never came. I held my breath till I finished the physics section, and I couldn't believe it. I actually didn't feel very different from how I would in the last half an hour of exams at school. That last half hour would be the best time of the whole exam (if I had to choose)—I would feel elated like I was taking the victory lap during a marathon. Not that I would know how that really feels, though.

I knew it wasn't a good idea to measure your results before the actual results came out (especially not during the test), but I was sure I would be *up there*.

When the invigilator gave the 15-minute, I was in the middle of double-checking my answers. I felt a tap on my shoulder.

Ignore, ignore. Focus on the test.

'Avani?' Riya whispered behind me.

Maybe there was some other Avani they were mistaking me for.

'Avani, turn to the chemistry section. Do you know the answers to the fourth and tenth questions?'

I didn't reply, but I did actually know those answers. I was already done with my chemistry segment since it looked the easiest. Well, apart from some questions about the mole concept that I'd chosen to ignore for now.

'Help me out with some of the questions on maths too… fifth, ninth and eighteenth. Could you tell me the correct answer?'

she asked, handing her bubble sheet to me.

She literally threw it onto my desk from behind.

For a good minute, I was shell-shocked. Did that just happen? Did she just hand her answer sheet to me like that? What did she expect—that I would just fill it out obediently and hand it back to her, like the gracious and benevolent friend I was? I guess it was partly my fault for playing the part of the 'helpful, obedient friend'. Avik's words rang in my head. *Homework leeches.* It was a distasteful phrase for sure, but it really did ring true.

Staring at her sparsely filled bubble sheet, wondering how it all led to this, I could feel the disappointment in the pit of my stomach growing further and further. All I wanted was to make friends in coaching so I would feel like I used to back in school with Parnika, not become a doormat for people to use and throw any way they liked.

Maybe I used them too, in a way—in order to fulfil my compulsive need to feel normal again. Like I used to in school.

I could fill her questions out and she could help me with the questions I don't know, I heard a creeping voice in my brain. But that immediately felt wrong. It wouldn't sit well with my promise: my self-imposed ultimatum of scoring at least 150 on this test.

I looked away from my table and around me to make sure there were no invigilators around who could throw me out. After the coast was clear, I handed her back the sheet.

After a few quiet seconds, I heard a loud whisper. 'Avani, you didn't mark anything!'

I didn't reply.

I figured that this was the silent end of our 'friendship'.

Did I feel scared about being alone moving forward, not having a group to sit next to for once? Yes. But I'd been doing it this week as well. It didn't feel *that* scary. It actually felt more peaceful.

Big Day

After handing the paper to the invigilator, I stretched my neck, and boy, did it crack. As I was stretching my back (yeah, everything was cracking after sitting in that medieval torture device for three hours), I saw something out of the corner of my eye: Riya and Smriti talking to another girl—who would usually sit in the front, quietly and obediently listening to the lectures.

I guess I won't be missed.

∽

Walking out of that building, I felt vindicated and actually happy for the first time since I'd joined Hellen. The test went really well! I think I answered almost all of the questions. Maybe non-med wasn't that bad once you studied properly. Maybe Dad was right, I *could* do it. I *was* good enough.

With a hop in my step, I started making my way towards my car, ready to tell Mom and Dad about how great my test went. I wanted to celebrate the fact that I finally felt more normal. Maybe this was what I needed, some patience and some time for everything to settle down.

'Oye, Avani!'

I turned back. Shiv was standing a few metres away from me, leaning against a wall, with his hands in his pockets, still looking as cool by himself as he did when his posse surrounded him. Usually, his presence left me flustered. However, today I was too carefree to let it affect me.

'Oh, hi, Shiv,' I walked closer to him, wondering if this was the commencement of our 'date'. In *The Sims 3*, the formula for a successful date is pretty straightforward: a dinner at the bistro (if I felt fancy, otherwise the diner) and then hanging out in the junkyard.

He smiled at me, and I stood awkwardly, not knowing what to say next. We walked over to a bench. I didn't sit, though.

So, we both stood next to the bench, looking awkward as hell, staring at anything but each other. What was I supposed to ask him? What was his favourite colour? Wait, I already knew that. This was so much easier on text.

'So, how was your test?' He asked with his hands in his pockets.

This was the first time we talked about anything academic since starting coaching. It felt like uncharted territory.

'I think I did pretty decently,' I didn't tell him that I had managed to answer about 55 questions out of the 60. That was 'pretty decent' in my book. 'How was yours?'

His eyes met the concrete floor. 'Not as great as I would have wanted.'

Was it possible? Was it possible that I was *back*? The old, smarty-pants, goody-two-shoes Avani was back? Wow, I couldn't believe it. I was finally *better* than Shiv again. I was also disgusted at myself at how happy this made me.

'It's okay, Shiv. This test is the first of many. There's always room for improvement. You're such a smart dude! I'm sure you'll do better next time.' I tried my best not to sound patronizing.

He looked up at me, a half-smile on his face. 'Yeah, you're right. Thanks, Avani.'

'So...how's life?' I said.

He smiled weakly. 'Living without your family is very different from what I'd imagined, to be honest.'

'How did you imagine it?'

'Well, I had thought it would be similar to my real home. But it's nothing like that. You know, not having your family around can be very lonely. You basically have no one to talk to or joke around with. If you and your roommate don't get along, it is much worse. Plus, the food sucks. No one's there to give you your favourite yellow dal when things get bad,' he chuckled at himself, rubbing his eyes with the backs of his hands.

I had so many questions. How was *he* lonely? I always saw him surrounded by his posse. But it didn't feel very appropriate to ask further. I'd already made him cry on our first date. *Great.*

'Do you want some of my parantha? Mom packed an extra one in case I got hungry in the middle of the test.' I chuckled to myself. It wasn't as if I could eat the parantha while taking the test. I don't know what she expected.

'I don't want to be a bother, Avani,' he shook his head.

'Nonsense. Here you go,' I said, handing him my tiffin.

'Are you sure?' he asked, looking at me with misty eyes. How could anyone say no to that?

'Of course. There's some *aam ka aachar* on the side.'

As I sat there, watching him eat the only parantha Mom had packed for me, I realized I'd judged him wrong. He wasn't this perpetually cool, unwavering genius rock star. He was kind of like me. The thought made my stomach do a flip.

'Thanks, Avani,' he said, handing me back the tiffin. 'Tell your Mom she makes a crazy good parantha.'

I don't think Mom would ever know the circumstances under which this parantha was consumed. She'd actually combust if she knew.

'Yeah,' I said, my eyes wandering to Avik in the background, carrying a heavy plastic bag in his hand.

His smile faded, being replaced by a look of nervousness. 'Avani, I wanted to say something.'

'Just a second, Shiv,' I said, hearing a loud thud.

I don't know how it all happened, but the next thing I knew, I was crouched on the ground, trying to help Avik pick up his paraphernalia off the ground.

'Hey, are you okay?' I asked as I looked at Avik, also crouched on the floor, trying to collect as many things as he could.

'Yeah, I'm fine. The plastic bag tore,' he said.

I'd expected thick, scribbled-on olympiad-preparation books, in accordance with his 'hobbies'. But instead, as I helped him put back his stuff into his bag, I found something completely different.

'Um, you have a lot of sci-fi books,' I looked at the loose sheets of paper strewn on the ground, 'And is this sheet music?'

He snatched those papers away from me, getting up quickly. 'Okay, thanks, Avani. Why don't you return to your lovey-dovey conversation with your *boyfriend* Shiv?' he snapped, spitting out the word 'boyfriend' as if it was a hairball.

'Hey, I was just trying to help,' I said, backing away from him. 'Besides, Shiv's not—'

Wait, how did he know Shiv? Avik's not from Chandigarh and this was his first year at Hellen. Was Shiv that popular?

'No one asked you to help, you know? Stop trying to be Mother Teresa. There's no way you're a saint, considering the number of times I've seen you talking to that loser,' he gestured towards Shiv.

What the hell? Did he just say that?

'Yeah, I'll go running to my loser boyfriend, and you should go running to...hell,' I retorted, my voice breaking. I wasn't very good at comebacks. The best ones usually came to me a few days later in the shower.

My eyes started to fill with tears. I fought back the urge to start sobbing like a three-year-old. I walked away in an arbitrary direction as fast as I could, wishing that these tears would disappear. Why was I even crying? He didn't say anything egregiously hurtful.

After I'd regained my composure, I went to the same spot on the bench where our 'date' had been paused. Shiv was now surrounded by his nerd posse. All of them had gathered around the bench with the test paper in their hands. The way they were standing in a circle with papers in their hands, it was almost like they were having a séance. All that was missing were some creepy candles.

'Oye Avani, is everything alright?' Shiv asked, turning away from his circle of friends. I could feel their eyes on me. How could Shiv say he was lonely? He sure didn't look the part, surrounded by his Shark friends.

'Yeah. I'm fine,' I said in the most stable voice that I could manage. His friends were all shooting glances at me.

Right then, Shiv was at the top of my list of favourite people at Hellen (even though that list was only just created by me). Why was I letting Avik ruin this 'date' for me? Why was I letting the way Shiv's friends were looking at me ruin this? I had to be more confident.

'Sorry for the interruption. Where were we?' I said.

'Uh...' Shiv mumbled. 'I was gonna ask you something important.'

'Oh okay.' I stared at his unsure expression. What did he want to ask me?

'I...' He trailed off. I quickly glanced at at Avik, who was standing a few metres away, trying to get his scooter started. I wasn't going to help him this time.

'Yes?' I asked, bringing my gaze back to Shiv, who had been looking intently at me this whole time.

His tone changed as he crossed his arms. 'Now I finally realize the truth in what my brother said. I really hardly get any time for my hobbies.'

Huh? He seemed like he was going somewhere else. I decided to play along, though. 'What are your hobbies, anyway?' I asked, wondering if he had similar studious hobbies as Avik.

'I loved sports. Cricket, football, basketball—you name it, I've played it,' he said, smiling. I was just glad he wasn't crying anymore.

'I do remember you playing basketball during PE back in school. Weren't you the captain of the team at one point?'

He chuckled. 'Yes. I was. It was pretty awesome, actually. I used to stay back after school and play with my teammates. Well, that was before the Hellen foundation course classes started.'

'Oye, Shiv! Guess what, that answer was right! You got it right, bro!' a guy from his posse called out to him, waving the question paper in his hand.

'Sorry about them,' he said, gesturing for them to wait.

'It's fine if you want to go talk to them. We can catch up later,' I said with a resigned tone in my voice. I didn't want to hold him back.

'Okay, see you later. It was nice talking to you,' he said, giving me a half-smile, and then turned back to his posse.

I tried to force a smile, then power-walked in the direction of my car, my sweet, safe haven from all of this madness. Who knew that a simple three-hour test could be so draining for reasons completely divorced from the test itself?

18

'Congrats on the Wreck—Rank'

I spent the rest of my night not studying one bit. It was a Sunday night, I had just sat for a big test and had a super awkward first date—I deserved to treat myself. I indulged in one of my favourite activities—playing *The Sims 3* and living out my fantasy life. What is my fantasy life, you ask? Well, it's kinda obvious. A single woman in her young adult years, living in a metropolitan city—Bridgeport to be exact, for all *The Sims 3* players—in a penthouse (with a hot tub, obviously) with a best friend flatmate, a golden retriever as a pet, having an exciting and cool job that pays well. Replete with a huge bookshelf, good internet connection and a personal chef, of course.

Avik would probably baulk at the sight of me playing a *video game about imaginary characters*.

Ugh, why did I think about him?

I shot a quick text to Parnika before I went to sleep.

Avani: Guess what happened today? You'll never believe it. I participated in a particular social activity that rhymes with 'late' (which you usually are to most events, LOL).

I know it sounded like a clickbait title, but the gossip about my date was too juicy for me to divulge at once.

By the time it was time to go to Hellen again on Monday, I had blocked out everything about Avik, Riya and Smriti. I had thought about Shiv for a while. Okay, more than just for *a while*. I was looking forward to finally being in the same batch as him and Parnika for once. Funnily enough, Parnika hadn't even read my message yet.

The maths teacher, Shruti ma'am began the class by saying, 'The results of the grand test will be displayed on a bulletin board outside the building by today evening. All the students who rank 100 or less will transfer to the Shark batch from the next class; students who rank between 101 and 200 will stay in Dolphin; and the students who rank above 201 will transfer to the Octopus batch.'

I sighed. I was happy she didn't use words like 'upgraded' or 'downgraded'. Those words made me feel like I was a crappy old phone that desperately needed an upgrade. I don't know why, but that's just where my mind went.

Well, this was it. My last time in Dolphin, which meant no more Shruti ma'am. I was kind of starting to like it here. I would finally not be lying to my dad about my batch. I could finally be a 'Smart Kid' again. I could be one step closer to my goal of being in the top 1 per cent. My heart raced at the thought of being in the same class as Shiv and Parnika again. Maybe Parnika and I could finally be close again. Maybe Shiv and I would actually become good friends or maybe something more.

After class, I approached the bulletin board, now populated with a few sheets of paper. Taking a deep breath, I scanned the list, reading all the names carefully. A few familiar ones popped out quite soon.

Rank 4: Shiv.
Wait, didn't he say that his test went badly?
Rank 10: Avik.
Rank 50: Parnika.
Rank 95: Riya.

What the hell!

Rank 98: Smriti.

Just then, I spotted it.

Rank 170: Avani. Score: 151/360.

My heart dropped. Maybe this was some other Avani. Maybe someone else had the same name as mine. Of course, that could definitely be a possibility. No way I did this badly. I'd attempted 55 questions out of 60, for God's sake!

After scanning the list of 300 students twice, I confirmed that there was no Avani other than me. Thanks, Mom and Dad, for giving me such an uncommon name.

That meant I would stay right where I was—in mediocrity. I wasn't saying goodbye to Dolphin. In fact, I would be saying goodbye to my dreams of joining Shark. My dreams of being one step closer to being in the top 1 per cent.

Even Riya and Smriti managed to get more marks than I did. Guess I was the real loser all along. How would I look at them ever again? How would I look at *anyone* ever again?

'Hey, Avani! What are you doing there?' Shiv called out. He was standing beside me, grinning stupidly.

He was the one person I did not want to see after this. I took a few steps away from him. I felt my balance falter as I slipped down the stairs at the entrance.

'Oh my God, Avani! You okay?' Shiv held my arms, preventing me from smashing my head on the ground. I looked at his astonished face looking back at me.

As soon as I regained my balance, I shrugged him off, my heart beating in my ears, 'Yeah, sorry. You scared me.'

'Well, I saved you too, didn't I?' he said, winking at me.

His wink made me want to hurl.

'Yeah, thanks for that. By the way, I thought you said you didn't do well on the test?' I asked in the most nonchalant way

I could manage.

He let out a blaring laugh. It almost sounded obnoxious, like Parnika whenever she talked with her new Shark friends, 'Yeah, I'd missed a question in the chemistry section.'

Was that the definition of tests going badly—missing a single question? Well, then I guess I was a living train wreck. 'Congrats on the wreck—rank,' I managed to say.

It wasn't that I was jealous, per se. I felt betrayed, more than anything. How could he do so well? Where did he find the time? He texted me *every single day*. Sometimes I wouldn't even respond because I was too busy doing some assignment, and later, I'd feel bad for not replying to him. Ugh, I was such a fool. He seemed almost normal yesterday on our date, talking about his loneliness and his love for basketball. I felt like I could identify with him. Now I was the farthest possible thing from him.

'So, will I see you on our next date sometime soon?' He asked, a smug smile on his face. Or was I imagining it?

I was overcome by the panic trifecta—sweaty hands, a sinking feeling in the stomach and a racing heart. You're too smart, and I'm too dumb. We come from opposite worlds. Like Romeo and Juliet, in a twisted, Indian way, non-med edition. There was no way we could be 'together'. Why did he even want to hang out with me?

He just stood there, head cocked to one side, looking at me with a slight smirk on his face. I can't believe I tried to *console* him yesterday on our date when his test went 'badly'. And now he goes and gets the top rank and then acts so nonchalant and cool? I don't know why, but I just wanted to punch him.

'Oh my God, Avani. What was your text about?' Parnika said, popping out of nowhere.

'Huh? Oh,' I said, looking shell-shocked, almost falling down again.

'Oh hey, Shiv,' she said, draping her arm around his neck.

'Parni, don't scare Avani. She almost fell down the stairs right now,' he said. 'I caught her, though.'

'You did?' Parnika turned to look at me, a mischievous glint in her eyes. Both of them seemed so tall, graceful and smart. Meanwhile, I was a talentless munchkin who kept falling off the stairs and needed to be saved.

'Yes, he did,' I said, pressing my lips into a thin smile.

I wanted to continue my 'cool charade'. I wanted to look like an unbothered smart kid, but the proof was in the pudding. My rank was right there on the bulletin board, quite literally in black and white.

'Avani, you okay?' Parnika asked, removing her arm from Shiv's neck. She turned to Shiv. 'I'll talk to you later, bro.'

She took me aside to the parking lot. I was still in a haze of my own self-deprecating thoughts.

'What happened, Avani? You look so sad. Is everything okay with you?' she said, bending down to my level as if I was a little kid, putting her hand on my shoulder, a slight frown plastered over her face.

'Stop it, Parnika. Just, for the love of God, stop being so perfect!' I said, shrugging off her arm.

'What's gotten into you?' she took a step back.

'Why do you even care about me?' I said, tears welling in my eyes.

'What are you talking about, Avani? You're my best friend. Of course, I care about you.'

'No, you don't. I think you're just friends with me cause you feel bad for me. I'm just the formerly smart kid, and I wasn't even that smart back in school! You and Shiv, on the other hand, you both are perfect.' I slumped onto the hood of the car behind me and slowly fell to the concrete parking lot road.

'That's not true, Avani. You should know that,' Parnika sat cross-legged in front of me on the concrete parking lot. Why was she doing that? She was going to spoil her mint-green trousers.

'It is, Parnika. I ranked 170 in the grand test, whereas you and Shiv did so well. I'll never be good enough. I'll always be trailing behind you guys, stumbling and falling along the way. I fail to understand why Shiv asked me out on a date. What is wrong with both of you?'

'Wait. Shiv finally asked you out?'

'Yes, we went on a date too, but I don't know why when obviously *you* are the better one for him! You completely ignore me whenever we're all together,' I said, my voice cracking.

'Avani, come on. Stop spouting nonsense. I could never like Shiv like that, and I'm sorry if I ever ignored you.'

'You know I was the one who cheated in that chemistry test?' I blurted out a bit too loudly. Some people turned to look at us.

'What?' she narrowed her eyes.

'Yeah, I was the one you Shark people talked smack about that day. But you were right. I am squandering my parents' money. I should never have taken non-medical.' I buried my face in my hands, roughened by the loose concrete and dirt on the road. Great, another addition to my already perfect skincare routine.

'Avani, I didn't know it was you,' she spoke with a guilty expression on her face.

'How does it matter? What you said was right,' I stood up, turned around and sprinted towards my car, which was parked a few metres away.

'Avani, wait!' Parnika called after me.

It was a wonder I didn't trip and fall again. I'd rather have scraped my knee than be caught in the arms of Shiv.

I stared out of the window at the massive Hellen building as the driver manoeuvred the way out of the parking lot. I stared at where Shiv and Parnika probably were, now surrounded by their posse, most likely talking in their usual, loud, smug way.

I was the same scared girl from January. The one who couldn't handle the truth, the one who easily ran away from difficult conversations, the one who couldn't even score well on a small test—I, the pretender, was finally coming undone.

19

Indian Inadequacy

I could barely get through dinner without feeling like I would start bawling my eyes out. Soon enough, the tears fell and mixed with the ghee on my roti. This had to be the lowest thing I'd ever done when I was sad—definitely, the grossest.

'Avani? Are you fine? What happened?' Mom asked, her voice panic-stricken. I'd never seen her that way with me before, apart from the time I had an asthma attack when I was nine.

That was the point when I started full-on silent-wailing—the type where you cry, but no noise comes out. The horrible feeling of absolute dread for the future started to sink in.

'What happened, Avani? Did someone say something to you? I swear if it's that girl Riya—she doesn't give me good vibes,' Mom said.

'I just—I don't know what will happen in the future,' I said in between my sobs.

'No one does, Avani,' Dad said, handing me a handkerchief from his pocket. Why did he always carry those things, anyway? Just in case he burst into tears, like me? Oh, who was I kidding?

Dad was nothing like me. No one was anything like me.

'No. You guys will continue with your life and your jobs till you retire or till I leave, and then you'll relax. Probably go on vacation. You have it all set out—unlike me,' I said.

'What does that mean?' Mom asked.

'I thought I had figured it all out. I had made my goals and everything. But now I don't know if I'm made for this.' I shook my head, feeling dizzy from doing so. Ugh, why did everything make me feel worse?

'What's *this*?' Dad asked, 'JEE coaching? I thought you were getting along quite well. You seemed—'

'Happy? Well, guess what, Dad? Appearances can be deceiving. I was going through so much. I still am. I tried my best, you know—the 'best' you expect of me. I tried my best to adjust to the fast way of learning and all the tests and the competition. I tried my best to make friends. I tried my best to score well on the tests and make you guys proud.'

I took a deep breath. Was this too dramatic? Was I being too emotional? I didn't care.

'I tried my best to be optimistic, you know. I've been studying so hard for the past few weeks—harder than I ever did at school. I tried to adjust to the place. But—' my eyes filled with tears again, blurring my vision. 'It wasn't good enough. I'm not good enough for non-medical or coaching. I just don't fit in.'

Dad said, 'But you've done so well in school! You should think you are good enough for anything, let alone non-medical coaching.'

'I—I'm not who you think I am,' I said. 'I'm never going to be the best. Not anymore. I'm not even in the best batch, Dad. I lied when I told you I was with Parnika. She's better than me. Even Shiv, this random guy from school, is better than me. Also, can you believe I cheated on a test because I was too scared to face the truth that I didn't know the answers? I am such a poser! I don't deserve anything.'

'What are you even talking about, Avani? You didn't need to do all that,' Dad asked, the tone of judgement apparent in his voice. 'You've always been a top student. You *are* the best.'

'Hey, let her speak,' Mom said, giving Dad the stink-eye.

'I'm *not* the top student at Hellen, okay? It's not like school. I studied hard for the grand test, promising myself that I'd leave Hellen if I scored less than 150 marks. I got 151 marks out of 360. Even after working so hard, I did so poorly.

In school, I was a big fish in a small pond. Here, I am in a pond full of 169 bigger fish than me. And the fish keep biting each other, and the pond is on fire. What am I going to do? I feel like I've always been hanging by a thread, and now that thread has finally snapped, and now I'm drowning,' I said, wondering if I was making any sense. I probably wasn't. Why would dumb Avani make any sense?

I felt like I was going to die in this terrible feeling of inadequacy and uncertainty that comes with being a student in India. It was horrible. I was staring into my future, so many paths stared me back, and I just stood there. Not fitting in anywhere. Frozen.

'Avani, I think you are too tired. You should sleep. We'll think about this tomorrow with a fresh mind,' Dad said.

'No, I'm *tired* of running! I'm always avoiding my problems, sometimes to the extent of not being able to make a *huge life-changing decision* till the last moment. I'm sick of hiding the truth from everyone, especially myself.' I got up, slamming my hands onto the table. 'The truth is this: Mom, you were right. I am not made for this. I want to quit. I'm terrible at non-med. If I'm not even in the best batch in my 300-student coaching centre, there's no way I have any chance of being at the top in the whole country. There are probably a million people better than me. I—I'm wasting my time and your money. If I keep going, I'll probably end up in a terrible engineering college and die alone in mediocrity there. I'm probably not even good enough for the worst college,' I mumbled the last part. My worst fear had taken the shape of words and had been thrown out into the world. There. I was tired and scared.

Not being the best. Failing. Being alone.

They were both silent for what seemed like an eternity. Then, Dad spoke, 'Avani, this was just one practice test. You can't give up like this. I know you. You're much better than this.'

I was growing frustrated. 'No, I'm not. I was never the person you think I am. I might have been good at school somehow, maybe I was just lucky, and maybe school was easier. I've been working so hard for the past few weeks, and it didn't get me anywhere. I'm so tired. I don't think I can do this for even one more day, let alone for the next two years. I want to quit.' I murmured, leaving the room without looking at their reactions. I really didn't care what they thought of me anymore.

A part of me wished they'd thought I was not 'smart' from the start. That would have made everything so much easier for me.

I wanted to block out the feelings—the terrible, nausea-inducing thoughts, but I knew I'd been avoiding them for too long. I had to face them at some point.

Shiv and Parnika and all the other Shark people were just *better*. And if they were just *better*, it meant I would never be better *than* them, no matter how hard I tried. And this whole thing was about the competition, wasn't it? If I wasn't winning, what was the point of participating? It would be foolish. This is a game I was destined to lose.

I don't want to do something where I feel like a loser all the time. And right now, I definitely felt like one. What was I doing? I was such a fool, thinking I had a chance. I should have known. Nothing I do could ever make any difference. I was doomed from the start. Should have never chosen this path. Why did I think I could prove myself wrong? I was not made for this at all.

'Open the door, beta,' Mom lightly knocked at my door.

'No, I'm about to sleep,' I croaked.

It was near 11.00 p.m. There was no way I slept that early, and she was fully aware of that.

'Avani, I want to see you,' she knocked loudly on the door with her ring. Ugh, I hated that noise. I was afraid she would break down the door (completely possible), so I reluctantly unlocked it.

She was standing in the doorway, holding a cup of milk. I had been lying face-down on the carpet (my amazing skincare routine, which is why I have at least three pimples living rent-free on my face at any given moment), trying to think myself out of this crisis (or maybe more into the crisis?).

'Mom, I really don't want to—' I said, lying back down on the carpet, waiting for her assault of words on how I was spoiling the carpet with my tears.

'It's okay. I won't talk about it,' she handed me the cup of milk. 'Drink this. You'll feel better. I put your favourite chocolate powder in it.'

I got up, careful not to drop the milk, and sat down at the edge of my bed, staring down the cup, hoping for something crazy to happen—like a sea nymph jumping out of it and taking me away. Mom joined me, seating herself next to me. Her warmth radiated off of her to my arm.

'Mom, what am I going to do?' I mumbled.

'You are going to drink this cup of milk. Then, I am going to read you a bedtime story and tuck you into bed.'

I stared at her, the corners of my lips curling up a bit, tears welling in my eyes for some reason. 'Are you serious?'

She had to be joking, surely. Even though I knew she didn't kid around.

She looked at me, the strange, sad look back in her eyes. 'I don't know which book you are reading these days. *The Hunger Games*?'

Indian Inadequacy

I was silent for what seemed like an eternity. 'Nothing. I haven't read since I started coaching.'

'Oh, my poor baby,' she said, her voice breaking as she put her arms around me. 'You deserve so much better, beta. You don't deserve to feel like this.'

'I feel like I made a mistake by choosing this stream, Mom. I know you didn't want me to take non-med anyway; you don't think I'm strong enough for it.' I mumbled into her shoulder.

'You are such a brave girl, Avani. So strong and resilient. I always knew that.' She broke off our hug, her eyes pools of water never overflowing. 'I just didn't want you to get hurt… I didn't want you to feel like you are feeling right now. I know it's a tough road, and I don't want you to get hurt, beta. You're my baby. I want to protect you.'

'Would you call it getting hurt if you are the only one hurting yourself?' I asked, unable to see a single thing due to my tears.

'That's the worst kind.'

'What should I do, Mom?' I said, burying my face in her shoulder again.

'You should take a break.' She patted my hair. 'I'm going to get your e-reader from your drawer. I'm sure it has some battery left.'

She really kept her word. She tucked me into bed, blanket all the way to my neck (I liked being swaddled as an almost adult, who knew) and sat on the side, reading out *The Great Gatsby*. I didn't understand half the words, but Mom's voice lulled me right into the warmth I wanted to melt into all this time.

'I love you, beta,' I thought I heard her say right before I fell into the deep warmth of sleep.

She loved me even after I had admitted to being a cheater, even after I told them how terrible a student I was—even after I had turned out to be such a failure.

20

Vacation

For the first time in many months, when I woke up, my mind wasn't full of tasks I had to finish before heading to Hellen. I didn't feel the overwhelming pressure of achieving my self-imposed goals. Instead, it was a quiet bliss of nothing. The poor score, crying on the roti and telling my parents that I was far from the best—I could feel the panic rise, but strangely it was not as much as I expected it to be. It felt freeing. I wasn't the best, and now my parents knew it. And the world didn't burn down. In fact, my mother told me she loved me for the first time in my life.

'Good morning, beta!' Dad said, his mouth stuffed with toast. It was kind of adorable but also gross at the same time. 'You feeling better today? Toast and boiled eggs are on the kitchen counter.'

'Good morning, Dad. Yeah, I feel somewhat better today.' I responded as if a month-long fever had just broken, and it was the first time he had seen me on my feet in a while.

I took a seat at the dining table opposite him. In Mom's absence, Dad would 'cook' breakfast.

'Great. I could see you were a bit caught up in your emotions yesterday night,' he said, focusing solely on stuffing a boiled egg between two pieces of toast.

I was quiet for a while, trying to find the right words that would get to him. 'I wasn't being emotional, Dad. I was speaking my truth. This is what I feel every day. It just came out in front of you yesterday.'

'What exactly do you feel?' he said, finally making eye contact.

'Long story short, I'm having a tough time in coaching. I'm not in the best batch, I don't have any friends, and I feel hopeless about my future most of the time, especially when I get bad marks compared to my old friends from school.. It's overwhelming, trying to meet all the standards of being the best,' I said, staring him right in the eyes. There was something powerful in being so direct.

'Why didn't you tell us this before?' he said, putting his sandwich down on the plate.

I didn't expect him to ask me. This was a first. Usually, he pronounced some judgement his genius brain thought was apt for me.

'Because I didn't want to disappoint you. You have this image of me in your mind, and I wanted to live up to it. I guess, I have had a similar image of myself in my mind.'

He looked at me, his expression sombre. I imagined him saying something impertinent like, 'But you *are* a good student. You *will* be a topper one day.' But he didn't. He didn't say anything for what seemed like an eternity.

'What are you going to do now?' he said, his voice restrained.

'For the long run, I don't know. Today, I want to take a break from coaching,' I said, for once, vocally confident about my decision.

'Uh…okay,' he replied. I could feel the hesitation in his voice. Like he was holding himself back from saying something, perhaps how he expected more from me or that he was disappointed in me.

But I tried not to care. I had to stand my ground. I had to be honest. I needed some time away from the mess.

Today was a Tuesday, a full-fledged day at coaching with chemistry and physics lectures. I should have been getting ready for class. Instead, after Dad left, I walked to the living room, switched on the TV and put on a show. There is nothing like some unmistakable American humour to make you forget about the world's problems.

It felt like such an act of resistance. Like I was doing something immoral. But thinking of going back to that coaching centre, surrounded by so many students, made me want to hurl.

I must've parked myself on the sofa for long enough to forget I even existed because when my mom finally came home from college, I had lost all semblance of time or even sense of self. Suddenly remembering everything again almost gave me a headache.

'Avani,' Mom walked into the living room. 'Want to go shopping?'

'What?'

'Let's buy you some new shoes and jeans,' she said, taking off her 'outside shoes'.

'What about lunch? It's almost noon.'

'We can stop by your favourite coffee place—Indian Coffee House. And Softy Corner for dessert.' She walked up the stairs to my room, and I followed her.

'Are you serious?'

'Yes! Come on, get dressed.' She walked to my wardrobe, 'Here, wear this top and these jeans. Ugh, I think we need to buy you some cute tops too.'

I put on the dark green top with pink flowers, which had previously been stashed in the back of my closet and paired it with the flared jeans that Mom had picked. It certainly looked better than what I usually wore to Hellen—any of the five t-shirts I owned paired with one of the two mom jeans. Hey, they were comfortable *and* trendy.

As we entered Sector 17, I was a bit taken aback. I wasn't sure of the last time I'd been here. Even though it was noon on a Tuesday, many people were still around. I saw a group of boys, probably around my age, hanging out at the Softy Corner. They looked like they should've been at school. Actually, *I* should've been at school too. I'd almost forgotten about the normal outside world—people sitting on benches, laughing with each other, buying clothes and showing them to their partners or friends. There was a whole world out there, not worrying about grand tests or how smart they looked or whether they were ever going to be in the top 1 per cent.

'Where do you want to go first?' Mom asked, slinging her purse across her body. Wow, she was serious.

After two hours of trying clothes on in different stores, I was able to find a few tops and a couple of pairs of jeans that I loved. Then we went to the Indian Coffee House, and we were just getting ready to order some good South Indian food when I happened to glance at my watch. It was 2.00 p.m. If I were at Hellen, I'd have already started with chemistry by this time.

'Stop glancing at your watch, Avani. You're on a break today.'

'Thanks for taking me out, Mom,' I dug into my masala dosa. 'I don't really remember doing this with you before.'

'Probably because you are much closer with your Dad,' she said, passing me the coconut chutney. It was weird hearing her say the truth out loud. I wonder if she felt bad.

'I've wanted a closer relationship with you all my life, Mom,' I said, looking down at the coconut chunks in the pastel green chutney.

'Really? I just assumed you didn't like me,' she said, fidgeting with the potato filling in the dosa. 'There would be many reasons not to.'

I looked at her. 'Are you serious? I only got through the last one month because of my conversations with you. I *love* hanging out with you, Mom. I love you.'

She finally met my gaze, her eyes a bit misty, 'I love you too, Avani.'

After a while, I asked, 'I had a question, though. What about all the judgemental looks when I'd be reading fiction, playing games or sleeping too late?'

She sighed, 'I'm sorry for that. I now realize it wasn't the right approach to take. I should've been more liberal, like your Dad.'

I smiled. 'Don't sell yourself short. Those looks of yours got me to do my homework well before the deadline countless times.'

∽

I couldn't help but reflect on our conversation from today and last night during the car ride home. My relationship with Mom had grown and changed so positively over the last few months. Now, she was my biggest cheerleader.

We got home around 3.00 p.m., and Mom had to leave for college again. I lounged around on the living room sofa till I fell into a deep, comforting and dosa-induced slumber. By the time I woke up, it was 5.00 p.m., and as I waited for Mom to come back, I found a yellowed and surprisingly well-written chemistry book on the living room bookshelf. When I heard Mom unlock the front door, I looked up from the book, taking some time to mentally adjust to the non-text world.

'Oh my God, you scared me, Avani! I thought you'd be asleep,' she dropped her tote bag on the ground, all the contents spilling out of it.

I scrambled off the couch to help her with the papers that had flown under the furniture. I'd always wondered what teachers carried in their mysterious tote bags; turns out, it was mostly papers.

As I picked up her papers, I was reminded of the day of the grand test when I had helped Avik recollect his mysterious accoutrements. As I stacked the papers neatly, tapped them against the floor to line up the edges and brought them to the dining table, one particular letter caught my eye.

It was a form to request childcare leave. I stared at it, reading the words quickly, but it didn't make any sense.

'Mom, what is this?'

'I...uh, I'm thinking about taking a short leave from my job,' she mumbled.

'What? Why?'

'So that I have more time for you. I don't want you to go through this alone. You need someone with whom you can talk about these things, about your feelings.'

I was immediately overwhelmed by guilt. 'But Mom, I'm not a baby. People go on childcare leave when they have a baby, right? Besides, what's the point of sacrificing your career for me. I mean, look at me. I'm not the best. I won't be like Shiv or Avik or Parnika.' She didn't even know two of those people, but I think she got the gist.

She sighed. 'Avani, beta, you need to stop comparing yourself to these people.'

'But isn't JEE about competition? And doesn't the very spirit of competition lie in comparing? I *have* to compare, and I accept that I'm not as smart as them,' I said, the pit in my stomach growing deeper.

'Do you think you're smart?' she asked.

I hesitated, 'Yeah—I—I think so. I mean, I wouldn't have made it this far if I wasn't.'

'Exactly.'

'But everything is so competitive. How am I supposed to put everyone else aside? There are currently thousands of students in

India studying harder than I am and who will do better than me on the entrance exam. This is a fact I accept to be true. Isn't it?'

'Yes. It's true.'

My heart sank. Did this mean she didn't think I was smart? I took a deep breath.

'But that doesn't take away from your smartness, Avani. Other people's academic achievements should not bring yours down. The world is competitive. It will continue to be competitive even after your admission into a college or even when you get a new job. You won't be able to survive if you keep making yourself feel small like that.'

'So, you mean I can have a better rank than Parnika or even, Shiv one day?'

'You can. But even if you don't, that doesn't make you any less of a person than them. Competition is important, but your happiness and personal satisfaction are more important. And if your happiness depends on your relative performance in these tests, well, then your moods will change so fast that you wouldn't know what's going on. Marks may matter, but they shouldn't be the only thing defining your happiness.'

I was astounded. I'd never heard Mom talk about happiness before.

'Why does my happiness matter? These IIT people aren't going to look at my happiness level,' I mumbled.

She chuckled, but she didn't look a bit amused. 'You think you'll make it to the IIT exam if you don't care about your happiness? You think you'll be able to achieve all your future dreams if you don't care about your happiness? Your happiness is the most important thing, Avani. More important than any exam will ever be.'

'I still don't know if your taking a break from your job will solve that. It might just make me feel me feel more miserable and guilty,' I said.

'Okay, let's not talk about that right now. Anyway, it's not your decision what I do with my job,' she said, the strict, familiar tone returning to her voice.

I sighed, 'Okay.' I was still so mortified. What would my mother tell her co-workers—that she's taking an extended leave to take care of her almost-adult daughter, who, by the way, isn't even that smart anymore?

'What are you reading?' she asked, gesturing to the book on the coffee table.

'Oh, did you know this book had been lying on our bookshelf all this time? It's a book on physical chemistry.'

Her eyes lit up, 'This was one of my course books in college. I remember referring to it a lot because it explains the concepts so well.'

'Yes, I know! The practice books they give at Hellen aren't anywhere as good as this. I feel like I've hit the goldmine.'

She smiled at me, 'You like science.'

'Yes. I like studying it. It's so complex but logical at the same time. It's fun when it starts to make sense,' I said. 'I like it even though it doesn't like me.'

'You don't like the competition,' she added.

I stared at her, astounded how she could sum up my entire experience at Hellen in just two sentences. *I like science. I don't like the competition.*

'Do you like the teachers at Hellen? Do they teach well?' she sat down next to me on the sofa. I could smell her moisturizer. It smelled like cherry blossoms.

'Yes. Most of them are way better than school teachers. They know their stuff and take all our questions, whereas the school science teacher would freak out if we asked her about something that wasn't straight out of the textbook. She would use the "out of syllabus" excuse and move on. The teachers at Hellen don't evade questions like that. Even though I'm not in the best batch.'

'It's okay, Avani. As long as you keep the passion alive, you'll make it someplace where you're happy. Just focus on yourself.'

'I'll try.'

'You know, your whole comparison habit has given me an idea. Why don't you keep a tally of every time you catch yourself comparing yourself to someone else? It might help you break the habit.'

That night, I lay in my bed reflecting on everything that I'd learnt in the past few days. I rummaged in my drawer, trying to find the previous list I'd created just when I'd filled the stream form. I started making some amendments to it, cutting points which didn't make sense to me anymore and adding new points.

Avani's Guidebook for Surviving Hellen

1. Just as I was at White Meadows, I want to be at the top of the class at Hellen. I will do the best job I possibly can; anything less would be unacceptable. I have to beat the odds and be in the top 1 per cent.
2. ~~Perform on par with Shiv and Parnika. Try to become even better.~~
   Even though I am preparing for a competitive entrance exam, I don't have to compare myself to others constantly. I should just focus on myself and my progress.
3. ~~Prove to Mom that I am not a delicate or weak person who cannot survive JEE coaching.~~
   I am done trying to prove anything to Mom because she accepted me even at my lowest point.

> 4. Prove to Dad that he was correct—that I am as smart as he thinks I am.
> 5. I will not shy away from doing things that I want but seem scary. I can't be afraid of failure anymore. Don't ever be left wondering 'what if...'
> 6. I will be honest about who I am to myself as well as others. It isn't worth it to hide my feelings, especially in front of my parents. I don't have to pretend I'm a smart kid.
> 7. It is good to take a break sometimes. It gives me a new perspective.
> 8. My happiness is the most important thing.

I still wanted to be the best. But now, I would try to approach it differently. I was going to focus more on myself and less on others, be more honest about my feelings and value my happiness the most.

I carefully folded this list and stashed it in my bedside drawer. Today, I was calm, even though tomorrow would, most definitely, be a shitshow.

21

Putting the Past Behind

It was a Wednesday. I put on my favourite clothes—the deep-blue flared jeans that I had bought yesterday and a rainbow tie-dye t-shirt. I resolved to put more effort into my appearance, if only just for myself. It had a confidence-boosting effect on me. I had felt it yesterday during our shopping spree. Now, maybe I was starting to understand why Parnika was so into fashion. I cringed at our last conversation. I had never had an outburst like that in front of her—even though she was my best friend, I was considered the more 'stable' one, the quiet one. I was usually the one listening to Parnika rant passionately about various issues, such as vanity sizing in fast fashion brands. It definitely felt weird, unloading all my emotions like that on her—on anyone, for that matter.

As I headed downstairs, Dad called out to me from the dining room, 'Avani, it's noon. Where are you going now?'

'To Hellen,' I replied, looking at myself in the hallway mirror. The dark circles were darker than ever, but I could also see a look of determination. Maybe that was just my bloated face from eating out yesterday.

'Oh!' he looked surprised. After all, I had to keep my resolution: I had scored above the benchmark I had set for myself, even if it was only by one mark. 'Could you come here for a moment? If you have time?'

I could discern the delicate nature of that last sentence. He was walking on eggshells around me or maybe he was angry at me. Who knew at this point?

'Sure. What's up?' I said, taking a chair opposite him at the dining table. The table was strewn with crumpled papers that someone had tried to flatten and restore to their original shape. 'What's this?'

'This is your question paper for the grand test. You threw this in the trash,' he said, looking at me through the frames of his glasses.

'Uh...' I did throw it in the bin out of anger like I had thrown the chemistry test on which I'd cheated and the talent hunt test that I'd flunked. I'd rather forget those tests ever existed. 'Yes. I do remember doing that.'

What else was I supposed to say?

'Why?' He asked.

'Because I had no use for it,' I said, knowing that wasn't the complete truth. I was compelled to add to it after a minute of uncomfortable silence. 'It reminded me of how incapable I am. I got angry, crumpled it up and threw it away.'

After some consideration which involved him turning the paper over a few times, he began, 'Instead of judging yourself so harshly on the basis of your performance on these tests, you should take them for what they are: a yardstick for how many questions you were able to answer correctly.

'But the questions you got wrong shouldn't make you feel bad about yourself. Instead, think—without judgement—why you got them wrong. Revise the topics for which you weren't able to attempt the questions. Don't just throw out the test paper and move on. Learn from your mistakes. That's what these practice tests are for.'

'Okay. I can do that,' I said. Although this conversation was reminiscent of the ones we'd have back when I was in school, when he'd help me create study plans for school exams, it was different now. I was embarrassed that Dad knew I crumpled up that test paper in anger. I wonder what he thought of me, knowing that I wasn't a perfect daughter, that I was a person who could get frustrated or angry and do things that perfect people probably didn't do.

'Here. Keep it someplace safe,' he handed me the previously crumpled paper that I think he had ironed smooth for me.

'Thanks, Dad. This is really good advice,' I said, nodding at him, trying to look professional. On the inside, I was dying of shame.

'I wish you had been honest with me, you know,' he said, looking at his hands, placed one on top of each other on the dining table.

'Sorry, Dad.'

'You don't need to apologize. I should've been more sensitive,' he nodded at me. Even now, he was diplomatic but straightforward. But I could imagine it took a lot for him to say that.

Honestly, I was taken aback by the reactions of my parents. I'd expected them to be so caught up in my marks as Riya had anticipated her parents would react. I thought they'd openly express their disappointment and anger about me not being in the best batch and having cheated on an exam, but they didn't seem to care about any of that. Even Dad seemed to take it somewhat better than I'd anticipated. What he suggested to me was definitely going in my guidebook.

∽

After the grand test debacle, my first class was quite lonesome. Maybe because I still felt a bit bad I hadn't been 'promoted'.

Maybe because Avik wasn't there, even though I never sat with him during lectures, I felt comfort in knowing that there was someone in the room who *knew my name*. He was definitely in Shark now—and good for him. I didn't ever feel that jealous of him. Maybe it was because I knew about his dad, and I didn't envy him for that at all. Maybe it was because I considered him my friend, even if he didn't reciprocate the same feelings.

After class, I sat at a cafeteria table, killing some time before my driver arrived. The cafeteria was a cold, despondent place with poor lighting—like the rest of the classrooms in Hellen—and a sad display of overpriced junk food. The entire place smelled like day-old cheese sandwiches. I saw Riya and Smriti sitting a few tables away, talking animatedly. They were in Shark now. Sure, that could have made me feel horrible and jealous and bitter, but for some reason, today, I was fine. I didn't care. At least their parents would be happy with them. Smriti would have probably got her laptop back.

As I sat there, people-watching, suppressing the usual instinct to compare my scores with everyone I laid eyes on, I saw Parnika. She was sitting alone at a cafeteria table, staring at her phone, quite like me—which was peculiar. She was usually found tagging along with Shiv and his posse. I got up from my lonely table and walked over to her. When I got a closer look at her, I was shocked some more at her appearance. She wasn't wearing her signature bright colours. Instead, she wore sweatpants and a grey, long-sleeved t-shirt. It was basically a cry for help that only I was capable of recognizing.

'Hey, Parnika,' I said once I stood behind her. Her eyes were glued to her phone.

She didn't look at me. I glanced over her shoulder and saw that she was going through the website of a foreign university's undergraduate programmes.

'What're you doing?' I asked, taking a seat next to her.

She quickly put her phone away. 'Nothing! Avani, hi, I didn't see you there,' she said, surprised.

'That's fine. How are you doing?' I said, folding my hands on the table. I glanced at her nails. They looked like mine. This was bad. Real bad.

She looked at me with a fake smile. 'You know. I'm fine.'

'Really?' I asked. The last time Parnika was dressed like this was the two weeks following when she scored 15 out of 20 on a maths test back in ninth class.

'What about you?' She asked, clearly deflecting.

'I'm good,' I said, trying to think of more things, not wanting the conversation to come to a halt, where it definitely would, given Parnika's visible condition. 'Actually, I didn't get promoted to Shark. I really wanted to. I worked hard for it but didn't get it. So, yeah, I've been a bit off for a few days.'

I guess I was on my honesty bender, and it felt really liberating to just say what was on my mind.

'Oh. I see,' she said, her expression unreadable. Maybe she was mad at me for my uncharacteristic outburst?

'Look, I wanted to apologize for my behaviour on Monday. I shouldn't have said all those things. I guess I feel a bit insecure. Anyway, I'm sure you didn't mean what you said about Dolphin either.'

She continued to stare at me silently.

'So, maybe we can put this behind us and move past?' I prompted.

'I thought a lot about what you said, too,' she finally said, shifting in her seat. 'I concluded that, yes, I do agree with what I said. I do think that you Dolphin people don't work hard enough. I think you're bitter and desperate to be like us. Your outburst on Monday proved me correct. So, I'm not sorry.'

'What?' The blood in my veins felt like it stopped moving for a second. I stared at her as she failed to meet my eyes, instead choosing to focus on the sad sandwich display.

'You have to make sacrifices in order to succeed here, you know? You have to completely dedicate yourself to being the best,' she said, exasperated. 'You can't just get by so easily.'

'What do you mean?' I asked. Maybe she was trying to give me some twisted advice.

'You have to work hard. Hard work is not just mindless studying, you know. If you really want to succeed here, you'll have to give up things you're actually passionate about.'

I looked at her, speechless. Where was she going with this?

'Forget it. You wouldn't understand,' she said with a melancholic sigh.

'Did you just tell me that I'm not working hard enough?' I blurted out, choosing to focus on her words and not the sadness behind them.

'Maybe you got by in school somehow, but it's a whole different world at Hellen, and clearly, you can't keep up,' she said, matter-of-factly. The flash of that dismal expression on her face was now replaced by one of contempt.

I didn't know what to say. She was right.

I was mortified. This was my real fear all along—my friend— my *best* friend recognizing what a failure I had become. This is the situation I had wanted to avoid at all costs.

But for some reason, it didn't bother me as much as I thought it would have. At least, not as much as it bothered me when *I* said those things to myself. Maybe only I had the prerogative to say such scathing things to myself.

'I do agree that I'm not doing too good at coaching right now. But what do you think I should do?' I asked, hoping this conversation had some positive note that she may have wanted to reach.

Without missing a beat, she finally looked at me and said, 'Quit. That's the only option. What's the point of doing something if you're not the best at it?'

'Maybe because I know I'll get better. I want to work hard and get to the top. Also, I feel like I'm learning a lot, and not just about studies,' I said. The chances of this going anywhere good were abysmal, but I had to defend myself.

She shook her head, chuckling to herself, 'I don't get you, Avani. You're a bit sad to look at, you know.'

'You know what, Parnika?' I said, getting up from the table, 'I don't care what you think of me. I know I'm good enough. I'll get there.'

Part Three
The Final Struggle

22

There Is No Try

It was nearing the end of July. I looked outside the car window at the mango groves near the industrial area, prodigious trees laden with yellow, green and red ripe mangoes. New leaves, which had sprouted with a parrot green colour sometime in May, were now almost the same hue as the older ones, only a shade lighter. The mango-picking season was in full force. Some men were climbing the dark brown trunks of these trees swiftly with ease; others were doing the same cautiously and slowly.

The last three months had really gone by quickly, in what felt like the turn of a page. The seasons had changed from spring to summer and now to monsoon. The rest of April went by the same, with me getting used to being alone in Dolphin after that first grand test failure. I didn't even try to make any new friends because there was no point.

May was a bit depressing because I tried hard to do well in the grand test, and although my rank improved by a lot, I had, once again, failed to get into Shark. Shiv, Parnika and Avik had topped as usual. I tried to ignore their achievements but struggled. The whole situation was embarrassing for me, sure, but I'd isolated myself from everyone, so there was really no one left to make fun of me. Only *I* could ridicule myself, which I did, of course, but I quickly moved on. I heeded Dad's advice and tried to learn what I could from my mistakes.

June was better because I just tried to pretend that I was the only person left in Hellen. When I'd look at the noticeboard for the grand test ranks, I'd start from the bottom, thereby preventing the accident of ever seeing my topper ex-friends' names. And guess what, I was almost on the cusp of getting into Shark. We were also given a week-long 'summer break', in which I decided to treat myself by playing *The Sims 3* for 12 hours straight on each of the five days of the week. The following weekend was spent recuperating from said self-indulgence. Yeah, it was not pretty. But I didn't regret it a single bit.

July had been good to me so far. Mom's childcare leave officially began in the first week, so we were able to spend a lot of time together. She took me to the local ice-cream parlour every time I had a bad time in class, which was a significant motivator for me. And guess what? I finally got a good enough rank in the last grand test and got into Shark. One step closer to my goal. However, I felt that my dad was way happier than I was.

∽

'Dad, why do we have to go?' I whined.

'Well, it'll be good for you. She's a great teacher, and she'll definitely give you some guidance so you can improve yourself further,' he said, looking out the window at the auto repair buildings in the industrial area.

Dad had arranged a meeting with the Shark batch's senior-most chemistry teacher, who had taught us the mole concept, for some 'guidance'.

'I don't like her a lot. She always taught too fast for me to understand,' I murmured.

She was literally the reason I had cried once—she was so scary. How the hell was I supposed to have a normal conversation with her? What if she knew that I'd cheated on her test all those months ago? I started breaking out in anxiety sweats.

'Avani, you're starting your classes in the Shark batch next week. You'll have to deal with a lot of such teachers,' Dad said brusquely. Or maybe I imagined it.

She had called us to her house, which was nerve-wracking in itself. I'd never been to a teacher's house in my life—wait, that wasn't true. I lived in a teacher's house. Well, a teacher on sabbatical, anyway.

Her place was quite opulent. She even had a fancy waterfall at the entrance of her house. Wow, she must be bringing in the big bucks. Her living room was filled with photos of her with students, many of whose faces were being stuffed with sweets by their parents. They all seemed very happy. Like they'd learnt the secret to living a happy and fulfilling life.

It was definitely getting into IIT and not that. But were the two related?

'Hello! Please come inside.'

On seeing the haggard man greeting us, my heart stopped. It was the Hellen version of Filch. The same guy who'd caught me cheating in that first chemistry test. Oh my God, did he remember me? I was so busted.

Although, he didn't look like he remembered me. I'm sure he would've said something if he did or maybe he was waiting for the right moment to strike and destroy me.

'So, Avani, your father told me that you recently got upgraded to the Shark batch?' she asked. Oh my God, she said my name. She knew my name. I was not expecting to freak out so much, but I felt like I was meeting a celebrity. I couldn't believe she was an actual human being. And that she was a person who had made my life hell at one point.

'Yes,' I managed to say.

'What was your rank in the previous grand test?' she asked.

'Seventy-five,' I said, with a jolt of pride rushing through me.

She gestured for Hellen Filch to get something. 'Oh, that's great. I'm sure you'll do well in Shark. It's full of the smartest students in the city.'

I half-smiled, feeling the lump in my throat. Smartest students in the city? That didn't scare me at all—nope.

Her assistant came back with a stack of papers. I peered at them—my name was on the sheets. She spread out the papers on the coffee table before her and closely scrutinized them.

'So, here I can see—you scored 204 out of 360 in the previous test. Yes, this test was easier than the previous one, where you'd scored a 180. In the one before that, you got a 175. Hmm...the one before, you had a 151! Seems like a decent improvement!' she looked at me, smiling. Wow, she was *actually smiling*.

'Thank you, ma'am,' I said, dying of happiness on the inside. She thought I was smart!

'Our top 20 students always make it into an IIT, and the top 50 into a good National Institute of Technology (NIT). It's not always an exact number but an approximate according to the data for the past 10 years,' she said. Wow, she sounded exactly like she did in the lectures—only more human and less android. 'In order to get there, you must get at least 270 and above in the tests.'

'Okay,' I said, hoping she would tell me how I could get there. Would I ever be able to get there? From her words, it seemed like I was going to neither an IIT nor an NIT. Where was I going? To a deep dark pit at the bottom of the earth?

'Do you have a study group?' She asked, looking straight into my eyes. I felt so exposed.

'Umm...no,' I said, having mental flashbacks to how all my friendships went up in flames back in April. I was somewhat of a pariah at the moment.

'You must form a group with students who are keen on

studying. The most important thing for getting to the top is clearing your doubts, and many times, peers can help each other in that regard more than the teachers. Now that you're in the Shark batch, there will be a lot of dedicated people working alongside you who will be happy to include you. It can make all the difference in getting a top rank. And if you're not already studying six hours a day, you *must* increase your study time.'

'Six hours after my classes at Hellen?' I asked.

'Yes, obviously. If you can do more per day, that's even better. But you *must* study consistently, at least six hours per day.' She looked at me like I'd asked her if grass was green.

'Actually, ma'am, I get so tired after returning from Hellen. I find it difficult to study for more than three or four hours,' I said.

She scoffed, 'You must study a lot more than what you're doing right now. Self-study is the way forward. Three or four hours may have been fine when you started out in Dolphin, but now you've been here for a long time. You should've adjusted to the long hours by now. After all, the JEE Advanced exam is also six hours long. You need to be able to maintain that level of concentration.'

Dad said, 'Yes, I agree. I also had to study for hours back when I was preparing for engineering entrance exams. She is right, Avani; studying after classes on your own is essential.'

They didn't know that when I started out, I hardly did any self-study. I would be so tired and overwhelmed. Somehow, I was able to bring it up to three to four hours a day and was proud of myself for doing so. And here they were, looking at me smugly, asking me to double my time, like it was nothing.

Her assistant brought out some mithai and tea for us. Usually, the sight of food would make me feel comforted and calm. But here, it was kind of having the opposite effect. I looked around the living room at the walls clad with newspaper clippings of various students being fed the same mithai, and I felt so out of place, so unworthy. The negative voice in my head popped up. I would probably get demoted to Dolphin again. This seemed like a fluke.

Nope. Bad Avani. I wasn't going to disparage myself like that.

'You must work hard, Avani. To get into an IIT, students dedicate themselves completely to their studies. Everything is optimized for that one goal,' she said, chomping down on some kaju katli.

What was I supposed to say to that? So I just nodded.

'Take these Hellen grand tests seriously. They are reflective of the real JEE exam. There's a mega grand test coming up in a month. This will include most of the eleventh class syllabus. Students from all over the country are invited to take this test, and it's what Hellen is most famous for. We usually have over two lakh participants. You must score well in it,' she said.

'Yes, ma'am,' I said, weakly smiling. 'I'll try.'

'There is no try. You *must* do it. There is no other option,' she said, smiling back at me, almost menacingly.

Nope. I wasn't scared at all.

23

A Second First Day

On Monday, my heart raced as I walked down the dimly lit basement hallway, trying to locate the new Shark classroom. I had a thousand different thoughts running through my mind. Would the classroom be better? Would the seats be softer?

I'm sure Avik and Shiv would've become best friends, and Parnika was probably in their little group as well. They were all perfect for each other. Smart, cool, capable of studying more than four hours a day—no, stop, Avani. Don't compare.

I had been making a lot of effort to focus on myself. And for the most part, it worked, and I was stable. I didn't compare myself much since I didn't talk to anyone at Hellen. I just attended the lectures like a machine and came back home, did my assignments, prepared for tests, talked to Mom about my day and ate the delicious food prepared by her—rinse and repeat.

I just hoped getting into Shark didn't ruin the stability.

Although I'd been attending classes at this coaching centre for almost four months, I'd never been inside the Shark classroom. It was quite similar to the Dolphin one, in the sense that it was windowless, bare-walled and depressing. Additionally, it was in the basement—which only made it look worse. The word 'Shark' was written in big letters above the projector screen. I was also given the fabled folder with a photograph of the vicious sharp-toothed, cold-blooded animal on it.

Even though dividing the students into batches named after aquatic animals was lame and borderline discriminatory, it still felt like an achievement to be in Shark. I'd finally made it to the top of the ladder at Hellen. I was getting closer to being in the top 1 per cent, being the best—my number one goal. I had resolved yesterday that I would study longer and work harder than ever before. There was no try. I *had* to do it. I had to get the best possible rank in the mega grand test. Anything less would be unacceptable.

The girls' section in Shark was much smaller than Dolphin, just three rows. That meant there were a total of about 18 girls in a group of 100 students. I went and sat in the empty, non-reserved second row. The first row was already occupied by the toppers, all of them buried in their notes.

I scoured the section, trying to spot Parnika's bright clothes but couldn't. Maybe she was late? It sucked, but I hadn't made any effort to talk to her after our argument three months ago. She hadn't reached out either. There had been so many strange or funny moments in the past few months that I wanted to text her about—like the time a monkey stole Dad's glasses when we were out on a hike behind Sukhna Lake. But each time, I remembered what she had said to me and stopped myself. Now, though, I really wanted her back in my life—we'd never had a fight last this long. I also spent a lot of time trying to figure out the meaning behind her response to me as well—all that talk about her sacrificing the things she was passionate about. In any case, I was ready to apologize, even though I wasn't quite sure what for. My feelings, whatever I'd told her in that parking-lot outburst, I still held true. They were perfect, smart and sorted. I wasn't.

A group of roaring guys barged into the classroom. Shiv was in the centre, loudly talking about some formula I had only read yesterday night. He looked as if on top of the world. I hadn't talked much with him after that day he'd 'saved' me from falling down the stairs. He'd texted me a few times since, attempting to initiate a conversation, but I'd replied curtly, and, eventually, he got the hint. I did miss talking to him, even if most of our talks were about trivial things—it had added some flavour to my otherwise boring coaching life. But his 'betrayal' of scoring such good marks after complaining about his performance still stung, even though I knew he hadn't done it on purpose. I guess Parnika was right. I was a bit bitter.

A few minutes passed, and my eyes would flick to the door the second someone would walk into the class. Still, no Parnika. Where was she? Too eager to see her, I finally decided to walk out of the class and into the hallway, trying to locate her among the few groups of students who were probably trying to get some fresh air. But I couldn't spot her anywhere.

I decided to suck up my ego and send her a quick text.

Avani: Hey, Parnika. Hope you're doing well. Just got upgraded to Shark today, but I couldn't find you in class. Are you out sick today?

When I came back to the class, my bag was nowhere to be seen, and the second row was completely filled with students. I approached the girl sitting in my seat.

'Um, hi. Have you seen my bag? It has rainbow-coloured stripes. I was sitting here,' I said, pointing to her seat.

She had purple-rimmed glasses and looked like she'd smelt something putrid. Her mouth contorted, forming a face of mild disgust.

It couldn't have been me, I took a shower that morning. Mom forced me to, like always. Even though Mom's judging looks had, for the most part, disappeared, her strong insistence that I do basic human tasks regularly persisted. I was grateful for it.

'No, I have no idea.' She replied, not even looking at me. Instead, she opened her notebook and started revising the previous lecture.

'Okay, but I'm pretty sure I kept it here,' I repeated myself. I was no longer the non-confrontational Avani. I was going to stand up for myself.

She narrowed her eyes, finally looking at me. 'Look, I have no idea. Okay?'

'Um, okay,' I said, still lingering. I was trying to be confident and all, finally having made it to Shark, but this was my first attempt at it, leaving me a bit unsure on how to proceed.

'Are you even in the right classroom?' she said, gesturing to the huge 'Shark' written on the wall. I could feel the condescension dripping from her voice.

'Yes, of course,' I said, trying not to make my voice sound shaky.

'Are you seriously fighting with her over a seat? Ugh. Get a life,' the girl next to her looked at me and rolled her eyes.

'I'm—I'm not fighting. I just—I was here first. I can prove it if I find my bag,' I said, trying not to cry. I crouched in the aisle, trying to locate my bag, looking at people's feet. Ugh.

'Excuse me,' someone was standing behind me, waiting for me to move.

'I'm sorry,' I said, standing up, giving the guy some way.

A tired-looking guy with dazed eyes, dark circles and unkempt fluffy hair stood a few inches away from me. It was Avik. He was almost unrecognizable.

'Avik!' I said, 'How are you?'

He moved past without looking directly at me. Maybe he just didn't hear me over the chatter coming from the class.

I slid onto the third bench, i.e. the last bench for girls. I found my backpack thrown on the ground near my new crappy seat. I was pretty sure I didn't leave it there. Did that girl with the purple glasses throw it here or did it just slip and end up in the next row on its own?

This was not the congenial attitude I was supposed to have to form a study group. Damn it. I took a deep breath and tried to let it go. It was useless to worry about it.

We were waiting for the teacher, and I was already done revising my lecture, so I looked around the classroom discreetly.

My gaze quickly went to the boys' section and, without much thought, started to scan for Avik. It wasn't tough to spot him—he was sitting in the first row. I didn't know he was still a topper. I was happy for him, though. We hadn't talked at all after that strange confrontation on the day of the first grand test way back in April when he'd shouted at me for helping him. I wanted to, of course, but he got promoted to Shark after that, and as everyone at Hellen knows, Shark people don't talk to Dolphin people much. Since then, I hadn't even seen him, as our classes would be on different floors.

He didn't seem to be talking to anyone, not even Shiv—who was seated next to him. On the other hand, Shiv was talking animatedly with his neighbours, debating boisterously on the possibility of exceptions to Third Law of Motion (yes, I could hear it from where I was sitting).

'Hi, I'm Avani,' I said to the girl sitting to my left. I recognized her as the Space Girl—I mean, Meenal, from my first day at Hellen. 'Oh, hey, Meenal! Remember me? We were in Dolphin together back in April.'

She stared at me as if I'd just offended her. 'Sorry, I don't really remember much about Dolphin. I was quickly *up*graded, you know.'

Well, this was very awkward. 'Oh, no problem.' I had to be persistent. 'This is my first day in the batch, actually. What's the teacher like?'

'The teacher's good,' she mumbled, getting back to her notes.

I slumped back in my seat, and just as I did, the teacher finally walked in to put me out of my misery. Lo and behold, it was none other than the man who pointed me out during orientation, mentally scarring me for a few days at least: Sahil sir.

Any remaining excitement I had for being in Shark was slowly dwindling away.

24

Familiar Feelings

Three hours later, my mind was almost completely numb. I'd gotten used to the Dolphin pace. This seemed like a different ball game altogether.

'As you all know, if you have any doubts remaining, you can ask me after the class in my office.' Sahil sir said, getting up from his seat and leaving the class. A trail of students followed him, armed with notebooks in their hands.

Shiv, the first-row girls, Meenal and Bag Girl, were asking complex questions during the class. Their questions weren't like the ones I asked in Dolphin. Theirs were insightful and contextual and so detailed. I had doubts about their doubts—how funny (*not*). No one ever asked such complex doubts in Dolphin. This meant that they knew more—way more—than I did. The familiar feelings of comparison were starting to creep in again now that I was surrounded by the very people I had tried to avoid for the past three months. And I couldn't shake their superiority off, no matter how much I tried. They were smart and I wasn't.

How was I going to get better than what I was and eventually get to the top? I had to score well in that mega grand test (God, that sounds lame)—so many people all over India were going to be taking the test. As chemistry ma'am had said, it would be reflective of my JEE score. If I didn't, then all this hard work would be for nothing.

I was full of questions during the lecture, but I was frozen. My doubts were too basic—they probably weren't as smart as the others' were. I wrote them down in my notebook instead. Maybe I could go to his office—or I could ask my future study group. They wouldn't judge me, would they?

I scoured the room, trying to find a potential study partner. I used the process of elimination.

No girl who would shove your bag to the back row.

No boy who would be funny and kind one moment and then stop talking to you next.

None of the top 10 students. The comparison might kill me or at least my ego.

I walked towards the circle of the first-row girls. I recognized one of them as the only girl who was consistently in the top 10. They were all huddled together, talking quietly amongst themselves. I had a feeling they would be nicer than the others.

'I think the integral will be taken before the inner bracket's limit is calculated...' said one.

'No, that doesn't make any sense. I think it's supposed to be done this way...' the Top 10 Girl said.

'Hmm, yeah, I think you're right,' the other girl replied, scribbling in her notebook.

'Did you get a chance to revise that grand test question?'

'Yes, I had a talk with Sahil sir. The limit for that equation did not exist, so the question was actually invalid,' the topper said dismissively.

I couldn't believe it. They were so smart that they were even finding mistakes in the test questions. Whereas I was always just trying to get through the whole test paper with time to spare. I took a deep breath, trying to suppress the comparison.

'Hi, I'm Avani,' I said, butting my way into their circle. I had to give this my best. I'd just been standing awkwardly next to their circle for 10 minutes. I hoped that wasn't weird. It probably was.

'Hi,' one of them said, quickly glancing at me and then bringing her gaze back to her notebook.

They didn't look like the kind to entertain small talk for a very long time, but still, I tried. 'So, tough class, huh?'

Silence. Tough crowd as well, I guess. I didn't even know their names, but I had a feeling that if they had wanted to tell me, they would've.

'I think I heard the word "hyperbola" so much in this lecture that it stopped sounding like an actual word and more like a Hogwarts spell at some point,' I continued. The room was suddenly so quiet that I was made aware of my own annoying voice. Why was I making *Harry Potter* references all of a sudden?

'Oh,' one of the girls said. She'd been talking quite animatedly before I'd joined, and now she looked completely bored. Wait, so did all the other girls.

I jumped straight to the point, abandoning all hope about small talk and opened my notebook to my doubts page. They seemed like they were discussing each other's doubts anyway.

It kind of felt like a set of interview questions, them being the celebrities, but my ego was not the thing on my mind right now. The overwhelming urge to make a 'Study Group' was.

'I just had a few doubts about today's lecture. Did you understand the relationship between alpha and beta in the first question that sir had asked us?' I asked.

They all shook their heads side to side as if to say, 'We have no idea what you're saying right now'.

'What about—the question about recognizing if a particular complex number equation represents an ellipse? That was too confusing.'

Blank. Completely blank.

'The triangle inequality concept for complex numbers? I didn't understand the reasoning behind it. How come the inequality holds true only under certain conditions?'

The topper spoke up on that one, 'Yeah, sir didn't explain the complete concept. He assumed we already knew it since we were given the module assignment a week ago. The concept was like this...'

She then proceeded to give a very long explanation full of jargon I hadn't even heard of before this conversation.

'Oh, okay. Thanks for the help,' I said, too awkward to ask her to explain the said jargon. I could feel the group getting restive, so I shut my notebook, 'Nice talking to you guys.'

I waited for a reply, maybe something like, 'Nice talking with you as well, dear Avani! Welcome to Shark!' would've been nice, but who was I kidding. I slowly turned around and walked off in a random direction just to get further away from them.

When I was at a safe distance from them, I saw them chattering away with each other, just as they were doing before I'd interrupted them. I was hoping they would chatter like that *with me.*

I felt like a little kid who'd been cast off to the side. Like I didn't belong here. Like I was imposing on them. I probably was. Why was I so awkward? Why couldn't I just be like the others?

I took a deep breath. The self-deprecation was coming back. It had almost vanished for the past three months, and I knew why. I'd avoided everyone by staying in my bubble back in Dolphin. I couldn't run away now.

My chemistry teacher's advice on making a study group was starting to seem like a death sentence for me. If I couldn't even *talk* to smart people, how could I become one?

I started walking to Sahil sir's room, hoping I'd clear my doubts with him instead.

Upon entering sir's room, I was surprised to see him being

hounded by at least 30 students, all surrounding his desk and asking questions in a way quite similar to an out-of-control press conference. Back in Dolphin, I would be one of the few students who would stay back after the lecture to clear their doubts. Here, I couldn't even see the teacher. The huge noisy group of people next to me were all arguing about modulus and locus.

I leaned against the back wall of the room, trying to listen in on the debate going on, but they were talking fast and with so much jargon that I wasn't able to understand much—it was like listening to a someone fluently speak a foreign language you'd been learning on an app for a few months.

Shiv was one of the debaters, talking determinedly with another person, the girl who was in the top 10. She was the only one who had given me an explanation when I'd asked doubts, and even though I didn't understand a single word of what she'd explained, I sided with her.

I stood and waited for a good 20 minutes, but the crowd didn't budge. Everyone was bombarding sir with questions.

There was no way I could get through the crowd. Not unless I crowd-surfed my way to the centre, but I doubt anyone would want to be subjected to that. Most of the guys weren't buff enough, and I wasn't Harry Styles. Not quite the combination for crowd-surfing.

'Excuse me,' I finally said to one of the boys standing nearest to me, blocking my view of the teacher. He didn't budge.

'Could you please move aside? I just need to ask a few questions. Please?' I spoke timidly that time. I was tired of being loud, trying to be heard—no matter how loud I tried to speak. I was drowned out by the chatter of all of the students around me.

I tried to enter the crowd from another direction but to no avail. I was invisible.

Looking behind, I saw a hound of people waiting for their

turn, most of them engaged in heated discussions with their friends, probably from their study groups. Ugh, they were definitely getting into an IIT.

My head was starting to pound, and I was sure my headache would take over my body by the time my turn came, and I wouldn't understand anything the teacher would explain to me.

∽

As I stood near the exit of the building and waited to be picked up, trying to placate my incoming headache by taking deep breaths, I spotted Avik sitting on the stairs, talking to someone on the phone. I tried my best not to overhear, instead, I focused my attention on the passing cars on the busy road in front of us.

'I'm sorry,' he said. 'I'm trying my best, you know.'

I could hear some shouting on the other side.

'It's not that easy.' He winced and closed his eyes, 'I won't end up like her. I promise you.'

Some more 'loud talking' from the other side.

He sighed. 'I'm sorry, I'm sorry. I'll do better next time. I promise.'

After cutting the phone, he proceeded to throw it down the stairs.

Wow, so smart. Was this guy supposed to be a topper?

'Ugh,' he said, seeing the wreckage beneath him. Luckily, it didn't look like a very expensive phone.

He covered his face with his hands. Was he...crying?

I stood there, frozen. What the hell was taking the car so long?

Something was definitely wrong with Avik. Especially now, his upset mood made me feel really uncomfortable. Something was off. But I didn't want to butt into his problems, especially after he'd told me off for being too 'helpful' that day after the first grand test. Though I guess I had eavesdropped (by mistake,

I swear), so technically, I had already butted in.

'No shattered screen. Hey, phone abuse is a real problem, you know? One in 20 phones report cases every day. Don't become a statistic,' I said, going down the steps to collect the pieces of his phone, attempting to put them together. 'Luckily, your phone looks like it is from the 1980s. It looks like it will be okay.'

I offered him his phone, which now lit up like nothing ever happened to it.

He extended his hand to take it, and for a second, our fingers brushed. His hand was freezing. 'Thanks.'

I sat down next to him on the steps, maintaining a respectable distance of a metre. It was 7.00 p.m. The days were getting shorter, and mosquitoes were everywhere. A streetlight flickered in the lonely parking lot in front of us.

'I thought you were doing the best. You're sitting in the first row.' I mumbled, staring at his side profile. I could see some tear lines on his cheek in the intermittent glow of the streetlight.

He looked at me in shock, as if he just realized I'd overheard his entire conversation.

'Sorry, I didn't mean to overhear,' I said, full of remorse.

He shook his head, quickly wiping his cheeks with the back of his hand. 'No, it's fine. My rank slipped in this test.'

'Oh. What is it now—five—10—20?' I asked, a familiar sense of bitterness creeping into my voice. I didn't want to be bitter, he definitely didn't deserve it, but I couldn't help it after the day I'd had.

Slightly smirking, he asked, 'Are you mocking me?'

'No, please, do tell. I haven't been paying much attention to others' ranks recently,' I said, trying to hide the resentment and turning it into comedy, at least as much I could manage.

'Oh, is that the case?' he chuckled. 'Probably for the best.'

'So, what is Avik the Topper's rank now? I'm dying of

curiosity,' somehow whenever I talked to him, my most witty, sarcastic self—which wasn't even that witty or sarcastic—came out. It was the best I could manage in a real-time scenario.

'Fifteen,' he sounded hesitant as if he was revealing a bad secret.

'Are you serious? Is that supposed to be bad?'

'Well, I was ranked second before. So...'

'Oh my God, you "smart people" are so *whiny*. First Shiv, and then you? You guys really don't have any sense of self-awareness, do you? I can't even—'

I stopped myself. What was I doing? Why was I saying all of this? Maybe from remembering Shiv's smug looks with his 'bros' or from Bag Girl's horrid treatment of my cute rainbow backpack.

Avik was looking at me intently, 'No, please go on. I want to hear the rest of it.'

He looked serious about it. Well, at least he wasn't crying anymore.

'Okay, since you asked for it. Here you all are, with your perfect lives: ranks in the top 10s, complex doubts and finding mistakes in the tests and still whining about your rank slipping by a few numbers, whereas there are people like me whose rank never crosses 50. Get over it.'

'Yeah, I'm whiny. You're whiny too. You just whined to me, like I whined to you. I think if you're telling me to get over myself, you should also be telling the same thing to yourself.'

'What?' I did not expect such a deep analysis of a teenage rant.

'You just complained to me about your rank not crossing 50. But what about the kids whose ranks never cross a 100? Would they feel the same way you do about me?'

'I—' I trailed off. He had a point. Past Avani, whose rank was always in the 100s, would feel that way about Present Me.

'We all have a right to be whiny, you know. Everyone has

some crap or the other going on in their lives. You can't really judge someone by their rank or their level of smartness.'

'Says the smart dude with the perfect life: ranks in top 10s and who is definitely going to an IIT,' I mumbled.

He chuckled, 'I could say the same about you. You have such a cool dad and a nice car. Purely judging you on that basis, I would say your life is perfect.'

'I'm sorry, what?'

'You judge others on their rank or relative smartness on an MCQ test, and I judge others on the quality of their dads and their cars,' he said.

'Are you serious?' a giggle escaped me.

He started laughing, 'It's sad but true.'

'That was my dad's government-issued car, and it isn't even that good. Plus, my dad has been acting like an—never mind. Yeah, things are not as great as they seem for me. You, on the other hand—except you breaking your phone for some reason, everything else seems great.'

He shook his head. 'No, that's not the case at all. You know, my family situation is kind of messed up right now.'

'What do you mean?' I asked, not really sure if that was the polite thing to do.

'Well, my sister ran away from home. And now my parents are really just dependent on me to succeed.'

My jaw dropped. 'Your sister did *what*?'

He half-smiled. 'I know, that sounds crazier than it was. It happened two years ago. She was in twelfth, pursuing IIT coaching like me. She couldn't handle it; besides, her passions lay somewhere else. She's okay now—she's studying graphic design at one of the best colleges for it in India. I talk to her all the time—but my parents don't, and they don't want me to talk to her either. I miss her a lot. And I can't believe she left me alone to deal with my parents. I can't blame her, though.'

Oh. Was that girl with whom talked to on the phone his sister? It all made so much sense now. I wanted to know more—why she left, why his parents made his life difficult. But this seemed like a sensitive topic. He would tell me if he wanted to. I felt I had already pried enough.

'I'm sorry. That must suck,' I said, moving a bit closer, putting my hand on his shoulder, trying to console him. I wasn't really sure if it was working.

He sighed. 'Yes. It does suck. Sorry, I have never used that word before. Everything sucks!' he exclaimed, throwing his arms in front of him.

I laughed, putting my hand on my chest as if pledging to something. 'Avani, at your service, expanding your dictionary one semi-curse word at a time.'

'I'm your proud student, Avani,' he said, smiling back at me, folding his hands and bowing a bit as if he was saying namaste.

We stared at each other, our eyes crinkled with smiles. I don't know why but most of our conversations either involved laughing or crying or both. It was weird, but also, I liked it. I liked how we'd started talking as if there was no three-month gap in between. As if our last conversation hadn't ended up with him shouting at me for no apparent reason.

My smile faded as I remembered that day. Was this the right moment to confront him about that? I cared too much about our friendship to let it slide, but he seemed to be in a difficult place right now.

My heart sank as the car approached me. I guess the decision was already made for me.

'There's your expensive car,' he chuckled.

'It's not even the same car,' I rolled my eyes, but with a smile on my face for once. 'Bye. Take care.'

Familiar Feelings

As I went back home, I couldn't believe the conversation I'd just had, and with whom. Talking about 'life stuff' and 'feelings' was not something I did often, even with Parnika. Talking with Avik should've felt weird, given that he is one of the best students in the batch, but it didn't. I didn't see him as just a topper. He seemed more human to me. Maybe because of what he told me about his family or maybe because we started out together in Dolphin.

My mind shifted back to the present. What a travesty it was, trying to make a study group and ask my doubts. How would I ever get to the top without following the same steps others were taking? I had to score well in the mega grand test and get to the top 1 per cent. Anything less would be unacceptable. Like my teacher had said, there was no *try*.

I took a deep breath, bringing my focus to a cocker spaniel walking along the sidewalk with his human. Why couldn't I just be a dog? If I were a dog, I wouldn't have problems like these anymore. No more tests and the compulsive need to be the best. No more self-hatred and fighting said thoughts. Just going on walks with my human, who would give me food, a place to sleep and, most importantly, cuddles.

I wouldn't get to play *The Sims 3*, though—which I hadn't done anyway since the summer break back in June.

I couldn't even imagine a life without five-hour long classes and tests now. I was in too deep. What was I doing this all for? Just for the same things the dog wanted—food, a place to sleep and cuddles, of course.

I stopped myself from diving into existential thoughts. It wasn't going to be of any help. Instead, I turned on my phone's flashlight and opened my notebook. Might as well revise today's lecture.

And just like that, the car whizzed past the dog, leaving me alone with my notebook, trying to avoid the existential thoughts from pouring in.

25

'Why Do You Like Me?'

Tuesday was equally tiring, if not worse than Monday. I thought one maths class was bad on Monday. Well two equally long and harrowing physics and chemistry classes made it worse than I could have ever imagined. I had never thought this amount of intense focus was humanly possible, as even after two hours of the longest possible lectures, the toppers in the front row kept asking all kinds of questions. Meanwhile, I just wanted to crash my head on the table. Was I ever going to become like those people—full of energy, always alert and just perfect? Speaking of perfect, where was Parnika? She wasn't anywhere to be seen in class even today. It was usually not advised to miss Hellen classes, as it would be extremely difficult to catch up once back. It was the reason I'd see many sick students actually coming to class. It was gross, but it was what we were used to by now.

After class finally got over, I saw the same group of toppers gathered in the teacher's cabin, shoving their notebooks in his face and asking questions. How did they have the energy? Meanwhile, I felt like I was going to faint—I could still hear the chatter in my head, even after I was in the quiet hallway. I walked over to the cafeteria and ordered a tea for myself. It was nothing compared to my mom's, of course, but I needed the slight pick-me-up before I headed home for dinner.

As I sat there in the cafeteria at my usual table, nursing a cup of milk tea in my hands, I saw someone very familiar approach me. Why the heck did he want to talk to me?

'Avani?' Shiv stood next to the lonely table, towering over me.

'Hey,' I said.

'It's been a while since we talked,' he said, taking the seat opposite me, his tone willing me to elaborate on the reason why.

'Yes. It has,' I said robotically, not adding the reason. *I am super intimidated by you, dude. Get a hint.*

'So, how have you been?' He asked, flicking a strand of his hair out of his eyes. He had been growing out his hair, for some strange reason. I thought he looked better with short hair, personally. Not that anyone cares.

'I've been good. Avoiding people, mostly,' I said, with a laugh, looking at his generic polo shirt, not able to look directly into his eyes. Ah, like the good old days.

He laughed with me, 'Nice one.'

I don't think he realized I was being serious this one time.

'How are you?' I asked, finally willing myself to meet his gaze. I had to try to be confident, at least. I was in Shark now.

A weird, awkward silence filled our conversation. He seemed like he wanted to say something but was going over it in his head multiple times, similar to how I would be while hyping myself up to ask a doubt in class—but never actually having the courage to do it. Classic Avani things.

'Uh... I, um,' he mumbled. I'd never seen him look so terrified before. Was he okay? Did I need to call a doctor? Maybe he was having a brain stroke. Maybe all that studying was finally catching up with him.

'I've been meaning to say this for a very long time, but I wasn't brave enough...I like you,' he said, looking at me with his brown eyes.

I was quickly overcome by this nauseating feeling rousing in my stomach, and in just a span of a few seconds, it had spread all over my abdominal region.

'Oh...kay,' my stupid self mumbled. I continued looking at him, searching for any sign on his face that would indicate he was pranking me. Maybe this was a new form of hazing for Shark newcomers.

'So...' he trailed off. He looked so weird and shy all of a sudden. All that bravado had disappeared. It was then that I realized this was not a joke. He was really serious. I felt the same feelings of incapacitation take over me that I used to have back in my Dolphin days when I would talk to Shiv in person. One very familiar question swirled in my head and wouldn't let go of my attention. Why did this smart, popular, perfect guy like me?

'Why?' I blurted out.

'What?' He leaned forward in his chair, narrowing his eyes.

'Why do you like me? There are tens of girls in Shark who are better than me. You could like any one of them,' I said, staring him straight in the eyes.

It was true. I was actually nothing compared to the Smart Girls. Most of them always looked so sorted, whereas I would be trying to put myself together most of the time. Plus, they were naturally smart. I had to work extremely hard to be even half that smart. Why, in his right mind, would he choose *me*?

He looked irritated, not saying anything for a minute, 'I just like you. You're a nice girl. I like talking to you.'

'Sorry. I—I didn't mean to annoy you,' I said, trying to take a deep breath, but my breath hitched. Why did I seem to be regressing with each second that I spent in Shark? Why did I have to work so hard to stop my bitter, self-deprecating thoughts? Why weren't they stopping?

'It's fine. Maybe it was a bit of a shock, given we haven't talked for so long,' he said, putting his elbows on the table, shaking his head. 'I'm sorry, I didn't mean to spring it on you like this. It's just how I feel. You don't have to say anything if you don't want to.'

I looked at him. The most hopeless look clouded his face. I felt extremely guilty.

I was compelled to take away that hopeless look, to tell him that he wasn't the problem, I was. But I didn't know how to.

'I'll just leave now,' he said, in a resigned tone, getting up from the table.

⁓

When I got home, I was still lost in my thoughts. What could I have said—'Yes, Shiv, I want to be your girlfriend. I want to be with someone who gives me perpetual inferiority complex'?

I was pretty sure he'd have forgotten about me after not talking for these past few months. And then he drops a bomb like this.

'Avani, you okay?'

I looked up. Mom was staring at me, her eyes full of concern.

'You haven't touched your dinner. Here, let me warm the paneer curry,' she said, taking my plate to the kitchen.

If there was one thing I was grateful for, it was that I didn't have to eat lauki anymore. At least there were *some* upsides to this coaching arrangement.

I followed her to the kitchen. 'Where's Dad?'

'He's going to be late. Something bad happened at the office, so he is trying to fix it,' she murmured while tossing paneer cubes in the wok.

'Oh, but it's already 9.00 p.m. How late will he be?'

'I don't know, Avani,' she replied, sounding a bit exasperated. 'He didn't even come home for lunch. I'm so worried about him.'

'I'm sorry. It will be okay,' I said, patting her shoulder. I wasn't very good at this comforting thing, I could tell.

She sighed. 'Yes, it will. Thanks, Avani. I just get so worried about you two.'

'Why would you be worried about me? I'm perfectly fine.' Even saying that felt like I was going against every cell of my body.

'You may not realize it, but your face is a giveaway,' she said, handing me back the plate with fuming pieces of paneer. 'For example, a few minutes back, when you were silent, you looked like you were having an argument with yourself.'

'Oh, that is just the way I am,' I mumbled, taking back the plate of food to the table.

'Okay, if you say so.'

'Sorry, it's just that there are so many important things than what's going on in my head. Like Dad, for instance. I'm irrelevant.' I muttered the last sentence.

'No, you're not irrelevant. Avani, what happened?'

'I—you have to promise me that you won't judge me or scold me,' I said, my heart feeling like it was about to leap out of my chest. I could feel the scared part of me trying to hold myself back form saying anything. But I didn't want to hide my feelings, at least not in front of my mom. I used to do it before, back when I started out with coaching, and it was just really tiring to carry all these problems on my shoulders with no one to hear them. And anyway, I had a feeling she wouldn't judge me or scold me. She might have, a few months ago, but things had changed since then.

'Of course, I won't.'

'Well, this guy at tuition told me he liked me today. And I basically said no. But now I feel bad because I wasn't able to explain myself to him. And I think he deserved an explanation since he's my friend,' I said, putting it all out there but in very generic terms.

'Why Do You Like Me?'

'Why did you say no? What's wrong with him?'

I looked at her, shocked that she would ever go this route. I thought she'd say, 'Good job, kid. I raised you right.'

'Mom, are you trying to play me? Of course, I am not going to do that kind of stuff right now. I have too much on my plate, with studies and whatnot. And anyway, he's too good.'

'What do you mean, "He's too good"?'

I squirmed in my seat. The paneer I was chewing suddenly started to feel like rubber. I guess this was the price I had to pay if I really wanted to put all my cards on the table.

'He's this topper guy who always scores the best marks at Hellen. Like, seriously, everyone worships him. Once, he was whining after a grand test because he got one question wrong— one question! I don't understand how someone like him could like someone like me. I mean, *come on*. I am not one of those perfect, cute, topper girls and will never be. And you know what he said when I asked him why he liked me? He said it's because I am nice. Nice? What the hell? It bothers me so much. I know I'm not nice. Not with all the horrible thoughts in my head.' I put my hand on my forehead. 'I am so confused. Ugh, I am so weird. I'm so done with myself. I wish I could just turn it off.'

'So, the reason you don't like him is that he's too smart and seems perfect?'

'Yeah…I guess. I kind of hate him. I always feel less than in front of him. That's why I stopped talking to him. And the fact that he "likes" me because he thinks I'm "nice" is so infuriating! Why couldn't he have said I'm smart?' I could hear my voice break.

'Avani, why do you care what some random boy thinks about you?'

'Because I don't know. I guess his opinion matters because he's one of the smart ones.'

'So, you think he's a God, just because he's "smart"?'

I contemplated for a bit. 'I mean, I wouldn't say he's a God. But yeah, he's just so sorted and perfect. He's like a VIP. And I'm not even an IP. If that makes any sense.'

'Avani, you *are* important. You *are* good enough,' she said, walking over to my side, pulling me into a hug, stroking my hair.

'I used to think so, too, until I came to Shark batch. Everyone else seems so perfect here,' I mumbled into her shoulder.

'When you look at it, he's just a guy who scores good marks in MCQ tests. Isn't it true?' She pulled away to look at me.

I nodded.

'Avani, your self-worth isn't related to your marks or your ranks. Like I told you before—your happiness shouldn't depend on the comparison. You're so much more than that.'

'But Mom—it's so hard to actually implement that. Since I've moved to the Shark batch, I see all these perfect students asking complex doubts, getting more marks than me, and they seem so sorted. They'll all definitely make it to an IIT. Seeing them makes me feel so small, so incapable.'

'I can assure you, no one is perfect. Not even this guy. It's okay that you don't like this guy. You're allowed to have that feeling. But you shouldn't feel inferior to anyone. You shouldn't allow someone else to determine your worth. You are *you*. You are more than a sheet of paper, a number, a seat in a class in an educational institution.'

'What am I defined by, then?' I asked.

'Nothing. You define yourself based on the core values most important to you. That's the beauty of life,' she said, smiling at me.

Quite confused about this whole self-worth concept, I decided to instead shift my focus on something else Mom said.

'So, you mean to say, even Shiv would have his own share of problems? He's not perfect?' I asked, my mind immediately going to Avik's family situation.

'Yes. I'm sure if you got to know him well, you'd see things from a different perspective.' She added, 'Oh, was it Shiv who asked you? Meh, you could do better.' She chuckled.

'Mom! I told you, I'm not interested in this kind of stuff. I have never been, and I probably never will be.' I started squirming in my seat at the thought of 'liking' certain people.

'Oh really? When I was your age, it was much different for me. Let me think, there was Rahul and—'

I quickly got up from the dining table and ran towards the stairs. 'La la la la, I can't hear you! Thanks for the advice, but now I'm out!'

26

Not Going to Lose

'Avani?' Dad peered into my room. It was 12.30 p.m. on Wednesday. I should've been getting ready for maths class, or at the very least, not hiding under my bedcover.

I tried to pretend I was asleep, but I think the fact that my phone was still on and lying a few centimetres from me on the bed gave it away. I had been looking at memes to distract myself from my upset stomach, obviously. Definitely not thinking about the Shiv situation from yesterday or the myriad of my Hellen-related problems.

'Don't you have class in 15 minutes?'

'Yeah,' I said from under the covers.

'Are you okay?' he asked, sitting on the bed next to me. Our relationship had transformed somewhat into what Mom and I used to be like. Distant. Was it because he was disappointed in me?

I wanted to say, 'Yeah, just feeling a bit funny in my tummy. Maybe it's because I'm too nervous to go to class and look stupid in front of all the smart people, including the Top 10 Girl, Bag Girl, Shiv, Avik and, of course, how could I forget the teacher.'

Of course, I didn't say that. Instead, what I said was, 'Yeah, of course. Was taking a nap.'

I never took naps. When I went to sleep, I properly committed to it—an eight-hour-long commitment. Any less, and I was sure my brain would malfunction.

'Did you make a study group yet?' he asked, leaning over to switch on the light.

I was trying to do the bare minimum of making it through the class. The Study Group thing had failed spectacularly. There were two options—I could either lie to Dad and pretend like I was on track. Or I could do the more difficult thing.

'No. It's been tough. People aren't as friendly as I'd hoped. Or maybe I'm not trying hard enough. It's probably that,' I said, getting up from bed with a sigh.

'I'm sure you're trying hard,' he said.

'Yeah,' I said meekly.

'What happened, Avani? I thought you were improving,' he said. 'And because of that improvement, made it into Shark.'

'I don't know, Dad. I'm trying to do my best, trying to not compare myself, but it's hard,' I said, a bit exasperated, unsure how to explain everything to him without it seeming like an info dump.

He sighed. 'I understand. Well, as long as you're trying your best, I'm happy. I'm proud of you, beta.'

Dad was finally *proud* of me because I was finally in Shark. Mom was on parental leave for me. And look at me—my first week at Shark was halfway done, and I couldn't even ask a single question in this new class without thinking myself out of it, and I hadn't been able to make a study group of any kind. I felt like I was here by mistake. I felt so guilty.

After Dad left, I paced in my room back and forth for a few minutes, trying to make myself feel normal again. I wished at least my body could be normal: steady breathing, no pain in my chest and no constant lurching in my stomach.

Nope. I was done with the self-pity. I was going to do what I could to get where I wanted to. And I wanted to stop feeling like this.

Putting on a pink top with frilly sleeves that Mom had bought me on our recent shopping spree (I was really channelling my inner Parnika, and it kind of looked good), paired with jeans and sensible sneakers, I pulled myself together. I quickly put all my relevant books in my backpack. I was going to do one thing right today, and nothing could stop me.

I practically ran up the stairs to the classroom, and even though I was out of breath and about to die, as soon as I spotted an empty seat in the second row, I knew that it was all worth it. After making sure that there were no signs of any other occupants, I glided into the seat and parked myself there—deciding not to move even if there was a natural disaster.

During the middle of the lecture, Shiv was asking a maths doubt about something that I hadn't even heard of before. The same disappointing feeling grew in my stomach. *You're not smart enough.*

'Any more questions?' Sahil sir enquired. The class was silent. My heart was beating faster than it did when I went running (which was once a year, probably). 'Or shall I continue?'

I looked around. All hands were down. I don't know what it was, maybe the fact that my dad had said that he was proud of me in the morning or that talk with Mom yesterday about self-worth (which I still didn't fully understand) but I found the strength in me to do the most ridiculous thing ever. I slowly raised my hand.

'Sir, I wanted to ask a question.'

As I asked my well-rehearsed doubt, I could hear my own voice cutting the expectant silence of the room. My voice, usually quite low, came out in a weird, high-pitched tone, like I was about to cry. The class was silent. My eyes were on the teacher, but I could feel everyone's eyes on me. The toppers—Shiv, Avik, Top 10 Girl, and still no Parnika, by the way.

'Sure, let me go back to the slide.'

He went back to the relevant slide and explained the concept again. He didn't look as excited answering my doubt as when he answered the other students' questions—did that mean my question was too basic or I was too dumb to understand a simple concept? Maybe I should've tried harder to solve it on my own before asking. I bet I just wasted everyone's time by asking my dumb doubt.

'Okay, sir, I understand. Thank you,' I said, my voice returning somewhat to its normal state. As the lecture went on, I fell into the wormhole of overthinking. What did everyone think about me? They probably thought I wasted a good five minutes of their time that could have been spent in a much more fruitful manner had I not squeaked out my dumb doubt.

My heart was still racing for the next five minutes after I asked my doubt, and it was only then that I realized that I didn't actually understand what he'd explained to me. The whole fuss of asking my doubt in front of everyone else had gone to waste. I bet Shiv didn't get so self-conscious. He was probably made of steel and didn't think in circles as I did. He was so much better.

Ugh. What was wrong with me? Why was I so quick to compare? Why was I like this?

After class, I got up from my seat and stood in front of the teacher's cabin. I looked at the other students through the glass, all of them hounding him with questions like they were reporters and he was a politician who'd just delivered a controversial speech. I wished I could go inside and be like them. I wished I could be stronger, less self-conscious and just better. But I wasn't. I was me.

I'd never felt so alone before.

I sat on the steps, waiting for my car to come. Looking at the cars passing by on the busy street, I wondered what it would feel like to just run away. My heart fluttered at the thought of just disappearing, but the familiar thoughts of self-doubt set in. Where would I go? What would I do? How would I live? I would still be the same person even if I ran away. The only way to make this situation better would be to change my reaction to it. I remembered Mom's words from yesterday: you shouldn't feel inferior to anyone. You shouldn't allow someone else *to* determine your worth. You are *you*.

I was more than my 'dumb doubts'. Who cared what those smart students thought of me? They were no one to determine my worth.

Suddenly, it was like I was on autopilot. I shot a quick text to Mom, telling her I'd be half an hour late. And just like that, my legs—clad in the super-trendy jeans that Mom had bought—carried me. They took me all the way to the teacher's cabin, where the same overconfident kids were surrounding him. But I didn't care. I wanted to try. I wanted to try to be brave, even if everyone thought I was stupid. Even if *I* thought I was stupid.

In front of me, the battleground was full of eager students holding their heavy textbooks and notebooks in their hands. I was closer to the exit than anyone else.

Still, I stood my ground. I didn't think I was going to be able to wrestle my way into the crowd because, let's face it, I didn't have the physical prowess to do that, no matter how motivated I was. So, I stood there. Waiting, revising my doubts over and over again like a prayer.

It took half an hour for the crowd to reduce to a small group. That group had Shiv and Avik and the topper girl in it. My heart started beating loudly. But I didn't move.

I listened patiently to their painfully esoteric questions. The teacher was chattering in technical jargon to the group. I nodded along, pretending that I had the same doubt and totally understood what he was saying. In fact, the reality was that the only thing that

I could hear was the throbbing of my heart and the growling in my stomach and a voice in my head shouting, 'You're not good enough! You'll never be good enough. You don't deserve to be here. You're going to lose.'

'No, I'm not,' I mumbled.

'Yes? You have a doubt?' The teacher looked at me, 'You've been standing here for a while.'

Oh, God. I spoke out loud. Everyone was looking at me expectantly as if I was someone equally important as them. I was. *I* determined my worth.

'Yes, sir. I did.' I tried to speak in a calm, composed way. Not like my world was completely imploding.

'Go ahead. You can ask your questions.'

'Okay. Um, my first doubt was…'

I pushed the loud, annoying voice somewhere back in my mind. I pushed it aside and brought my focus to what he was saying. Whenever I had a follow-up question, I asked that too.

What was the worst that could happen? The Smart People were going to laugh at me? Would the teacher ridicule me? Parnika already did that a few months ago. I realized it didn't affect me as much. Even if they laughed at me, at least I would gain some knowledge. I would clear my concepts and get closer to my goal of being at the top of the class. Getting laughed at for asking my dumb doubts was better than not asking those doubts and remaining in the dark. It wasn't going to make me feel any worse than the voice inside my head already made me feel. So, I asked—forgetting anyone else was standing next to me, judging me. Because they didn't have the right to affect the way I viewed myself.

∞

27

My Chemical Romance

When I was finally out of sir's room, I felt victorious. My heart was still thumping, my hands were sweaty and shaking, but I had a huge smile on my face. I was so proud of myself. I did it. I was proud of asking those questions, but I was prouder for beating my worst thoughts. I was worthy. I determined my own worth. Who thought asking doubts in a room full of very studious people would lead me to understand that?

Soon enough, though, the excitement wore off and tiredness set in. I could feel my eyes ache and my backache as well, from standing so long. My mind, which was previously racing, had now slowed down to a halt, the only thought being 'give me food right now'. I didn't know just asking doubts could be that exhausting. Or was it exhaustion from fighting my own thoughts?

It had become dark outside, as I found out when I exited the building alone. I couldn't spot my driver anywhere, and the whole environment outside felt kind of eerie, so I decided to check out the Hellen cafeteria. I wasn't a huge fan of it either, but at least it was well-lit.

'You look like you've seen a ghost,' someone spoke from behind me as I stood in the line at the counter.

'Huh? What?' I turned around. My Chemical Romance was blasting through one ear of my earphones.

Avik said, 'Are you okay?'

'Yeah. I'm totally fine. Great,' I said as I suppressed a yawn. Not like I just overcame a very big life hurdle. Not like the super-important mega grand test was coming up that I definitely wasn't prepared for.

'You're listening to a song called "I'm Not Okay", so I don't really think you are okay.'

'What?'

'Well, if you wanted honesty, that's all you had to say,' he sang softly.

What the hell was happening? I was too shocked to say anything. Was he really singing? And why did he know such an obscure song in the first place? I mean, if you liked MCR, you probably knew the song by heart, but otherwise, it wasn't a song to be played on the radio or one that was blasted at weddings.

'What the heck?'

He shrugged. 'It's a good song. It's a good band. My favourite album happens to be *The Black Parade*.' I felt like I was in some bizarre alternate-reality, non-canon sequel to a depressing novel.

'But you—you're a—' I trailed off. *A nerd, a topper, a machine.* You shouldn't know all of these things. Even my 'cool' classmates from back in school didn't like them. I'd never met anyone who knew about them and liked them.

'I'm a what?' he narrowed his eyes.

'Nothing, never mind,' I shook my head.

'No, please enlighten me,' he had a similar smirk on his face from when he encouraged my teenage rant.

'I just didn't expect you to be into music.'

He looked at me with suspicion and narrowed eyes. 'Everyone likes music. Only sociopaths don't like music.'

'Well…' I said, giving him a look back.

His mouth curved into a smile. 'Wait, you actually think I'm a sociopath?'

'Well, that day in the car with you and my dad, you said all this robotic stuff about your hobbies being taking competitive exams and not being into anything remotely standard. You seemed like a bit of a machine back then,' I said, adding, 'or maybe I'm wrong, and your hobbies are completely standard. Who am I to judge, right?'

He fell quiet. We both bought our food from the vendor. Both of us ordered some flavour of the overly sweet 'healthy' juice boxes. It was the quickest, cleanest way to fill your stomach. Everybody knew that, even though you'd be consuming mostly sugar.

'I'll pay,' he said, taking out his almost-flat wallet.

'No.' I was faster in taking out the cash, as I always kept some in my pocket.

He glanced at me again when I handed him the drink.

'You're like a ninja with the cash. You should've let me pay,' he said as we walked towards an empty table. It was the table where I'd usually sit alone, waiting for the mid-class break to get over, scrolling on my phone. It felt weird to have someone else sit at the lonely table with me.

'No, it's fine,' I said, glancing at his very flat wallet.

He seemed conscious of where I was looking, quickly putting his wallet back in his pocket. 'Um, so I am not a machine. Just to be clear. There is a heart under all of this stuff,' he said, gesturing to himself, clad in a button-up shirt and a denim jacket.

I chuckled. I automatically spoke, 'Oh really? Where was your heart the day you said all of those randomly mean things to me?'

I guess today was the day I was finally confronting him. I really hoped this wouldn't go as poorly as my last conversation with Parnika did, which took place coincidentally at the same table we were sitting at now.

'Oh. That day,' he had a remorseful look on his face as he

remembered all the things he had said that day. 'I'm sorry for my attitude that day. It was not excusable behaviour at all.'

I stared at him, not knowing what to say. *It's okay, but your apology won't change anything about how I had felt that day.*

'I was just trying to help you, picking up those sheets and books that you'd dropped. And you were so unnecessarily rude,' I said. I couldn't remember the last time I stood up to someone like this before. I would usually say, 'It's okay', and move on. Maybe I just didn't care enough. Or maybe I never felt so self-assured before.

He nodded. 'I'd tell you the truth, but it's better to just show you. Can I have your phone? Given my phone is from the 1980s and could not render a video even if a gun was held to it.'

I handed him my phone, chuckling at his idea of a gun being held to a phone. His analogies were always a bit off. Was he going to show me some embarrassing video of his? Maybe he had an irrational fear of dropping things.

'Here, give me your earphones.'

I handed him my worn-down earphones after wiping them on my jeans. He plugged them into my phone, putting on a YouTube video. 'Listen to this.'

I wore the earplugs, staring at him. He looked at me expectantly.

On the screen, a not-so-tired-looking boy with fluffy, straight hair, holding a guitar, smiled at me. 'Hey guys, I'm Avik, and this is my YouTube channel. Today I'm going to cover a song practically everyone should know. Also, there's a tutorial on how to read the sheet music at the end! So, stick around.'

He then starts strumming in a perfect rhythm and starts singing. 'Hey Jude, don't make it bad.'

It was so good. I was mesmerized. Usually, when someone makes me listen to a song, I'd politely nod along even if I didn't like it. He didn't even have to make me be polite. I was nodding along to the music, appreciating the congruity of his voice with his guitar.

'That's me in ninth class. It was my favourite song back then. Before my 'emo' phase in tenth grade.'

I could make out the facial similarities, but the boy in the video looked sanguine, bereft of the worry and frustration that frequently reflected on his face now.

'You're really good. What other songs did you cover?' I said, smiling. How did this explain his behaviour from that day?

He nodded, his expression uncertain, handing me back my phone. 'Well, people poked fun at me. My own parents did, too. So, that's the only video.'

'Why—why did they make fun of you?'

'Well, to quote my dad, "You want to spend your life singing and dancing now? What next, you want to join the circus? Stop reading sheet music, go focus on your maths assignment instead."'

'Oh, that—'

'I literally taught myself to read sheet music from watching tutorials. I had already completed my maths homework. I don't know why he—anyway, so yes. I do like to hide my "interests", just out of self-preservation,' he said, with air quotes. 'Especially around grownups.'

He didn't want me to see the stuff that fell out of his bag that day. Sheet music and guitar tutorial books. He was afraid my dad or I would judge him like his own dad. That's why he'd started listing out all those hobbies of his in the car.

'Avik, I would never judge you for your interests. Even if you sucked at guitar and singing, which you definitely *don't*, I wouldn't judge you,' I said, feeling the irony in my bones. I definitely judged myself when I sang poorly in the shower.

'Thanks, Avani,' he said, nodding. 'That means a lot.'

I looked at the view count, my eyes almost popping out of my skull.

'It has 150k views, Avik. Did you know that? You're basically a viral hit at this point.'

'Oh. I didn't know that,' he stared back at the screen indifferently, almost scornfully. I seemed much more excited at this discovery than he did.

'Look at the comments. "Such a shame that there is only one song on this channel" and "Petition to hunt down this boy and make him record more songs in his buttery voice." Okay, that last one is kinda weird. I hope you have some kind of security system at your place.'

'Leave it, Avani,' he gave the phone back to me, his eyes lingering on the screen for a bit longer. 'It's best to focus on the present, not dwell on the past.'

He looked forlorn. He looked like he wanted to see more of those comments. He didn't look like he wanted to 'focus on the present' at all, whatever that meant? Studying 10 hours a day?

'What about now? You must be still playing.' I asked. 'There's no way you could ignore talent like that.'

He really was so much more than I thought. 'No...I don't. This is irrelevant now. All I do is study and try to sleep.'

At that moment, I could see the well-defined bags under his eyes. The same bags that didn't exist in this YouTube video.

'I don't think it's irrelevant. I could see you were happier back then,' I said.

'Well, Avani, things have changed since then. I need to leave. Bye,' he took his juice box with him and left me hanging. I couldn't believe it. He pulled an Avani Escape on me. I'd been beaten at my own game.

∞

28

Confrontations

I spent the rest of the week and the weekend catching up on lectures, doing assignments and strictly trying to adhere to the six-hour per day self-study minimum as prescribed. If I couldn't make a study group, I could at least try to achieve the next goal. I could come back to the study group thing later, is what I'd told myself. I also managed to ask doubts in class a few times with minimal self-loathing. Apart from the impending doom of the mega grand test, which was in two weeks' time, and the overwhelming pressure of my main goal to be in the top 1 per cent, things were really looking up.

On Monday, by the time I was done with tuition for the day, I was starting to feel sleepy. Perhaps because I'd stayed up till 3.00 a.m. last night trying to finish the assignment, which wasn't even discussed fully in class today. Ah, the bane of my existence: when I work hard on assignments and they don't even get discussed. I was walking out of the teacher's cabin after asking my doubts and let out the biggest yawn possible. And it was at the moment that I was mid-yawn, stale coffee breath probably emanating from me, that I saw Shiv standing with his group in the hallway.

It was time for me to make amends, no matter how stupid I may look. Shiv had been shooting glances at me all throughout the past week ever since I 'declined his offer', and it was making me feel guiltier each time. I loitered near his group for a while, checking my phone and typing random words in my Notes app, trying to appear as inconspicuous as possible.

'Yeah, bro, the upcoming mega grand test is supposed to be the most important. It's half-syllabus, bro,' the guy wearing a beanie said. I wondered whether his hair was just submerged in sweat due to the humidity that came with mid-August monsoons, and he was too afraid to take off the beanie at this point.

'Uh-huh,' Shiv said, his eyes glazed over. He seemed to be looking straight ahead, although nothing, in particular, was to be seen at the point his eyes were directed.

'Bro, Sahil sir's class today was the coolest, right? I mean, the way he talked about Imaginary Numbers was so different!' The same beanie guy exclaimed.

Shiv didn't look like he gave two hoots about the whole lecture.

'I got to go now, bro. Catch you later,' Shiv said, walking away from the beanie guy. Aw, I felt a bit bad for the beanie guy now. He was left standing all alone.

I ran after Shiv, trying to catch up to his long steps. 'Shiv?'

'What, dude? I'm not really looking to talk about goddamn Imaginary—' He turned around, a look of faint surprise on his face. He looked duller than ever before. 'Oh. It's you.'

'Shiv. I just wanted to apologize,' I said, trying to catch my breath from my short sprint. Wow, I was really unfit. 'I was a bit rude. I know we've been friends for so long. It wasn't fair, the way I acted.'

He didn't say anything and kept pacing forward with long strides.

'Oh really?' he said dismissively.

'You look so sorted and smart, whereas I am struggling like *hell* most of the time to just keep my head above water. You just seemed to effortlessly score the best marks in class.' Also, I wanted to punch him when he topped the first grand test after complaining about his test going bad. But I didn't mention that.

He finally stopped, looking at me, completely lost.

'What I'm trying to say is, I always felt inferior and jealous of you. I guess that really clouded my thought process, and that was the reason I found it hard to talk to you sometimes, and that is why I reacted the way I did last week. I guess I just found it hard to understand why you would like me, given my inferiority complex,' I said, cringing so hard at myself. But I felt like I owed it to him. I felt like I could finally breathe. He deserved an explanation.

'So, what you're trying to say is, you don't like me because you think I'm too *smart*?' he asked, his mouth contorted into a confused frown.

'No, I didn't quite say that—'

'Leave it be, Avani. Just say it straight—you don't like me. That's it. You don't have to make up a story to make me feel better,' he said, turning away from me and walking too quick for me to follow.

'Shiv, wait! That's not true.' I tried running after him, but I was quickly too out of breath to catch up. Wow, I really needed to work out more.

∽

As I tried to come to terms with what had happened, I realized I was in the familiar halls of Dolphin batch classes. They would be having their physics class right now. I peeked at the group of students, trying to recognize any of my past classmates and immediately spotted Parnika's curly hair—though it didn't have the usual panache or, more literally, the usual volume.

What was she doing here?

I observed her as closely as I could from the entrance to

the classroom. She had one hand on her forehead and seemed to be looking down at her phone on the desk while the same monotonous voice of the teacher from my Dolphin days droned on and on.

What was happening? I took out my phone and texted her again.

Avani: Parnika, I can see you. You're looking at your phone.

Her head immediately shot up, looking at me standing at the entrance. She smirked.

Parnika: Wow. Stalker much?

Avani: Can we talk after class?

Parnika: I'll do you one better.

She simply walked out of the classroom with no regard for the teacher. The teacher looked dumbstruck for a couple of seconds, unsure of whether to exercise his authority, but immediately resumed his lecture once she was out of the classroom.

'What's up?' Parnika said, casually leaning against the hallway wall.

'Parnika, what the hell was that?' I quiet-yelled at her.

'What?' She looked unbothered as if nothing special had happened.

'How are you? I haven't seen you in class.' I chose to change the subject. This was all too much for me to comprehend.

'Yeah, I know. I'm okay.' She nodded. 'I actually got demoted to Dolphin.'

Parnika got demoted. That was impossible. She was so smart. She'd been at Hellen forever. She was so good at it. She had figured out the game. An apathetic part of me thought, 'good riddance'.

After passing such mean comments at me, I shouldn't have cared much. But, of course, I did—she was my best friend. Coaching had always been a big part of her life. I wonder how she felt.

'You look like I died and this is my apparition,' she chuckled dryly, rolling her eyes. 'It's fine. Whatever. This coaching shit is getting old now. Do you want to get some coffee or something?'

'Coffee? Don't you remember, it's so dehydrating and bad for your skin?' I said, reiterating the same words she'd told me once when I tried to take her to a coffee shop last year.

'I don't care. Not anymore,' she shrugged, looking at the floor. I could see the same apathy on her face as I used to see on Riya's and Smriti's faces. Like they'd rather be somewhere else but here.

'Parnika, I just wanted to apologize for my outburst all those months ago. I was really going through a rough time, and you didn't deserve it,' I said, still trying to maintain eye contact with her, even though she was still looking at the ground.

'It's fine. I already forgot,' she said, giving me a half-smile. 'Honestly, I'm the one who should be apologizing. My rank had slipped to 50 in that first grand test. I was kind of like you, freaking out after seeing that. I had left everything I was passionate about just to focus on my studies. So, that day in the cafeteria, I was just really projecting my own issues onto you.'

'Oh.'

'But what you said about me is wrong. I'm not perfect at all,' she said, sinking to the ground in the empty hallway. 'I hate this place. I hate my life. I hate who I've become. You know, I never even wanted to do coaching. My dad persuaded me to go to these foundation classes in sixth grade, and he was so happy to see me that I really couldn't ever say no to him. But this is not my dream, Avani. I haven't felt so apathetic in my life ever before.'

I crouched down to the floor, looking her in the eyes. 'Who

do you want to become?'

She looked at me, astonished as if she'd never been asked this question in her life. 'I don't know. Someone else—anything, but not this,' she said, gesturing to herself and our surroundings.

'I'm sorry, Parni. I didn't know you were going through so much,' I said, pulling her into a hug.

'Please don't use that lame-ass nickname that Shiv gave me. He's so stupid, I swear to God,' she said, somewhat returning back to her normal self.

I chuckled, thinking of his clueless face as I poured out all my insecurities in front of him just a few moments ago, 'Yeah, he kinda is.'

'Tell me something interesting. I know something happened,' she said, a mischievous glint in her eye as she skipped along the hallway. Wow, it's like her whole demeanour changed.

'You've got to buy me a cold coffee then. And you'll get one of those healthy green juices. I really don't like what coffee does to your brain, as much as you didn't like what it did to your skin,' I said, as we both walked towards the cafeteria as I explained to her the juicy details of my date with Shiv and his 'confession'.

29

Trying My Best

'Avani, you should go to sleep now. Your big exam is tomorrow, you need to get a proper night's sleep,' Mom said, peeking into my room at 12.00 a.m. I was sitting at my study table, notes from each subject sprawled out on my desk as if they were a tablecloth. A very anxiety-inducing tablecloth.

The past two weeks had gone by very quickly. I spent most of my waking hours trying to solve one question or the other, figuring out why I was getting a particular answer wrong and, of course, attending classes and trying to ask all my doubts from the teachers amid the chaos created by the front-row toppers.

The only goal in my mind was that I had to score well in tomorrow's mega grand test. I *had* to reach the top. There was no try—even if I had to forgo basic things like sleep. But Mom's insistence on putting me to bed was unbeatable. She only went away after tucking me in.

I thought it would be easy to sleep. After all, I had spent the whole day, actually the whole week, studying extremely hard. But at 1.00 a.m. in the morning, anything seemed easier than going to sleep. Even solving that calculus question I'd left behind looked easier. Should I get back up and solve it?

I stopped myself. Mom was right. I should have been asleep in order to rest up for my super important test, which was technically today. Instead, I was tossing and turning, a million thoughts racing through my head and switching pillows every 10 minutes because, apparently, each of them made my neck hurt.

What a great way to spend Saturday nights. How much would I have loved to sleep at this moment and not be worrying about Hellen-caused things?

I lay in bed, trying to focus on other, less stressful things. Then I realized that I didn't have many relaxing hobbies left anymore. I hadn't played *The Sims 3* in months. Everything I had been doing in the past few months since joining Hellen had been made into a challenge. Attending classes every day, studying at least six hours per day, trying to keep up with the pace, trying to stop the constant barrage of self-deprecating thoughts in my own head, gathering the courage to ask questions in class where everyone is out to win. I was trying to do my best every day—study longer, worry lesser. Only because I had resolved to do the best job I possibly could, anything less would be unacceptable. Because if I didn't do the best job, then what was the point of it all?

As I tried to lay still and will myself to sleep, for the first time, I noticed how much my body hurt from all the tension I had been inflicting on it. My back ached from sitting all day, my legs were sore from not using them much, and my eyes were constantly tired. Was it really all worth it? When would this struggle, this competition *stop*? It didn't seem sustainable.

I finally got up from bed when I heard the birds chirping. It was 5.30 a.m. My test was at noon. I was so out of it. How could I do my best? I walked down to the living room, trying to calm myself. To my surprise, the room was lit, and Dad was sitting on the sofa, tying his shoelaces.

'Avani, what are you doing awake so early?' Dad looked up.

'What are *you* doing so early?' I asked him back.

'I was just leaving for a morning walk,' he said.

Of course, my sorted Dad was so perfect; he got up before

the birds to go on a walk.

'Were you not able to sleep last night?' he asked, studying my dishevelled appearance.

I guess the dark circles under my eyes gave it away, 'I wasn't.'

I expected him to ask more prodding questions because the probability of him knowing how I felt was extremely abysmal.

'Okay. Come on, put your shoes on,' he said encouragingly. The same encouraging voice that used to make me feel okay before school exams. The same voice that told me he believed I could be the best. Was I going to let him down?

Too tired to protest, I did as he said, and we both walked out of the house. It was now 6.00 a.m. As we walked the empty roads, I observed my surroundings carefully. The sun hadn't risen yet, but there was a faint glow in the sky. The morning air was pleasant and sweet. I could actually smell the ripe mangoes and pollen in the air. Only a few cyclists—milkmen, newspaper boys—were on the road, making me feel like I had been transported back in time. The birds chirped incessantly and melodically, almost inversely reminding me of the familiar, non-melodic buzz in the classroom before the teacher would walk in.

We walked and walked, crossing empty roads until we made it to Sukhna Lake. Apart from a few dedicated morning walkers, the concrete walkway was mostly empty. When I looked in the distance, I could spot the blue hills from behind the Lake Forest looking at us imposingly, as if we were mere specks compared to their staggering size.

'Dad, why are we here?' I finally broke the silence. We hadn't spoken at all since he'd asked me to put on my shoes. At this point, we'd crossed Suicide Point, and my heart was racing, trying to catch up to Dad, who was a notoriously fast walker.

'Avani, beta, I think you're too hard on yourself,' he said, finally stopping, allowing me to catch my breath. 'Your mom and

I have seen you awake at 3.00 a.m. on most nights, toiling hard, sitting at your desk. Do you really feel you need to do this much?'

I chuckled inadvertently. 'Look who's talking.'

'What do you mean by that?' He put his hands on his hips, looking at me with a confused expression. Oh, you have got to be kidding me.

'Dad, you're always pushing me to do my best. You're the one who pushed me to take non-med because you believed I could be the best, that I could succeed. I still remember your disappointed face when I told you about all my lies. You only said you were proud of me when I got into Shark. So, please don't put this all on me,' I said, out of breath.

We both sat down on the stone divider between the concrete pathway and the slanting rocks that led to the lake. The sun was rising now and it gave the lake a beautiful, almost divine golden sheen. It was kind of the polar opposite of that day in January when I'd confronted the Stream Question. Had I changed since then?

'I said I was proud of you because I saw you trying *your* best, Avani. I didn't ever want to pressure you to be the best. I'm sorry if you ever felt that way because of me...' he said, looking at me with an unreadable expression.

'It's not your fault. It's me—I'm the problem. I'm at fault. Maybe if I was inherently smarter and more resilient, I would not struggle so much. Maybe then I would've gotten to the top by now,' I said, bringing my legs close to my chest and hugging them.

'The truth is, Avani, life doesn't come easy to anyone. No one is inherently smart or resilient. It only comes when you struggle and face challenges like you have been doing for the past few months.' My dad must've heard my voice shake because his energetic eyes now shone with sadness. I didn't want to see myself like this either.

'But I'm tired now.' I mumbled, placing my head on my folded knees, feeling the weight of my brain. 'And I'm still not the best.'

'That's okay.'

I turned to look at him, not believing his words. 'How is it okay? All this hard work I've been doing is to be the best, as you expected from me. My main goal so far has been to get to the top 1 per cent. Only then I'll be able to make it to an IIT. I should never be okay with not being the best.'

'Avani, let me give you one example, okay? Maybe it'll be clearer then. I knew someone who, ever since he was a little boy, wanted to take the civil services exam and become a civil servant by joining the Indian Administrative Service, or IAS, as most people call it. That boy worked hard his whole school life. He even became a mechanical engineer before taking the entrance exams for civil services. You know what happened to him?'

'What?'

'He failed to be the "best". He failed the preliminary exam once. Next year, he failed the subsequent exams. The year after that, in his last possible attempt, he cleared the exam, gave the interview, but failed again. That year, he'd also taken the Indian Forest Services exam, which he cleared. But he wasn't able to achieve his lifelong dream, and there was no chance he ever could in the future. You know what he did, then?'

'Did he move to Mexico and start living among the alpacas?' I asked. That's what I would've done. Actually, now that I thought about it, what would I do if I really didn't make it to IIT at the end of these two years? I shuddered at the thought.

Dad chuckled. 'Well, I was upset for a while. A few months, at the very least. I was sad that I wasn't in the "best" class of civil servants, that I had failed to fulfil my childhood obsession. But you know what happened then? I slowly got over it. It took time, sure, but through this experience, I learned perhaps the most important lesson in my life.

'I realized that life was about more than an exam. I was more than a piece of paper, a number or a job. Sure, all of these things are necessary. We need a job to get by, which I had got, by the way. But as I moved on in my life, I experienced all the things life had to offer. I met your mother. We had you soon after. We had a decent house, which we decorated as we pleased. Sure, looking at IAS officers in meetings even now, I do still feel a bit envious of the career I could've had. But I don't care about it now.'

'Why not?'

'Because I'm where I want to be. I did achieve my dream of being a civil servant. I like my job. I love my family. I love my life. The prestige of the job I do, as determined by the public, does not hold water to any of the things I actually value in my life,' he said.

I looked into his eyes as he tried to hide his tears by focusing on cleaning his glasses on his t-shirt. It was his life story. My dad wasn't the perfect person I thought him to be. He wasn't bulletproof. He was just like me.

'What I mean to say from this story of a boy is two things,' he said once he'd composed himself. 'First of all, life is not solely about achievements. Your life will not come to a halt if you aren't able to accomplish your one goal. If you don't get into an IIT, you will go somewhere else. You will do something else, something great in your life that matters to you. Everyone does. Life moves on and so will you.

'Secondly, even if you fail, all your hard work isn't for nothing. That boy—he—oh, forget it. You must've figured it out by now. *I* learnt a lot, taking the same exam thrice. Of course, I learned numerous facts about India's geography, governance and society, which still help me in the job I do. But also, I learned many life lessons: how to have faith in yourself, how to stop comparing yourself, how to be *kind* to yourself, even if faced with failures,' he spoke the last sentence carefully.

'Don't you ever wonder about the what-ifs? *What if I worked harder, I could've cleared the exam?*' I asked.

He pondered for a moment, quite seriously. I'd only seen him this serious when he'd be talking with his subordinates about where was the optimal location to plant trees in a certain forest. 'I did, initially. But then I realized that I had done my best. The best I could do at that particular time. And that was enough for me to forget about the what-ifs.'

'Oh.' I tried to hold on to each word of his.

'You're trying to do *your* best. You're doing whatever you can at the moment to get where you want to be. And that's enough,' he said, almost reflecting my thoughts.

'So, you mean to say…even if I bomb in the final exam, even if I get a bad rank, as long as I believe I tried my best, it's fine?' I asked for reassurance, although I think I'd figured it out. It would be fine. Dad was fine.

'Yes.' He smiled at me with his familiar, reassuring smile. I could see tears glistening in his eyes through the golden, pure rays of the morning sun.

'You don't have to *be* the best,' he said. 'Just do *your* best. Whatever you can at the moment. Even if it is just existing, that is enough.'

His first point reminded me of what Mom had said a few weeks ago to me about self-worth: 'Self-worth is determined by whatever matters to you the most.' Dad's words were, 'You will do something else, something great in your life that matters to you.' Did getting into an IIT matter to me? Thinking about it deeply, clearly, I realized it did matter to me somewhat, but something mattered to me more. I just wanted to do my best to prepare for the entrance exams so that I didn't regret not working harder in the future. I just had to do *my* best, whatever I could at that moment.

'Thanks, Dad,' I said, feeling like I was starting to choke up as well. We really looked like two weirdos at Sukhna Lake sobbing at 6.30 a.m., but I didn't care.

'I'm proud of you, beta. I'll always be proud of you, no matter what you do or don't achieve,' he said.

30

The Top

The two days after the mega grand test were holidays for Hellen students. I think they said it was for letting the students recuperate, but mostly I didn't believe that, given it is Hellen after all. I think they had a large number of students sit for the mega grand test countrywide and, therefore, wanted some time to compile the results.

After coming back from the early morning Sukhna Lake walk on Sunday, comforted by all of Dad's words, I'd fallen into a deep sleep. I was only awoken by Mom 30 minutes prior to the test so that she could quickly feed me a paneer parantha and some chai. I took the test, and after it, I completely hibernated for the rest of the day. I'd spent Monday and Tuesday revising some lectures, sprinkled with a healthy amount of *The Sims 3*. Oh, who am I kidding? When it comes to that game, there is no possible 'healthy amount'. I played four hours each day and enjoyed every second of it. My character was now finally moving into a Victorian-style mansion, which I'd spent hours meticulously designing.

On Wednesday, as I descended the stairs to the maths classroom, I almost walked into a tall, long-haired boy standing alone at the bottom of the stairs. He was leaning against the hallway wall, tapping his foot as if waiting for someone.

'Shiv?' I asked once I reached the bottom of the stairs.

'Avani, can we talk?' He stood up straight, looking at me

with an earnest expression. A group of his friends were talking amongst themselves a few metres away. Why wasn't he with them?

'Uh… sure,' I said, walking in the hallway, always a few steps ahead of him. We *were* cat-and-mouse.

'I just wanted to apologize for the way I reacted when you tried to explain yourself to me. I realize I haven't been clear about most things in my life with you.'

'Okay…' I mumbled, not really sure where this conversation was leading.

'Avani, you're my only good friend here. I loved talking to you, even if I was only asking you about small things about your life. It made me feel normal. I don't really get to talk like that with anyone anymore,' he looked at the ground, probably trying to find a piece of gravel to kick like I remember he used to.

'I am?' I asked. 'What about your bros?'

He sighed, looking at his group. 'They don't really see me as a person, more like a source for solving their maths doubts. You, on the other hand, treated me normally. I am constantly surrounded by them. But they're not my friends.'

'What?' That made no sense. He always looked so chummy with them.

'You are,' he said, looking intently at me. I still wondered how he could maintain eye contact so well. 'You entertained all my small questions. You listened to me talk about how much I missed my family and didn't make fun of me for being clingy. And I'm sorry if I made you feel less than. It wasn't my intention.'

I nodded, still feeling embarrassed that I had disclosed my deepest insecurity to him. 'I know.'

After a familiar awkward pause, he continued, 'I guess I told you I liked you because I saw you hanging out with Avik a couple of times, and it made me jealous, especially because you started ignoring my messages around that time. Avani, that guy isn't good news.' Shiv's expression changed. He looked very serious now.

'Why do you sound like you hate him?' I asked, crossing my arms in front of me.

'I don't hate him, but he's always talking on the phone with some girl. I assumed that was you, obviously.'

'What? I don't even have his number,' I said. Avik had never asked for my number, and I hadn't asked for his, either. Maybe he was scared of his dad finding out or something, even though there was nothing to find out.

'That's even worse, then. He's two-timing you. Now that I think about it, I heard him call someone called Shanaya.'

'That's his sister, you dumbass. Why do you even know all of this about him?' I almost choked on my own words. I would've never spoken so boldly before.

'He's been my roommate since I joined Hellen,' he said, looking a bit taken aback at my cursing, probably. Huh, it wasn't even a proper curse word.

'Oh,' I said. What kind of twist was this?

'So, Avik's not your boyfriend?' he asked quietly and pensively.

'No! And I'm not really interested in obtaining one in the near future.' I looked at him, hoping he'd catch my drift. 'I think Avik and I could be termed as friends who met under strange circumstances and then sort of...stuck together.'

Thankfully, he did, for once. He nodded quickly and said, 'Of course, I understand.'

'You know, Avik's not so bad once you learn to see past his strange sense of humour,' I said, as we started walking to the classroom.

'Yeah. He's a pretty good guitar player too, you know?' Shiv said.

'Really?' I asked. I thought Avik had told me a few weeks ago that he was done with it because 'things have changed now', whatever that meant.

'I just wish we can still remain friends,' he said, gesturing to me and then himself.

Looking at his hopeful face, I smiled, saying, 'Of course, we can.' I eagerly await your next "trivial" question.'

He smiled back.

∽

Flustered at Shiv's revelation, I entered the maths class, which was buzzing with anticipation over the marks and rank announcements. My stomach started filling with a habitual sense of dread. It was almost a reflex now. They would sometimes distribute the answer sheets for grand tests rank-wise, always starting with the best rank.

I was smushed between students in the non-reserved girls' row, waiting for the teacher to arrive. And it definitely didn't help, when the first thing that Sahil sir said as he entered the classroom was, 'I'm distributing the answer sheets for the mega grand test, in which we had a record number of participants this time—three lakh students. I'll be announcing the all-India rank, along with the Hellen rank.'

His assistant appeared with a stack of OMRs, the same ones we had filled for each Sunday grand test. Ugh, this was killing me. I could feel a stomachache creeping in. It spread across my entire abdominal region, and I felt like disappearing. And to top it off, Sahil sir was the one distributing it. That meant he would *see* me. And see how dumb I actually was, like how he'd predicted back in orientation.

'Shiv, Hellen rank, 3, and all-India rank, 102. Congrats!' Sahil sir exclaimed.

No, Avani, stop. I'm not dumb. Marks do not define me. I remembered my parents' words as I tried to establish what really mattered to me. Doing my best at the given moment. I had done my best in this exam, whatever I could manage at that time. I didn't care about the result. I didn't care about what anyone thought of me based on this result. I would only continue to try my best the next time around. After all of this suffering and toiling over notes, I had learnt something way more important than any formula. There was a try. My life did not stop at this exam. There was more to life. Life moves on and so will I.

As I was having this extensive, life-changing internal dialogue, someone poked me on my arm.

'Ow! What the—' I looked to my left at the girl who injured me.

Then I realized everyone was looking at me. I didn't even say anything this time!

'Avani, Hellen rank, 15, and all-India rank, 917.' Sahil sir repeated.

I was on autopilot after that. I found myself standing up in my seat and walking a long distance in the aisle to the dais in the front of the class, where Sahil sir was standing, beaming at me.

'Congrats, Avani,' he smiled at me. 'You've shown a tremendous jump, all the way from a rank in the 70s. You must've worked very hard; even without our foundation classes, you've managed to score such a good rank! I guess I am proven wrong after all.'

'Thank you, sir.' I felt like I was giving my acceptance speech after getting an award at a ceremony—although sir had done most of the talking.

He smiled genially and continued with the rest of the distribution and rank announcement. However, I paid no attention. I went back to my seat and stared at my OMR sheet in astonishment. I had gotten three questions wrong—that was it. I took a few deep breaths, trying to steady the feeling—whatever I was going through. Was this excitement or something else?

My first thought was one of elation. Oh my God, I got such a great rank! I can't believe it! I worked hard, believed in myself and finally achieved my number one goal. I was in the top 1 per cent.

My second thought was kind of a negative analogy of my disbelief. How the hell did I manage to pull that off? It must be a mistake. What if I mess up on the next test? Then I wouldn't remain in the top 1 per cent. I realized now that this would never end. This constant competition, this race to be at the top. I *was* finally there. But what if I still lose in the next test?

I looked around at the toppers sitting in the front row. Did they feel this too? After looking at Shiv and Avik's tired faces every day, after talking to them, I think they did feel the same pressure. It was never going to feel better. It was only up to *me* to determine how I felt. My self-worth really couldn't depend on these marks or ranks—otherwise, I'd always be at the mercy of how I'd perform in the next test or the test after that.

This might be a game I would 'lose' at the end. But I wasn't afraid of playing it anymore. Because I was going to give my best, whatever I could manage at the moment. Whatever happens after that, I'd accept it. No regrets, no what-ifs.

∽

'Hey Avani, congrats,' Shiv was standing in front of the class, waiting for me. 'It's so cool that you scored such a good rank.'

'Uh, thanks,' I said.

'Hi,' Avik came up to stand beside me. He didn't have the same kind of tiredness that would usually cloud his face. His eyes shone a little brighter, his hair was a bit fluffier. What happened?

'Hey Avik,' I said, glancing at him, my voice feeling as unsteady as my heart. Shiv looked him down from head to toe. This was *so* awkward.

'Congrats,' he smiled at me, not aware that Shiv was staring daggers at him. Or maybe he didn't care. 'Although, for the record, I thought you were cool even before this lecture,' he gave Shiv the side-eye.

'Thanks, both of you,' I said. Now that I was finally aware of their dynamic, everything felt a hundred times more awkward than usual.

'By the way, Avik, Avani knows you're my roommate now. So, I'll be complaining to her about all the annoying things you do, like how you leave the curtains open before sleeping.'

Avik turned to look at Shiv with a rather amused expression on his face. 'Oh really? I dare you to do it.'

'Do you know, Avani? How much sunlight falls on my side of the room because of his habit? Please talk some sense into him since you're his friend and all,' Shiv said, rolling his eyes. I don't think I'd ever seen him so animated or passionate about something before.

Avik smirked. 'Well, you know what they say, keep your friends close but keep your enemies closer. This is all part of my grand plan.'

Shiv looked at Avik, contemplating the seriousness of his response. Shiv was seriously so clueless.

'Now you just wait and watch for the next part of my plan, Shiv,' Avik said, rubbing his palms together evilly.

'Very funny, Avik,' Shiv chuckled, but with a hint of fear in his eyes.

As I was waiting on the Hellen entrance steps for my car to pick me up, I looked around at my surroundings. It had been almost five months since I first came to this institution. When I started out, I really thought that I would've gotten used to the entire dreary ethos of the building by now. The way the 'en' part of the Hellen light-up board had not been fixed since the first time I saw it back in January. The bare, cold walls of the classrooms and the way the lighting made all of us look like ghosts, no matter where we were in the building. The reserved row system in the classrooms seemed like it was breaking some kind of anti-discrimination law. But I hadn't really grown to like any of that. Why should I? This place hadn't given me a lot, to be honest. Many of the teachers were good, of course. But I realized that it was really what *I* decided to do with what I was given. *I* had to take the initiative to understand the concepts. No one was there to hold my hand and walk me through it. I had to try to navigate my emotions and try to solve my own problems. White Meadows seemed so far behind now. I missed it, of course, but I guess I had to leave the training wheels behind at some point.

'Avani, hey,' Avik looked at me eagerly, with a slight smile on his face. He was sitting right next to me on the steps.

'What the hell? How long have you been sitting there?' I jumped in my seat.

'I just wanted to talk to you. Something good happened,' he said, beaming at me.

'Did you score a really good rank on this test, and is your dad finally getting off your back?' I said.

He chuckled, shaking his head. 'Nice one. I got a rank of 40 this time. It's the lowest I've ever gotten in these grand tests, actually.'

'Oh. Are you okay?' I asked, a cynical part of me baulking at how he thought a rank of 40 was 'low'.

'Yeah, of course. Can you give me your phone?'

I gave him my phone and watched his sanguine expression as he searched for his own name on YouTube. Was his 'happy' face just a coping mechanism for his 'low' rank or something?

'Watch this,' he said, handing me the phone.

I peered at the screen as it loaded the video. It was a recent version of Avik, dark circles and all, saying, 'Hello, guys! Welcome back to my channel. Sorry to you make you all wait for two years. I read your comments from my last video and really appreciate your kind words. Today I'll be covering one of my all-time favourite songs, 'Here Comes the Sun' by the Beatles.'

He began the song's optimistic initial plucking sequence on a slightly worn-down acoustic guitar, though still sounding as melodic as it could with Avik's dexterity. Soon he started singing and strumming along, his voice still as sweet, and his expressions still as serene as the cheerful singer I'd seen in his previous video.

'Sorry about the strumming. I know it's not the best,' Avik murmured to me during the second verse. 'You can blame me or my second-hand guitar. I just bought it online recently.'

'Avik, what are you talking about? You're really good.'

He smiled to himself.

Once the song was over, I asked him, 'You'd told me "things have changed" when I asked you if you still played the guitar. And then left quite dramatically.'

He chuckled. 'Yeah, I guess I felt a bit resentful seeing my past self all happy and carefree. You know, it was right before my sister left coaching and before the entire family drama happened. I thought about what you said about my happiness being important. I don't know why, I couldn't get my happy face from that video out of my mind.'

'Okay...' I said, wondering where he was going with this.

'Things have changed since that first video, definitely. But the more I thought about it, I realized that I still deserved to be happy. Don't get me wrong—I'm fine with the coaching here. But why should I have to give up my passion for the sake of 'sacrifice', if it could bring me that much happiness? After that, it was like I was on autopilot. I ordered the guitar online. I looked up some of the sheet music. I would play a while before going to sleep—even Shiv didn't mind much, for once. And you know what? I feel much better these days.'

He grinned at me as if he'd discovered the secret of life or something. My mind went back to those smiling students with their mouths stuffed with mithai at the chemistry teacher's place. Avik's smile was like theirs but a bit wider and a bit brighter.

'What about your "bad" rank?' I asked, putting the word 'bad' in air quotes. 'What will you say when your dad calls you up?'

He shrugged. 'I honestly don't know how it'll go. But at least I'm happier and less stressed now. I can only hope he understands. I do want to still prepare for the entrance exams. But on my own terms.'

Avik was such a force to be dealt with now. I almost couldn't believe it was the same boy who'd stammered speaking his own name in class. The same boy who cried, cursed and threw his phone out of frustration after talking to his overbearing father. If anyone deserved to feel even a bit happier, it was Avik Chaudhry.

∽

On the car ride home, I opened my backpack and took out a very important piece of paper I had kept somewhat neatly folded inside a notebook. I smiled at the list, looking at all the revisions and additions that I'd made in the months since January.

Avani's Guidebook for Surviving Hellen

1. ~~Just as I was at White Meadows, I want to be at the top of the class at Hellen. I will try to do the best job I possibly can, anything less would be unacceptable. I have to beat the odds and be in the top 1 per cent.~~
   I will strive to do my best at any given moment (even if my best is just existing through the storm) and accept whatever happens in the future.
2. ~~Perform on par with Shiv and Parnika. Try to become even better.~~
   Even though I am preparing for a competitive entrance exam, I don't have to compare myself to others constantly. I should just focus on myself and my progress.
3. ~~Prove to Mom that I am not a delicate or weak person who cannot survive JEE coaching.~~ I am done proving anything to Mom, because she accepted me even at my lowest point.
4. ~~Prove to Dad that he was correct—that I am as smart as he thinks I am.~~
   I have nothing to prove to my dad either. He believes I will succeed in life at things that matter most to me, no matter what happens in an exam. I believe that too.
5. I will not shy away from doing things that I want to do but seem scary. I can't be afraid of failure anymore. Don't ever be left wondering 'what if...'
6. I will be honest about who I am to myself as well as others. It isn't worth it to hide my feelings, especially

in front of my parents. I don't have to pretend I'm a smart kid.
7. It is good to take a break sometimes. It gives me a new perspective—sometimes even a new approach to solving a difficult calculus question that I couldn't crack before.
8. My happiness is the most important thing.
9. I will learn from my mistakes without self-judgement. After my mock tests results are out, I should try to revise the topics for which I wasn't able to attempt the questions or got the answers wrong. Don't just throw out the test paper and move on.
10. My self-worth is not dependent on anything or anyone. *I* define my self-worth, based on the values that are important to me. I am not a piece of paper, a number or a seat at an educational institution.
11. There is more to life than achievements. Life is more than just an exam.

Epilogue

I had been waiting at Indian Coffee House for what seemed like an eternity, checking the door each time I'd hear it open. Where were they? My stomach was growling with hunger. We'd all promised to meet the day after the final entrance exam, right at 2.00 p.m.—it was 2.15 p.m., and no one had arrived yet. I looked outside the window at the blinding afternoon sunlight of June. God, I really couldn't wait for the monsoons to arrive.

'Sorry. This one was taking *way* too long to decide which polo shirt to wear,' Avik said, crashing into the seat opposite to me, giving Shiv, who was a few steps behind him, the stink eye.

'Oh yeah?' Shiv plopped down next to him. 'Well, *this one* was warming up his vocal cords in the auto-rickshaw on our way here. Dude, could you have spooked the auto driver any more than you already did with your entirely black outfit? He probably thought you were possessed.'

'You guys really do bicker like an old married couple,' I murmured.

'Where's Parnika?' Avik asked.

'Probably late, as usual,' Shiv rolled his eyes. 'I remember her last day at Hellen, you know, almost two years ago, back in September. Wasn't it just a few days after that mega grand test? I only heard the rumours. Apparently, she came dressed in a pink jumpsuit that read "I QUIT!" and just strutted out of the physics class mid-lecture. She was never to be seen again at Hellen.'

Epilogue

'Talking about me?' Parnika finally arrived, clad in a beautiful, custom-made ruffled white dress with silver sequins. She really did look angelic. 'Of course, you are. Is there anyone else who is even worth talking about?'

'Damn, Parnika,' Shiv mumbled, trying to control his laughter. 'Are you getting married today or something?'

Parnika shot him a deadly look. 'No, idiot. I just sat for my final online interview. You know, so that I'm able to attend the fashion designing course I was accepted into in—'

'—London, England, Europe. Yes, we know,' Avik said, half-smiling.

'Parnika, I think you look great. And, of course, congratulations once again,' I said, smiling wholeheartedly at her.

She beamed at all of us. I don't think I'd ever seen her this happy before.

'Sooo, how were all of your exams?' she asked, studying our faces. 'I know the results will be out soon.'

I glanced at Shiv, studying his face. He probably looked the most tired of all of us. He'd grown out his stubble into a beard, and he never really did go back to his shorter haircut. His eyes had deep, pronounced bags under them, and his face was thinner than ever. But I could tell he was the happiest when next to Avik. Their friendship had really blossomed in the past one and half years. I wasn't exactly sure what the catalyst was, but I guess they formed some kind of a truce.

Shiv simply said, 'It was okay, I guess.'

I smirked. 'That's what he says when his exams go really well and he doesn't want to jinx anything.'

'Yeah, I'd seen him jump with joy once he'd come back to our apartment and had a look at the first answer keys. He's definitely getting into an IIT,' Avik rolled his eyes, clapping Shiv on the back so hard he almost choked. Shiv smiled meekly at

Avik, amused at his funny way of showing affection. I was just happy he didn't feel alone anymore.

'What about you, Avik?'

He had his classic half-smile on his face, but I could see he was tired too. Apart from his unkempt hair, which never really lost its volume—I never did figure out the secret to his hair, and he refused to tell me, saying that he couldn't reveal his 'beauty secret'—he, too, bore a similar tired, sleep-deprived look on his face. But it was different from the sleepy-eyed, dazed face I'd seen him often with prior to reviving his music hobby. He'd always smiled a bit brighter since then.

'You know, I'd like to think it went well. I didn't jump for joy as Shiv did, but I'm satisfied,' he laughed at himself. 'Honestly, I still can't believe my dad came around to me scoring "mediocre ranks", as he used to call it. So, after all that has happened, I think I'll be satisfied with wherever I get into. I think Dad will be too.'

'By the way, how's Shanaya? I haven't talked to her in a few months.' Parnika asked. After Parnika was introduced to Avik, she quickly learned of Shanaya, his sister, whom she called a trailblazer. She'd contacted Shanaya for advice after she had decided to quit Hellen.

'Oh, she's just finishing her final year of university now—she already has a job lined up at a social media company abroad. You know she has her graduation ceremony coming up soon. All of us are planning on visiting her,' Avik said.

Avik finally confronted his father's mounting pressure on him to 'succeed' at the end of eleventh class. To all our surprise, after his parents saw his YouTube videos—he'd recently uploaded a rendition of an old Hindi song, they seemed quite pleased with his performance and realized that he was happier if given a chance to indulge in his hobby. His father even bought him a beautiful, golden-brown guitar. He'd carry that thing around even to our classes, deeming it a 'suitcase with a very valuable item'. When things would get too stressful (which they did), he'd quickly whip it out in the cafeteria, which had become a sort of concert hall by the end of our two years. Avik even took all three of us to meet Shanaya once when she had come to Chandigarh earlier this year.

Shiv, Avik and I had become sort of a team at Hellen. Parnika was also a member, of course—but she had left Hellen shortly after this team was solidified, thereby limiting the time all four of us could spend together. Still, we would try to meet once in a while when Parnika'd get a break from her hefty international baccalaureate programme.

After she left, the remaining three of us would try to stick together at Hellen—never letting the other feel too lonely. Shiv would text me from time to time, asking me an infinite number of trivial questions that never did end—and I'm sure there were many more to come. Avik and I would have our usual rant sessions, where we'd try to one-up each other on who had the worse life situation. In that world full of nameless machines all trying to achieve the same thing, these friends of mine knew my name—knew *me*.

'Avani, what about you?' Parnika asked, smiling at me knowingly. She already knew. The two of us had constantly been in touch once she had left, probably more so than when she was in Hellen.

My coaching life after that first mega grand test had been way less turbulent than the five months prior to it. Sure, I would have my ups and downs in terms of ranks, marks and emotions. I didn't sit in the 'reserved row' for my entire 'tenure' at Hellen. I was even close to getting demoted to Dolphin once. I cried many times—after frustrating, tiring days and when I couldn't seem to go anywhere. I still had my self-deprecating thoughts, and I still doubted myself often.

But the thoughts that kept me going were solidified in my mind and also in the form of my 'Guidebook for Surviving Hellen', which I was constantly updating. Whenever I'd feel down (which was often), I'd glance at the points or talk to my parents, unafraid to share even my most anxious thoughts with them. They had probably worked as hard as I had in these two years. I persuaded Mom to finally go back to her teaching job when I began class 12 last year—though she insisted on going back full-time gradually, and began working part-time at first so she'd get enough time to take me out for ice-cream nights and shopping trips. Dad would tag along as well, and, of course, we had our walks full of his usual advice—study plans and pre-exam reassurances. I wouldn't say I've gotten fitter over the past two years, but I could at least walk to the banyan tree at Sukhna Lake without running out of breath.

'Well, I think it went fine. I really did try my best, whatever was possible at that time. I'm proud of myself for that. And I can't wait for the future.' I smiled.

Acknowledgements

Writing this book has been one of the most difficult and rewarding experiences of my life. *Teen Machine* is a culmination of a generous amount of support and guidance that I've been fortunate enough to receive.

I would like to thank my publisher, Rupa Publications, for believing in me and my editors, Saswati and Soumya, for giving me advice that has made me a much better writer.

I am forever indebted to my family for being my primary support in life, my parents, who endured me as I went through coaching, college and writing this book. I am so grateful to my mother, my closest confidant and best friend, who is always there to feed me a paneer parantha. My father, who is always there to listen to my worries and keeps a level head even when I can't, has my unending appreciation. I am thankful to my brother, who introduced me to the world of story-rich video games and is a surprisingly good listener. My biggest cheerleaders—Baba, Dadi, Nana, Nani, deserve the biggest shout-out.

I am incredibly grateful to my teachers, Ms Kunika, Ms Sangeeta and Ms Schafer. Their constant encouragement kept me writing.

Finally, thank you, dear reader, for picking up *Teen Machine*. I hope you enjoy reading it as much as I did writing it.